CassaStaR

Alex J. Cavanaugh

DANCING LEMUR PRESS, L.L.C.
Pikeville, North Carolina
www.dancinglemurpress.com

Copyright 2010 by Alex J. Cavanaugh
Published by Dancing Lemur Press, L.L.C.
P.O. Box 383, Pikeville, North Carolina, 27863-0383
www.dancinglemurpress.com

ISBN: 978-0-9816210-6-7 / 0-9816210-6-6

Printed in the United States of America

Cover design by C.R.W.

Publisher's Cataloging-in-Publication data

Cavanaugh, Alex J.
    CassaStar / Alex J. Cavanaugh.
    p. cm.
    ISBN 978-0-9816210-6-7

1. Space warfare —Fiction. 2. Science fiction. 3. Friendship —
Fiction. I. Title

PS3553.A964 C38 2010
[Fic]—dd22   2010927005

*For my loving wife who's
supported me all these years!*

Prologue

Slipping between two asteroids, the fighter continued in tight pursuit. The drone had attempted to elude destruction by hiding in the asteroid field, but the pilot was not about to lose his target. The teleportation device on board his ship still registered just enough power for a single jump, and he'd call upon its ability if necessary.

"There you are!" the pilot exclaimed, spying the drone's shiny surface against the darkness of space.

He sent his Cosbolt into a sharp nosedive. His navigator calculated their chances of catching the drone and relayed the information. Gritting his teeth, the pilot pushed his vessel even harder. Continuing on its course, the drone attempted to duck under a large asteroid. Fearing he would lose his opportunity, the pilot hugged the rock's surface as he closed the distance.

It'll be close! his navigator warned, the mental thought loud in his head.

Just as the nose of the drone disappeared from sight, the pilot fired, and two lasers sped toward their target. Sensing his navigator's growing panic, he pulled away from the asteroid just as his shots struck the tail of the drone. Recovering from his fright, the young man in the back seat confirmed the vessel's destruction.

Uttering a triumphant cry, the pilot eased back on the throttle. Gliding out of their tight arc, he realigned the ship and requested another target. A voice over the com cut him short.

"Damn, you're insane!"

Glancing to his left, the pilot caught sight of an approaching Cosbolt. He laughed at his comrade's observation, feeling pleased with his daring manuever. Guiding his ship closer, he fell into position beside the other vessel.

"Ease back, rookie," the other pilot suggested, his tone implying concern rather than a command. "It's just an exercise. What are you trying to prove?"

"That I'm the best!"

And if that doesn't get your brother's attention...? he asked, his question concealed from both ship's navigators.

Eyes narrowing, the young pilot tightened his grip on the throttle. Before he could form a response, his navigator announced the presence of another drone not far behind them. Snapping into action, the pilot made a sharp turn.

"Bet you a week's pay I get to him first!" he challenged.

The second ship veered as well. "You're on!" the other pilot exclaimed.

With a distinct lead, the young pilot approached the drone. Their target took evasive action and dove toward a cluster of small asteroids. The pilot fired one laser blast, hoping to catch the drone before it entered the tight arrangement of rocks. His shot just grazed the wingtip, and their target vanished into the cluster.

A lot of movement, his navigator warned.

Glancing at his screen, the pilot noticed the second Cosbolt had adjusted its trajectory. The other team intended to go around the asteroids and catch the droid on the far side. Unwilling to lose the bet, he made a rash decision. Feeling his muscles tighten in anticipation, the young man followed the droid.

That cluster's too unstable! the other pilot exclaimed.

I can handle it!

Swinging around a drifting asteroid, the young pilot requested assistance from his navigator. Guiding him under another rock, his partner relayed the location of the drone. The close proximity of so many asteroids blocked the galaxy's star, preventing proper illumination. The pilot relied on his navigator's direction, hugging the uneven surfaces as he flew around the giant boulders.

The drone came into view once more. A drifting rock brushed the vessel's wingtip, sending it into a slow spiral. Pressing forward, the pilot closed the distance. His thumb hovered over the laser's trigger, prepared to shoot at the first opportunity.

Swinging around another asteroid, their target regained control and dove. The Cosbolt followed and the pilot realized the drone intended to slip between two rocks. Determined his quarry would not escape, he conveyed his intentions just as the drone adjusted its angle and shot between the two asteroids.

We got him! he thought, pressing the button. Firing two shots, he requested teleportation coordinates.

His navigator hesitated but a split second before relaying a location. *Jump!*

The blackness of folded space consumed the ship for a moment. Entering space again, an enormous asteroid filled the pilot's view outside the cockpit.

Pull up! screamed his navigator.

Yanking back on the throttle, the pilot realized it wouldn't be enough. His mind touched the teleporter, but there wasn't enough energy for a jump. There was no escape.

I'll never fly with you now, brother, he thought as the Cosbolt struck the asteroid.

Chapter One

Straightening his jacket, Bassa adjusted the fall of the heavy fabric across his chest. He stared at his reflection in the mirror, conscious of the gradual changes in his features. The uniform was still a perfect fit, as he'd kept up his physique, but his face no longer reflected the same youthful qualities. Lines were forming around his eyes and the skin stretched across his chiseled features had grown rough. He wasn't sure at what point the subtle alterations had appeared, but he could no longer deny the inevitable. Bassa was finally showing his age.

"Still have a ways to go," he murmured, brushing aside the wavy locks that fell across his brow.

At fifty-nine, he was still considered in his prime. Cassans lived an average of one hundred and thirty years if they abused neither body nor mental powers. Bassa had served as a fighter ship navigator for almost eighteen years, a position that certainly took its toll on an individual. However, the past twenty years had been spent in a less strenuous manner. As the lead instructor on Guaard, he still flew daily but without the stress of deep space battles.

Satisfied with his appearance, Bassa retrieved his personal computer pad from the desk. In passing, his eyes caught the flicker of light through his tiny portal window. Shifting his position, he took note of the small, glowing orb in the black sky. The training facility resided on a dark moon far from the galaxy's star. Its light graced two habitable planets in the system, including his home world of Cassa, but the warmth of the sun never reached Guaard. The moon did not reside at the far end of the system, but it felt as if the inhabitants were on the very edge of existence.

Bassa exited his quarters and strolled down the short hallway. He paused at the lift, his gaze falling on the telepod's open door. New pilots and navigators were not permitted to use the teleporter pods until properly trained, but Bassa's rank granted him full access to the devices. The invitation to stretch his powers rather than his legs was too tempting, and he opted for the faster form of transportation.

Stepping inside the pod, Bassa waited for the gentle pop of the sealed door before visualizing his destination. Feeling the strength of the teleporter's power source, located in a compartment over his head, he tapped into the device's ability to fold space. The resulting jump was so brief that Bassa did not even notice its effects.

The door slid open, revealing the entrance to his office, which resided at the far end of the complex. Bassa strode across the hall and waved his hand over the press plate. The double doors moved aside without a sound and he surveyed his office. The wall over his desk was adorned with the Cassan fleet's insignia; the black, five-pointed star with double planets a sharp contrast to the white walls. His numerous medals and awards covered the two side walls, representing almost eighteen years of service as one of the top navigators. Two bookshelves occupied the far wall, and every book and file resided in perfect order. Bassa's large desk and chair were imposing figures in the spacious room, flanked by two smaller chairs for visitors. To the young and uninitiated, the room appeared daunting and intimidating, and it smacked of authority. That was exactly the impression Bassa wanted to impart as lead instructor on Guaard.

Before entering the room, he glanced at the wide bench just outside the double doors. Soon errant young pilots and navigators would occupy those seats, awaiting their turn in his office with growing anxiety. Bassa smiled as he pictured the nervous expressions of those foolish enough to warrant a reprimand from the toughest instructor in the fleet.

As soon as he was seated behind the desk, Bassa began reviewing the first set of simulator lessons. He and the other instructors made minor adjustments after every group passed through the facility, fine tuning and altering the flight patterns. The next batch of young men would arrive in three days and he wanted to prepare for their first week on Guaard.

Satisfied with the changes, Bassa turned his attention to the upcoming roster. He liked to familiarize himself with each young man and the skills he brought to Guaard's elite installation. Those entering the program arrived with over two hundred hours of simulator experience and were qualified for training in a fighter. Their skills were not in question, but rather their lack of actual experience. It was Bassa's job to prepare the young men for service in the fleet and the real dangers of space flight and combat. Guaard was the final checkpoint, and the lead instructor only certified those who met and exceeded his expectations.

His brief inspection of the incoming pilots and navigators was not to just size up the young men; Bassa sought not only those with heightened skills but ones who were potential troublemakers. In twenty years, he'd seen his fair share of rebellious individuals. Those with even one mark on their record were flagged and would undergo close scrutiny. Bassa expected discipline and obedience, and would not tolerate disregard of either quality.

Often it was not merely disobedience, but an arrogant attitude that gave cause for concern. A self-centered or cocky pilot was an even greater threat. He liked spirit, but it had to be controlled in order to be effective. Bassa's greatest challenge resided in such young men and he was twice as likely to require those individuals to repeat the entire course. Outstanding talent and skill combined with arrogance was what he most dreaded. Fortunately, those young men were few and far between.

Thirty new pilots and navigators were slated to converge on the facility in three days. The young men would arrive pre-paired, although the teams were not set in stone at this point. During simulator training, they were rotated as instructors attempted to discern the best combination. Bassa and his instructors would analyze the men and approve the final pairings. In order to properly function as a team, a high level of trust and familiarity had to be established between pilot and navigator. Without a strong bond, they were doomed in the field.

Bassa read through the history of each young man, making mental notes of potential problems. A navigator with a mark on his record was instantly flagged for observation. A pilot who'd barely passed the simulator test was also noted.

Either was a potential danger to the other members of the squadron. The instructors would monitor those two carefully, prepared to remove either if necessary. Otherwise, the remainder of the men appeared manageable.

Retrieving the files on the last team, Bassa flicked first to the pilot. The young man's image filled the screen and he caught his breath. Brows drawn, Bassa stared in disbelief at the fighter pilot's photo. The features and expression were all too familiar.

Eyes traveling to the lone picture residing on his desk, Bassa compared the two images. The young man in the heavy frame possessed the exact same characteristics, right down to the cocked eyebrow and partially concealed smirk. Bassa also noticed similarity in the eyes that could only be attributed to extreme confidence. There was no denying that the same unbridled spirit resided in both young men.

Bassa scowled at the thought and turned to the young pilot's record. There were no disciplinary marks, which surprised him, but an unusual amount of notes had been added over the years. The same words were repeated numerous times – possession of great skill marred only by attitude. The young man had excelled in every program, but his cocksure demeanor threatened to undermine those accomplishments at every turn.

Digging deeper, Bassa discovered that outside of his military record, the young man came with a load of baggage. His parents had died when he was a child, leaving him in the care of a much older sister who apparently couldn't handle the young boy. Shuffled from one facility to the next, he'd been in trouble more than once and his irresponsible use of mental powers and poor attitude were often cited as the cause. He'd managed to keep his record clean long enough to begin training for a position in the fleet. However, while no formal marks or disciplinary action resided in his records, there were enough cautionary notes to fill an entire log book. The young man was an explosive problem just waiting for an opportune moment.

A chime signified a visitor. Bassa had summoned his senior pilot instructor and he granted permission to enter. As expected, the tall, lanky form of Rellen strolled into his office.

He gave Bassa a proper salute, always respectful toward the senior officer, before a wry grin spread across his narrow face.

"Reviewing our next assignment?" Rellen inquired, pausing at the edge of the desk.

Bassa leaned away from his computer, his gaze still on the young man's image, which dominated the screen once more. "Yes," he said with resignation.

Rellen frowned at Bassa's response. Moving to the side of the desk, his instructor peered at the screen. His smile returned and Rellen emitted a chuckle.

"I see you've discovered 715's pilot, Byron," he observed.

"He's got some skill," Bassa admitted.

"And attitude! He'll provide you with a challenge, Bassa. Keep you from going soft!"

"Soft?" demanded Bassa, eyeing his instructor with skepticism.

Rellen's subtle wink was not unexpected. He relished pushing the envelope at every opportunity. Bassa rarely rose to the bait and felt annoyed with his quick reaction. This young man and the potential scenarios his presence could produce had clouded his thoughts.

"Well, you've never allowed this type to simply slip through the program," offered Rellen, crossing his arms and inclining his head toward the screen. "He'll either change or he'll fail!"

Bassa eyed the screen once more, his gaze slowly drifting to the picture on his desk. The similarity between the men was unmistakable.

He'll change or he'll wind up dead, Bassa thought.

Waving his hand in front of the press plate, Byron announced his presence when the speaker inquired and waited for his sister's response. The door did not open right away, which came as no surprise. Sighing, he turned to view the city, spread out across the valley floor for miles in every direction.

This was his first visit since his acceptance into the service. Byron had maintained contact with his sister but only through telecom transmissions. He'd felt obliged to keep Sherdan informed of his progress, although he was now past the need for supervision or her approval. He was sure his sister relished that fact as well.

Byron's sister had been absent for much of his life. After their parents' death, Sherdan had assumed responsibility of her younger sibling, but not for long. Byron's bond with her was fragile at best, and he'd rebelled against her authority. When he turned six, his sister decided she'd had enough and relinquished her guardianship. She shipped him off to a facility designed to handle troubled and abandoned children. Deprived of family and all he'd ever known, Byron was forced to survive by any means possible.

It was during those fourteen miserable years that Byron learned he could trust nothing but his own skills and wits. Sherdan's occasional visits did little to bolster his belief in people and he resisted all attempts to connect with her or anyone else on an emotional or mental level. Those in a position of authority bore the brunt of his anger and defiance. Despite his refusal to interact or bond with other Cassans, Byron's mind did not permit him to disconnect completely from the world. He relished knowledge and its potential to provide freedom, and he'd applied himself to his studies with obvious zeal.

By the time he was fifteen, his instructors began to notice his dexterity skills. They praised his talents and encouraged the young man to increase his proficiency. Byron had always excelled in his classes, but this form of recognition pleased him even more. Rigorous physical training soon occupied his spare time, reducing the occurrences of mischievous behavior. Byron had discovered a life driven by purpose as he contemplated the opportunities his skills could provide.

The day of his twentieth birthday he applied for military service. Despite his instructors' cautions that he might not gain admittance for another year, Byron was accepted as a trainee in the fleet. His high academic scores and reflexive skills, coupled with strong mental powers, earned him the right to apply for pilot training. Unwilling to compromise his potential, and determined to prove his worth to those who'd doubted, Byron decided to pursue the prestigious position of Cosbolt pilot. The two-seat fighter ship was the fleet's elite weapon of choice and the first into combat. Only the most skilled pilots flew Cosbolts. Confident in his abilities, Byron had applied himself to the program and finished at the top of his class. In two days, he would report to Guaard to begin the final stage of training, and he could not be more pleased with his accomplishment.

His triumphant thoughts were diverted when the door opened. A woman with features quite different from Byron appeared in the doorway. Sherdan regarded him with caution, her eyes scanning his face even as her mind probed his thoughts. Annoyed by the invasion of his privacy, Byron quickly shielded his mind. Sherdan frowned with obvious displeasure.

"Just as guarded as ever," she declared, her tone neutral.

"Did you really think I'd change?" Byron replied, offering a smug smile he knew would irritate his sister further.

"Of course not! That would be asking the impossible."

This time it was Byron's turn to scowl. He enjoyed exchanging words with his sister, but only when he held the upper hand. Judging from her sarcastic tone, Sherdan's expectations for her brother remained low. He'd struggled with feelings of inadequacy as a child and refused to be saddled with her poor opinion now.

"I didn't have to come here you know," he growled, prepared to beat a hasty departure.

His sister sighed and set her lips in a thin line. Offering a curt nod, she stepped aside. Feeling wary, he entered Sherdan's home.

Her new dwelling was much larger than her previous home. Byron's sister had recently bonded with a mate and shared his abode, although he did not appear to be present at the moment. Byron had never met the man and felt relieved. He could only imagine the image Sherdan had painted of her troubled younger brother.

Byron followed his sister into the food preparation room. Several vegetables lined the counter, their colors bright in an otherwise colorless room. He'd viewed so many white rooms as a child, shuffled from one facility to the next, that the surroundings caused Byron a sense of unease. He slouched against the counter and watched as Sherdan reached for a cutting knife.

"So," she said in a loud voice, her eyes focused on the vegetables. "Are you still in training?"

"I just completed simulator training," he stated with pride, still wary of Sherdan's tone. "I leave for Guaard in two days. In six months, I'll be certified."

Sherdan shook her head. "My brother, piloting a Cosbolt!"

"And why is that so difficult to imagine?" Byron demanded, grasping the edge of the counter with both hands.

"It requires a great deal of discipline."

"And you think I'm incapable? I finished at the top of my class!"

Sherdan ceased her activity and thoughtfully regarded her brother. Byron met her steady gaze, his fingers almost digging into the counter in an effort to control his anger. His sister might still doubt his abilities, but she could not argue with the facts.

"Then that is quite an accomplishment," she answered at last.

He sensed relief rather than pride in her tone and Sherdan's indifference stabbed at his heart. Outside of their blood ties, there was no bond between the siblings. Without further thought, Byron blocked that painful realization from his mind. He had wasted his time coming to see his sister.

"Were you staying for dinner?" she asked.

"No," Byron growled, leaning away from the counter. "I'm heading back tonight, so I need to go."

"I wish you well then," Sherdan replied, returning to her task.

Hands dropping to his sides, Byron stared at his sister. She paused in her cutting and turned to face him.

"You never really cared," he said, his words more of a statement than an accusation.

Sherdan set down the knife. "Byron ..." she began, her thoughts filled with exasperation.

"That's all right," Byron offered with a shrug. "Makes this all the easier."

Without waiting for a response, he strode toward the door and retreated from the unpleasant scene. If his sister asked Byron to return, he did not hear her entreaty, as his mind's shield prevented all mental voices from entering his thoughts.

His resolve to pursue a life far from Cassa was even more entrenched in his heart now. Most of his life had been spent without family or friends, and his last tie to this planet apparently never existed. No bonds or restrictions remained and Byron was at last free. Somehow, though, it felt a shallow victory at best.

Rolling his head to the right, Byron peered out the tiny portal window. The vast expanse of space appeared dark and uninviting. Even after two hundred hours in the simulator, he felt unprepared for the emptiness of endless space. Byron wondered if the unnerving sensation would affect his first actual flight in a Cosbolt.

"We're approaching Guaard," came a voice near his ear, and he felt a shoulder press against his own. "Do you see anything yet?"

Byron shook his head and frowned, his eyes still on the distant stars. If they were indeed drawing near the dark moon, he could not see it from his vantage point.

"We're probably on the wrong side of the ship," he commented dryly.

"Damn!" came the immediate reply, and he felt his seatmate's position shift.

Turning to confirm his assumptions, Byron discovered the young man leaning into the aisle in an attempt to see out the windows on the other side of the vessel. Trindel possessed a childlike spirit at total odds with his actual age. He viewed every new experience with wonder, and made no attempts to hide his zealous curiosity. Byron was eager to view their new home as well, but he was not about to reveal that fact to his navigator.

During his year of simulator instruction, Byron had endured seven different navigators. Three had lasted less than a week, while the others fared little better in his company. He'd run out of choices when the instructors placed Trindel in his cockpit. Sensing the desperateness of the situation and worried he would fail if no suitable partnership was established, Byron made every effort to work with this navigator. At first, he doubted their pairing would last, given Trindel's lighthearted and open nature. He finally came to trust the enthusiastic and often naïve young man, despite the differences in personality and style.

Once he'd accepted Trindel, their simulator flights drastically improved. Byron realized Trindel's hyperactive mind lent itself well to the many duties required of a good navigator. His partner was quick to project his thoughts, almost to the point of reckless inhibition, but that resulted in an incredible reaction time. Byron learned not to question those rapid judgment calls. Whereas the other navigator trainees' thoughts came across as commands, something he detested, Trindel's words were but suggestions and snippets of information. Byron responded better when he felt in command of his decisions. They had excelled as a team, completing the simulator training at the top of their class.

"You're right! Damn, why didn't we sit on that side of the ship?" exclaimed Trindel.

Byron glanced beyond his navigator to the seats on the other side. The young men were all staring out their windows, their body language expressing excitement. Obviously, they had a fine view of the ship's final destination. This fact caused Byron's navigator a great amount of distress, and anxiety emanated from Trindel's mind.

Byron took a deep breath. He had to be patient with his friend and suppress the exasperation that rose within his mind.

"Trindel, you're going to see it every single day," he offered.

"I know!" protested Trindel, glancing at his pilot. "I just want to see it now. I've never been off Cassa before."

Neither have I, Byron thought, his words audible only to his navigator.

Trindel ceased his desperate efforts to peer out the far windows and settled in his seat. *I just wanted to see our new home*, he offered, his head still turned.

Smiling to himself, Byron stretched his arms. It continued to amaze him that their pairing was a success. Trindel's overeager behavior had worn on the nerves of his previous potential pilots. Positioning him as Byron's navigator was likely an act of desperation on the part of the instructors, as both young men were running out of options at that conjuncture. Despite the differences in their personalities, as Trindel was outgoing and Byron introverted, they meshed well as a team. Byron had accepted Trindel's presence once he discovered the navigator's penchant for mischief and foolish antics, which mirrored his own rebellious inclinations. However, they wisely maintained a high level of precision and perfection during flights.

Glancing out his window, Byron realized the ship had altered its course. "Well, if you really want a view of the moon …" he taunted.

Byron felt Trindel press against his shoulder, the young man's excitement projecting loudly in his thoughts. Forcing his body deep into the seat, Byron leaned closer to the window in an effort to avoid being crushed. He really should've taken the aisle seat.

"It fills the sky!" Trindel exclaimed, his voice loud in Byron's ear.

On a direct course with the moon, the ship's current speed became apparent as Guaard loomed larger by the second. Craters and mountains were visible, but Byron could not locate the training facility. Judging from their trajectory, the complex was likely located on the dark side of the moon at the moment.

Trindel leaned back in his seat and Byron glanced at his navigator. His expression full of anticipation, Trindel grinned and winked.

"Welcome to our new home," he stated with pride.

Byron mulled over that statement. Guaard was just a dead moon orbiting a cold and lifeless planet. He doubted it would feel like home. Then again, Byron had never resided in a location he felt was home.

The transport ship soon landed, and from his vantage, Byron watched as the giant hanger doors opened while the vessel's progress slowed to a mere hover. The ship's pilots nimbly maneuvered the nose forward and the transport slid into the hanger. There was a moment's pause after the ship came to rest while the exterior doors closed. The walls began to move and Byron realized they were moving down a tunnel toward another set of doors. His eyes widened when the transport entered the main hanger.

Byron had not expected the facility to be so large. Room for a dozen transports existed in the massive building, and several vessels were in evidence. However, it was the rows of Cosbolts that caught his attention. Lined in perfect formation, the sleek fighters rested on the far side of the hanger. His eyes remained on the ships until the transporter's course took them out of view.

When the ship's movement ceased, the men were instructed to disembark and retrieve their bags. They were to then follow the escort and assemble in the receiving room. The facility's instructors were awaiting their arrival.

"Here we go!" Trindel exclaimed.

Rising to his feet, Byron followed his navigator. Trindel's eager steps were slowed by the process of thirty young men exiting the ship, but soon they were trotting down the ramp. The moment Byron's feet touched the hanger floor, he glanced in the direction of the Cosbolts. He was provided just a brief moment in which to admire the sleek fighters before instructed to secure his bag. Fighting the urge to defy his very first order on Guaard, he located his bag in the accumulating pile on the floor and joined the men waiting in line.

The last man had just secured his bag when the line began to move forward. They marched across the hanger and exited through a set of double doors. Turning to the left, the men entered a large room.

"Three rows of ten!" the escort commanded.

Byron's gaze fell upon five officers standing at attention on a raised dais, observing the men. The new arrivals began to fall into place as instructed. Byron paused, allowing Trindel to reach his pilot, and his moment of hesitation placed him at the far end of the second row. This pleased Byron, though. He relished his accomplishments and status as the best team but preferred to blend in as an individual.

Once everyone was in position, bags resting on the floor, the young men snapped to attention. Facing forward, Byron's gaze soon drifted to the five officers. They were all many years his senior although still in their prime. He sensed the elevated level of authority and knew they would not tolerate any foolish pranks here on Guaard. Judging from the stern expression on the senior officer's face, the next six months would be the most unpleasant of the young men's short lives.

Eyes scanning the trainees, the senior officer stepped forward, his hands behind his back. "You have been sent here for the final stage of Cosbolt training," he stated, his deep voice echoing in the large room. "And I will be sending half of you home before it's over."

He paused, his gaze traveling across the men's faces. Byron kept his expression neutral and eyes forward.

"For the next six months, we will instruct and evaluate each and every one of you. This facility boasts the most decorated officers in the fleet. To my left are Officers Char and Morden," he announced. "They oversee all navigator training. Officers Jarth and Rellen are responsible for the pilots.

"And I am Senior Officer Bassa," the man stated in a voice that smacked of authority. "I am in charge of this facility. I decide who becomes Cosbolt pilots and navigators and who goes home."

Byron involuntarily clenched his teeth. He refused to be sent home in shame. Too many years of his life had been lost at the hands of others for Byron to allow one man to decide his fate now.

The sound of a boot striking the floor returned him to the moment. Officer Bassa had stepped down from the platform. Slowly, he began to examine the line.

"There are no days of rest here," he announced. "You will train each and every day for six months. Time will be spent in the classroom, the simulator, and in actual flight. And just as in real life, one mistake will cost you. If your judgment proves faulty or you lack discipline, you will suffer the consequences."

Bassa moved as he spoke, inspecting each young man's appearance. He finished his statement just as he reached the second row. Byron was first in line, and the senior officer hesitated. With the man's final words ringing his ears, Byron felt the intense scrutiny of Bassa's gaze. Resentment rose in his thoughts as he realized Bassa probably knew of his chequered past. He quickly suppressed his feelings, lest the senior officer sense his negative attitude. Judging from Bassa's expression, he had already interpreted Byron's unguarded thoughts.

To his relief, Bassa moved to Trindel. His shoulders relaxed as the weight of the senior officer's scrutiny transferred to another man. Byron had just arrived and already he was tempting fate. He resolved to maintain a tighter rein on his feelings.

"You will be escorted to your quarters and then to the dining hall," Bassa was saying. "After the midday meal, you will be provided an extensive tour of the facility. Tomorrow, you will be expected to know the layout by heart. Those who fail to report on time ..."

Bassa paused at the end of the second row, his penetrating gaze falling on every pilot and navigator. The men silently awaited his next words.

"... will find themselves on the first transport home. Dismissed!"

All thirty men turned and began filing out of the room. Bassa remained in place, watching their departure. The other instructors fell in line behind the young men, with the exception of Rellen. He paused at Bassa's side and waited until the last person exited before speaking.

"Too early to tell," he observed.

Bassa nodded. "We'll know more by the end of the week," he replied, sensing a purpose behind Rellen's casual comment.

His senior officer nodded and moved from Bassa's side. Rellen hesitated, flashing his superior an inquisitive look.

"He bears a resemblance," he said in a low voice.

Bassa's gaze flickered briefly to Rellen. "Yes, he does," he conceded.

Taking a deep breath, Bassa considered that fact. The young pilot's appearance had caught him off-guard. In person, Byron was almost identical to his brother. Bassa's momentary hesitation was uncharacteristic and had been noted by his senior officer. Shocked by the similarity, he'd failed to take Byron to task for his obvious resentment of the scrutiny. Bassa would be careful to monitor future meetings and exchanges with the young pilot.

"And I fear his attitude is even worse," he admitted.

"We'll watch him close, then," Rellen replied with a nod.

Bassa remained in the receiving room after Rellen's departure, his mind mulling over the situation. He could not allow his feelings regarding Tal to interfere with the handling of this young man. Judging from his background information and unguarded thoughts today, Byron was capable of challenging his authority without assistance. If he were to maintain control, a higher standard was needed, and that applied as much to him as to Byron.

"Damn you, Tal," he muttered under his breath.

Chapter Two

The young men were joined by six others who'd failed the prior session. Pilots and navigators were given two opportunities to complete their final training, and out of the fourteen who'd failed the previous session, six returned to try again. Their presence sent a message to the new group that failure was a very real possibility at this juncture. Those not progressing past simulator training usually dropped out of their own accord; however, young men sent home from Guaard did not leave voluntarily.

Byron was already certified as a basic pilot, but flying transports or recovery ships did not appeal to him. He'd endured enough restraints on his life. He wanted the power and freedom a Cosbolt represented. Failure to achieve his goal was simply not an option at this point.

He was disappointed to learn that the first week would be spent in the classroom and simulators. Officer Bassa stated he wanted to view their simulator skills firsthand. The drills were difficult but not outside the maneuvers he'd already mastered. The classroom study covered new aspects of flight, but it was a small consolation. The absence of real cockpit time became the topic of choice over meals, but Byron refrained from adding his protests. He preferred not to call attention to himself unless it involved an achievement.

Byron and Trindel were the only team to achieve a perfect score on their final simulator test, and their precision continued on Guaard. While he despised personal, individual scrutiny, Byron relished the opportunity to show off his skills in the cockpit. As the week progressed, his confidence grew. Basking in the glory, he believed his team's abilities were beyond question.

By the end of the first week, they emerged from the simulator feeling triumphant. Not only had they completed another practice drill without error, but Byron felt he'd exhibited several complicated and daring moves in the process. Performing several jumps by way of the ship's teleporter, he'd emerged at the precise location every time. All targets were destroyed and they'd easily completed their task within the allotted time frame. In Byron's mind, their run was perfect.

Trindel removed his helmet, revealing curly locks now plastered to his head. "We're good!" he exclaimed, flashing one of his broad grins.

Byron removed his own helmet and tossed back his head. Running fingers through his straight, black hair, he caused the strands to stick out in an unnatural pattern. Grinning at his navigator, Byron straightened his shoulders with pride.

"No, I'd say we're perfect," he boasted, holding up his fist.

Trindel returned his gesture and they tapped knuckles. As one, the young men walked toward the control room. Byron predicted another report of excellence on his team's record.

Officers Rellen and Char were monitoring their flight today and awaited the men in the control room. Byron was surprised to discover Bassa also present. The young men snapped to attention, aware their casual posture would be viewed as unacceptable by the senior instructor. Bassa briefly noted their entrance, his gaze once again returning to the series of monitors in the control room. Rellen and Char remained seated but leaned away from the main panel. Byron waited for one of the men to speak.

"Adequate run," offered Bassa, his gaze still averted.

Byron had to suppress the indignation that arose in his thoughts. "Yes, sir," he replied in unison with Trindel.

Officer Bassa straightened his shoulders, a frown on his face. He turned to face the young men, his hands clasped behind his back.

"You performed numerous jumps," he observed, meeting Byron's eyes.

"I do what I feel is necessary to succeed, sir," Byron replied, ready to defend his decisions.

Bassa's eyes narrowed. "A good pilot cannot rely solely on the teleporter. You must learn to master maneuvers."

"Yes, sir," answered Byron, taking a quick breath. "We did perform twenty-seven unique maneuvers during that flight, sir."

He sensed a flash of panic from Trindel, but the feeling was quickly shielded. Bassa's eyebrows pulled together, reflecting his disapproval of Byron's unsolicited statement. Realizing he'd spoken out of turn, Byron felt annoyance rise in his thoughts. He didn't want to incur the senior officer's wrath but resented criticism of his skills. He'd flown perfectly today.

"Perhaps you'd prefer an opportunity to showcase those maneuvers," Bassa stated, his tone implying it was an order rather than an offer. "Officer Char, please run number 789 with the teleporter offline."

"Yes, sir!"

Unable to respond, Byron stared helplessly as Char punched in the code for the program. Bassa gestured for Byron and Trindel to return to the simulator, and they exited the control room with great reluctance.

Well, didn't take you long to annoy Bassa, Trindel commented privately.

Always start at the top, Trindel...

Byron knew he'd been too quick with his boastful words. Upon reaching the simulator entrance, he paused and glanced up at the control room. Byron grasped his helmet and placed in on his head before nodding at Trindel.

Regardless, we'll ace this run, he declared, not bothering to shield his thought.

In the control room, Rellen leaned away from the main panel and shook his head. Pivoting in his chair, he looked up at Bassa.

"Yes, he's damned cocky!" Rellen announced, a smile tugging at his lips. "Boy knows how to push it to the limit, too."

Still frowning, Bassa watched as Byron and Trindel entered the simulator and closed the hatch. His eyes dropped to the screens across the main panel and located the pilot's feed. Byron was already in position and preparing for the drill. There was no mistaking the look of confidence and determination on his face.

"We need to redraw the lines then," Bassa said in a firm voice.

He remained in the control room while Byron and Trindel performed their run. Their execution was not precision-perfect this time, but the men committed no errors and accomplished the objective within the allotted time. When the session ended, both pilot and navigator appeared quite smug.

"He's not going to make it easy for us," Char commented with a moan.

"It's only the first week," Bassa replied, turning to depart. "We will correct that attitude!"

Exiting the control room, he left the simulator area in haste. That final run had cut into the evening meal, although the loss of food did not concern him. Bassa preferred to spend the evening hours reviewing the day's performances, analyzing each team's weaknesses and strengths. Tonight he would require extra time to study Byron and Trindel's runs in detail. He would need every scrap of evidence if he intended to find flaws in Byron's next drill beyond multiple jumps. Cocky or not, the boy exhibited incredible skill as a pilot.

The following morning, the men reported to the classroom as scheduled. Byron was delighted when only an hour was devoted to instruction, and most of it focused on proper conduct in the hanger. Bassa concluded the session with a stern warning of the consequences of improper behavior or failure to follow procedures when in the presence of the fighter ships. After the previous evening's experience, Byron did not doubt his threat.

Trindel's eagerness secured them a position at the front of the line as they exited the lift. Officer Jarth led the young men into the hanger, emerging near the bay housing the Cosbolts. Byron noticed Officers Bassa and Rellen already waiting. Only officers were allowed access to the teleporters and the two men had obviously taken advantage of the device. Were he not so eager to view his ship, Byron might've resented the restrictions placed upon uncertified trainees. However, viewing the Cosbolts up close took precedence over all else.

The young men joined the senior officers, snapping to attention once assembled. Bassa surveyed the pilots and navigators, observing each one's reaction. For the majority of those gathered, this was their first time in the presence of an actual fighter.

"In the time remaining before the midday meal," began Bassa, his voice echoing across the empty hanger, "you will become familiar with your ship and the feel of the instruments. Do not rush through the opportunity to explore your ship at length. Use this time wisely.

"Officer Rellen will announce ship assignments," he concluded, stepping aside.

Rellen held up his computer pad, his eyes on the screen. "Surren and Arenth, ship number 479T. Ganst and Forcance, number 512T," he called.

The instructors gestured for those called to proceed to their ships. Byron waited while several other teams were called, anxious to finally touch his Cosbolt. Trindel's excitement threatened to bubble over, and Byron silently cautioned his navigator that he should reign in his emotions. Their names would be called soon.

"Vitar and Hasen, number 143T," Rellen announced, his eyes never leaving his computer pad.

Patience slowly eroding, Byron glanced at Officer Bassa and realized the senior instructor was watching him. Quickly averting his eyes, Byron suppressed his feelings of annoyance. He did not need extra duties or lessons foisted upon his team their very first day with the Cosbolts.

They were the last team assigned to a ship. Officer Rellen observed the men with intense curiosity as the moved toward number 715T, the last remaining unclaimed fighter in the hanger. Byron sensed his navigator's impatience but forced a slow and deliberate stroll to their Cosbolt. He didn't want to give Bassa or Rellen the satisfaction of knowing the wait had irritated him.

Trindel reached the ship first, his hand gingerly touching the wing. He hesitated, as if afraid, and turned to Byron. Seeing the elation in his navigator's eyes, Byron rested his hand on the underside of the wing. The metal was cold to the touch and it sent an invigorating shock through his fingers. Byron allowed a slow smile to spread across his lips and Trindel returned his grin with unbridled enthusiasm. With a gasp, Trindel turned and grasped the ladder.

No, Byron thought, sending his navigator a private message. *We have almost two hours. Let's show the instructors we're proficient and take our time.*

Trindel's mouth fell open, his eyes wide in protest. His shoulders slumped and he nodded, releasing the ladder. Taking a deep breath, Trindel moved toward the ship's nose. Byron elected to explore the ship's propulsion first.

Circling the wing, Byron ran his hand down the side of the vessel, delighting in the feel of the surface. He reached the engines and paused to admire the propulsion system. He envisioned the engines ablaze with fire, and the power required to thrust the ship forward in space fascinated him. Soon, that power would be at his disposal.

He continued around the far side of the ship, nodding at Trindel as they passed. Byron inspected the weapons system, which consisted of two rocket launchers under each wing and the laser directly under the nose. Byron glanced at the runners as he circled the front of the ship and discovered Trindel patiently waiting by the ladder. Byron smiled and gestured for his navigator to proceed.

Trindel required no further prompting and scrambled up to the platform. Byron followed more slowly, trying to exhibit some control. By the time he had a clear view of the cockpit, Trindel was already at his station. Flashing his navigator a wry grin, he swung into the pilot's seat and wedged himself into position. When he felt situated, Byron examined the console.

The displays were dark and no lights glowed in greeting. The controls showed wear from repeated use, the result of hundreds of potential pilots training on Guaard. The worn, metallic smell was unique as well. The simulator had reflected every detail of the panel, right down to the smallest of controls, but there was one critical difference. This was the real thing.

Doesn't look much different, Trindel commented.

Yes it does, Byron replied as he gripped the thrust. He felt the cold metal even through the padding.

It was then that he became aware of the teleporter. The device was self-sufficient and engaged at all times. Its power emanated from behind Trindel's seat, safely encased within the frame of the ship. It emitted no audible sound, not even a low hum, but Byron was keenly aware of the mechanism's energy as it rippled through his mind.

Closing his eyes, he focused on the device that would be his sole responsibility. Trindel was trained on the teleporter, but pilots were accountable for its operation. Byron's mind would connect and draw upon its power to teleport their ship. Locking onto the device's signal, he felt the surge of power in his mental abilities. In that brief instant, he now understood the skill required to teleport the ship to another location in space. All he had to do was concentrate and visualize.

Not planning on jumping us to the other side of the hanger, are you?

Byron opened his eyes and dissolved the connection. *Not just yet!* he answered.

Good, because I bet that would buy us a ticket home on the next transport, Trindel teased.

Byron chuckled as he envisioned the attempt of such a feat. Officer Bassa would be positively livid!

The teams were allowed ample time to explore their ships. Byron circled the craft one more time, his hands trailing across the cold surface, before joining the others as they gathered to depart.

The midday meal was consumed with haste. The men were eager to return to the hanger and their ships. The officers took their time, adding to the growing restlessness in the room. Byron did not hide his relief when the instructors arose and ordered the men to the hanger.

The flight crew was positioning the fighters when they returned. Byron was pleased to note their ship was placed in the front of the pack. Eager to experience his first flight, he suited up and returned to the hanger before the others. Trindel trotted out a moment later, out of breath from his hasty preparations.

Once the men had reassembled in the hanger, they received instructions on their first foray into space. Feeling his excitement mount, Byron forced himself to pay attention. He did not want to make a mistake now.

"Ships will launch in pairs," Bassa announced, his voice carrying across the hanger. "You will follow your flight plan precisely and return to the landing bay. Each ship will complete three runs this afternoon. Instructors will be circling the base and observing your flight."

Byron noticed that the officers were also suited for flight. His gaze traveled past the four instructors to the two fighters waiting by the launch tubes. The ships bore bright red insignias and the identifying numbers lacked the 'T' that marked the training vessels. Even in the darkness of space, it would be impossible to confuse the ships.

"Any deviation in your flight plan," stated Bassa, his voice redirecting Byron's attention, "will result in your dismissal. Understood?"

"Yes, sir!" the men replied in unison.

Bassa began to pace slowly in front of the men, eyes scanning the ranks. He gave Byron a cold stare before allowing his gaze to fall on the next man in line.

"This may be your first actual flight, but perfect execution and a precision landing are mandatory. Once you have performed your first run, your ship will be taxied into position for another run until three landings are achieved.

"Now, to your ships!"

Byron tried to conceal his excitement, but his pace was stretched by Trindel's eager gait. Upon reaching their fighter, the men ran through the exterior checklist before Trindel gave his pilot the honor of climbing the ladder first. As he reached the platform, he glanced at the other ships and grinned. Their Cosbolt was second in line, a far more enviable placement than dead last.

Once his helmet was in place, Byron slid into his seat and fastened the harness. Turning his attention to the control panel, he anxiously scanned the display. Confident none of the switches or dials had changed position during their meal, he poised his finger over the power button.

Ready? he asked Trindel

I'm ready!

Pressing the button, Byron grinned as the panel came to life. The various instruments and screens were a welcome glow. The lights were even more vivid than those of the simulator. Mesmerized by the sight, Byron stared in awe at the illuminated panel. An emotional burst of excitement from Trindel jolted him to life.

Preflight check, Byron announced, shifting his thoughts to the task at hand.

Running through each item on the list, pilot and navigator confirmed the proper operation of the ship's numerous systems. Signing off on the final check screen, Byron lowered the canopy and performed a final inspection on the cabin's pressure.

All clear? he asked Trindel, noting the instructor's ships were already entering the launch tubes.

Ready to roll!

Byron touched the com. "715T ready," he announced.

"Check, 715T, awaiting clearance."

He tested the seal of his helmet one last time before pressing his back against the seat and adjusting the position of his feet. His piloting skills would not be required until the ship entered the launch tube, as Trindel operated ground movement from his position. Until they received clearance and moved into position, he had nothing to do.

The lack of stimulus was calming, though. Discouraging Trindel's preflight nervous chatter had been challenging, but over time he had learned to be quiet. Byron had trained his navigator to shield his overactive mind before a flight, and even the prospect of actual flight had not loosened Trindel's mental voice. Alone with his thoughts, Byron's attention was once again drawn to the teleporter.

The mechanism's power was unmistakable. It echoed in his skull, vibrating every nerve. Byron focused on the device, allowing its potency to connect with his own mental powers. Feeling the strength of his mental abilities expand, he allowed his mind to absorb even more energy. The sensation was intoxicating. He felt capable of teleporting the ship across the universe ...

We're up! exclaimed Trindel.

Byron's eyes opened. The ships in front of them were rolling into the launch tubes.

Be ready, he replied.

Within minutes, they were given permission to approach the now-open launch bay. Trindel eased their ship forward, keeping pace with the fighter to their left. With incredible precision, Byron's navigator eased the vessel into the launch tube. It never ceased to amaze Byron that someone possessing Trindel's hyperactive nature was capable of handling such a delicate operation, but his navigator excelled in his position.

Once the second set of hatches closed, Byron fired up the engines and performed the final systems check. Trindel locked the vessel in place and their ship was ready to launch.

It's all you!

Byron smiled, his fingers tight across the throttle. The lights illuminating the launch tube beckoned, their glow leading to a dark point at the end of the tunnel. He focused on that patch of blackness and what lay beyond. That spot represented freedom.

"Launch in five seconds," control announced. "Prepare! Three ... two ... one ..."

The ship went from a stationary position to flight speed in less than one second. Byron's grip on the throttle grew even tighter as they raced down the tunnel, engines burning at precisely the correct level. The tiny speck of darkness grew and the tube's lights were only a blur ...

The fighter exploded from the tunnel in silence. Despite his exhilaration, which surged outward unshielded, Trindel held a fixed lock on their flight pattern and projected the course to his pilot. Byron maintained their gentle climb, the excitement of their first flight coursing through his body. The vastness of space stretched before him, its expanse immense. The simple route was obviously meant to provide new pilots a moment to gather their wits. Fearful the view would distract him from their assignment, Byron focused on the upcoming flight pattern change.

At the appropriate moment, he veered right. Following his navigator's instructions without question, he continued to circle to the right. As the landing bay came into view, he realized it was not the same one used by the transport. Four distinct lines guided approaching Cosbolts and he concentrated on the second stripe from the right. Trindel engaged the landing runners in preparation and gave the signal. Throttling back the engine, Byron prepared to enter the bay.

Perfect landing, perfect landing, he repeated.

He held the nose steady and ship parallel. Both sets of runners had to touch evenly and he refused to settle for a lopsided landing. A single, gentle bump assured Byron of his success. Throwing the engines in reverse, he slowed the ship's headlong flight. Trindel made adjustments from his position, assisting with the plane's movement on the ground. Operating as an experienced team, Byron and Trindel brought their ship to a halt on the exact mark.

Byron emitted a cry of elation, which was quickly seconded by his navigator. He turned off the engines, relinquishing total control of the ship to Trindel. To his left, he noticed the other Cosbolt's position two rows away and just over the mark. Byron grinned at the pair's mistake.

Think you just missed there! he called, his thoughts aimed at Surren, the pilot.

Didn't ask your opinion, hot shot! came the defensive reply.

Couldn't resist, could you? prodded Trindel, his tone one of amusement.

Byron chuckled, pleased with his taunt and satisfied with their first actual flight. His team had flown and landed with a precision worthy of their status.

Trindel taxied out of the landing bay and the relays pulled the ship into the hanger. They returned to the line of Cosbolts waiting to launch. The first two teams had already spread their enthusiasm among the young men, elevating the excitement. Byron preferred to gloat privately and only reveled in their success with Trindel. They still had two more runs to complete.

The final two runs resulted in perfect execution and textbook landings. Byron's confidence swelled and his elation threatened to emanate beyond the cockpit. He reigned in his emotions but did permit a smug grin to emerge as they returned to the hanger. The instructors could not fault their performance today.

Several teams were reprimanded for overshooting their mark upon landing, but none had veered off course or landed improperly. Byron felt a dismissal on the first day of flight would've been too harsh a judgment regardless. He liked to think that Bassa was not so coldhearted as to send a team home this early and dampen everyone's spirits.

Discussions during the evening meal centered solely on their first flight. The men were eager for tomorrow and the promise of a longer flight pattern. They also voiced displeasure with the harsh criticisms received. Sitting at the end of a table, Byron merely listened to the conversation.

"Well, if today was any indication, it'll be a long six months," mused Forcance, poking at the remains of his meal.

"Bassa sure is tough," Surren growled, cocking his eyebrows at the navigator.

"He expects perfection!" exclaimed Arenth, his dark eyes on the officer's table.

Surren leaned back in his chair and frowned. He was a large man and quite capable of exerting his dominance on lesser individuals. Conflicts with Surren were frequent, as he believed only his opinion counted. Byron found the pilot difficult and overbearing.

"I think Bassa gets off on pointing out mistakes!" Surren exclaimed, his wide nose wrinkled in disgust.

"Such as overshooting your mark today?" Byron asked, tired of Surren's attitude.

The burly pilot shot him a piercing stare, his eyes reflecting his contempt. Byron returned his gaze, aware that no one would side against Surren. Byron was not favored by the other young men and he relied on Trindel's friendly nature to remain integrated with the others. Of course, his outcast position was by choice. He was not here to make friends.

"Once Bassa sees your team's reckless antics, I'm sure he'll have plenty to criticize," growled Surren, his lips pulled back in a malicious smile. "I bet you're the first one to go!"

Feeling his defenses rise, Byron returned the pilot's threatening scowl. "Maybe you should go home before you embarrass yourself further, Surren."

"Don't worry about me, hot shot!" Surren announced with a laugh, rising to his feet. "Your first crazy jump will be your last."

"Maybe I'll just jump up your ass!"

Surren scoffed at Byron's rebuttal and departed with his tray. Irritated, Byron shoved aside the remainder of his meal and leaned back in his seat. He would not be sent home early, regardless of what Surren believed. Failure was not an option at this point.

"I'm not jumping up anyone's ass," Trindel murmured to no one in particular.

After three weeks of actual flight time, which involved formations and basic drills, Byron was pleased to hear the men would begin target practice next.

Despite Surren's prediction, Byron and Trindel's performance was flawless so far. They could hardly deviate from pre-planned flight patterns, though. Byron took pride in his perfectionist nature and was determined to prove his wasn't as reckless as his record suggested.

There was no time off on Guaard and the men began target practice the day after the announcement. The flight patterns were pre-assigned, but Byron did not mind. The simulators recreated true flight but not without omissions in experience. The knowledge that one's life hung on the brink of every maneuver made for a unique experience. Byron appreciated the opportunity to acclimate to the sensation and he was able to focus on his aim. His shots were precise and on target.

They advanced from one target to multiples while still following flight patterns. The last run of multiples, the teams were given free rein to select their own approach. The targets were set equal distance apart in a triangular form. The young men would be judged on their precision of flight as well as accuracy.

Slated to go last, Byron watched the other ships with interest as he and Trindel awaited their turn. The pilots varied in their course of attacking the targets from above or below, but every ship ran a zigzag course. There were a few notable maneuvers, but no performance stood out from the others. Never one to conform to standards, Byron opted to try something entirely different.

What's our approach? asked Trindel.

Byron smiled, sensing his navigator's adventurous spirit. *Out and back,* he replied, visualizing the projected path.

Sounds good to me!

Trindel plotted their course and they waited for the signal. "715T, commence your run!" commanded Officer Jarth.

Byron throttled forward, aiming for the nearest target. The metallic orb glimmered enticingly in the darkness of space and he set his sights on the object. The moment they were in range, he fired on the orb. A laser of light struck the middle of the glowing sphere. A green light blinked, signifying a direct hit.

Continuing in a straight line, Byron aimed for the second target. Pivoting ninety degrees, he fired at the orb without a moment's hesitation. The green light flashed and he pursued the final target. Byron angled their Cosbolt just enough to avoid firing directly at the squadron and hit the third target with ease. Adjusting their trajectory, he and Trindel rejoined the other ships and fell into formation.

"Interesting approach," Jarth commented over the com. "All ships, return to base. We'll reconvene in the debriefing room."

Maybe we should've tried something else? offered Trindel.

I had a reason for that approach, Byron stated, prepared to defend their course of action.

Good, because I have a feeling Bassa will want to hear it!

Once they'd landed, the young men gathered in the debriefing room. Trindel preferred to sit up front, but he remained by his pilot when Byron selected the back row. Wishing to avoid scrutiny, Byron always selected a position that would provide a view of the room. He and Trindel settled in their seats and waited.

The officers' ships were equipped with recording devices that captured the performances of the teams in training. These images flashed on the screen as Officer Rellen discussed each team. No team had missed their mark, although one team was reprimanded for a yellow light, which signified they'd barely grazed the target. No one received a glowing report, as perfection was expected at their level. Byron had learned to adjust his expectations accordingly and was not surprised.

However, the last drill was discussed in depth. Each team's run was displayed on the large screen, and Officer Jarth suggested corrections for every approach. When Byron and Trindel's performance was exhibited, Jarth paused.

"Team 715T tackled the targets with an entirely different approach," he stated, his tone neutral. "Your maneuver around the second target was acceptable, but it forced you to adjust for the last target. Time was not a factor in this drill, but that adjustment might cost you at a later time."

Several heads turned in his direction, but Byron kept his eyes on the screen. "I felt a direct shot placed the other ships in the line of fire, sir," he explained.

"That is true," Jarth conceded. "The safety of your comrades is a priority, but never anticipate a miss."

He managed a curt nod, but inside Byron seethed. He never expected to miss his targets.

"The other pilots elected to hit the targets in order," observed Bassa from the corner of the room.

Every head turned to face the senior officer as he stepped closer. Bassa stared hard at Byron.

"What made you select that particular route?"

The room's attention shifted to Byron. He gathered his thoughts and projected what he hoped was a calm demeanor.

"Sir, a direct course placed our ship further from the base and exposed," he explained. "By shooting the far target second instead of last, I placed our ship on a return course to the base and within safe proximity of the squadron."

Bassa nodded, contemplating Byron's response. "A logical approach," he conceded, addressing the men as a whole. "You must learn to think through every decision. The drills are repetitive for a reason. Learn the basics now so that when the time comes, you can make these decisions quickly and accurately."

He surveyed the room, his expression serious. Turning to Jarth, Bassa nodded.

"You are dismissed!" Officer Jarth announced.

There was a great deal of shuffling as the young men rose to their feet. Bassa watched Byron shoot his navigator a triumphant smile. Trindel did not speak, but his smug expression indicated private thoughts were exchanged. Bassa observed the pair with interest as they departed.

Rellen approached Bassa as the room emptied. "Think you may have boosted his ego to new levels," he declared.

"Jarth had already pointed out the only error in his approach," Bassa replied. "Overall, he did select the most logical approach."

Crossing his arms, Rellen regarded Bassa with skepticism. "Thought you wanted to keep him under control?"

"Considering he deviated from the others at the first opportunity, I'm sure Byron will provide ample occasions for rebuke."

Rellen nodded in agreement and departed. Bassa remained, still pondering Byron's actions and explanation. He would indeed require close observation!

Chapter Three

Moving targets provided a new challenge for the men. All had scored well during simulator training, but real targets proved more difficult. Blatant misses received sharp disciplinary words from the instructors and resulted in additional practice for the offending teams. The days grew longer as the men logged more time in space than during previous exercises.

Byron and Trindel didn't miss a single target, and their maneuvers were quicker and tighter than the other teams. None of the pilots were as adept at sharp turns or exhibited such precise movements. However, Byron's flying carried with it a dangerous edge. Bassa was concerned the others would attempt to emulate his tactics and was forced to point out the misjudgment of Byron's strategy on more than one occasion. He sensed resentment, although the young man was wise enough to avoid a verbal confrontation, but the last thing Bassa needed was a squadron of reckless pilots.

Small drones were employed for the next phase of training. The devices were programmed not only to evade the trainees but to pursue as well. This added a new dimension to the exercises and the teams were forced to adjust their plan of attack. The first day with the drones resulted in two teams failing the exercise entirely. This was not acceptable to Bassa and he voiced his displeasure at the debriefing.

"The first time this squadron faces an attacker and two teams are neutralized!" he exclaimed, fury enveloping every syllable. "That is totally unacceptable. Did you forget every shred of simulator training? If you can't avoid a drone then you don't stand a chance in real combat."

Bassa glared at the young men. The trainees appeared uncomfortable and the offending teams visibly sank in their seats. Officer Jarth had gone over the day's exercise, chastising the unsuccessful teams, but Bassa wanted to ensure they

ALEX J. CAVANAUGH

understood this outcome would not be tolerated. Often one ship would miss its mark the first time out with the drones, but never two.

"We will repeat this exercise again tomorrow with no errors, understood? Bassa proclaimed.

The young men signified their compliance with a loud 'Yes, sir!' Bassa scanned the room, his deep scowl reflecting disgust with the sloppy flying he'd witnessed today. His gaze fell on Byron, who appeared unperturbed. The pilot had performed his drills without errors, although his flying still bordered on reckless. Bassa opted to save that observation for another time and not detract from today's issue.

"Teams 512T and 639T, report to my office," Bassa ordered. "Dismissed!"

On the heels of that order, Bassa exited through the side door. Byron rose to his feet and his gaze fell on Trindel's wide-eyed face. Unconcerned with the fate of the errant teams, he gestured for his navigator to proceed him out of the room. Trindel was silent as they returned to their quarters, for which Byron felt grateful. He did ponder Bassa's words while he showered, though. Perhaps the first team would go home tomorrow.

He'd just slipped on a shirt when a persistent beeping signified a visitor.

Byron?

Trindel's tentative inquiry echoed in his head. Not surprised to hear his partner's thoughts, Byron instructed his door to open. Trindel's forlorn expression greeted him and Byron invited him to enter.

"I'll be ready in a moment," he said, dropping into his chair and reaching for his boots.

Trindel nodded and shifted his stance. "What do you think is going to happen to Forcance and the others?" he implored.

Byron shrugged with indifference. "I don't know. It's Ganst and Forcance's second error."

"Do you think they'll be sent home?"

Pulling on his second boot, Byron glanced up at his navigator and sighed. Trindel possessed such a tender heart. He hated to see any man fail. However, the fate of the two teams

47

was beyond their control, and Byron was far more concerned with his own team's performance to care.

"Trindel, we can't worry about them," he said, raising his voice to emphasize his point. "Just focus on our team."

"You don't care what happens to the others?" Trindel asked in astonishment.

"Not really."

His navigator's eyes widened even further. Byron could sense his answer bothered Trindel. Rising to his feet, he approached his friend and clasped him on the shoulder.

"Trindel, my primary focus is our team. My obligations are to you, my navigator. I can't control what happens to the others, so I'm just concentrating on our performance, all right?"

Squeezing Trindel's shoulder in emphasis, Byron anxiously watched for his navigator's reaction. He did not want to alienate Trindel. Few claimed friendship with Byron and it was imperative that he protect his relationship with this young man.

Trindel finally nodded with reluctance. "I suppose you're right," he admitted.

"I'm always right," said Byron with a wink.

Trindel smiled and the worry vanished from his face.

"That's better!" Byron exclaimed, patting his navigator's shoulder. "Now, let's go eat. I'm starving!"

Byron poked at the last of his meal, contemplating another bite. The midday meal was usually light due to their afternoon flight schedule, but he doubted he could finish. As of late, his strained nerves left Byron with little appetite.

"Not hungry?" asked Trindel.

Glancing briefly at his navigator, Byron shook his head. He stabbed at his food one more time before dropping his fork and shoving aside his tray. Across from Trindel, Byron heard a sarcastic chuckle.

"He's busy working on today's crazy stunt," came a deep voice, eliciting laughter from those present.

Byron scowled at Surren, annoyed by his glib comment. "No, I'm contemplating how many shots it would take to bring you down. I'm guessing one," he countered.

Arising from his seat, Byron grabbed his tray. Surren refused to relinquish the final word, though.

"At least I'm not the prime example of reckless flying!"

Byron did not reply, allowing his unshielded contempt for Surren speak for itself. Depositing his tray on the rack, he elected to retreat to the hanger and prepare for today's flight lesson.

Surren's parting words continued to grate on Byron's mind. He and Trindel never made errors and accomplished designated tasks in record time. At the moment, they were the only team without a mark on their record; a testament to their skill and ability in the cockpit.

Yet at almost every debriefing, Bassa found fault with their flying. They either performed a maneuver incorrectly or approached a target from the wrong angle. None of these corrections had resulted in disciplinary action or a mark on their record, but the squadron witnessed Bassa's verbal reprimand every time. Byron and Trindel had become the brunt of many jokes, and he was tired of the snide remarks.

He paused at the lift, his eyes on the teleporter pod across the hall. The units were off limits to the young men until they began teleportation training in the ships. Byron knew how to teleport, though. He'd stolen a few rides during his youth and understood how to operate the device. Every time he climbed in the cockpit, the ship's teleporter called to him. Unfortunately, Bassa had seemed adamant that the trainees not begin that particular lesson until the appointed time, and those drills remained a month in the future.

Scowling as Bassa permeated his thoughts, Byron entered the lift and requested the hanger's level. He was annoyed the senior officer had selected his team as the example for every questionable maneuver. Byron could not understand the constant criticism. His decisions weren't irrational nor did they place his team in danger. For reasons unknown to Byron, he'd become the senior instructor's prime target, and he was growing tired of the negative attention.

He suited up early and returned to the hanger floor just as the other men arrived. Byron ignored the stares and proceeded to his ship for preflight inspection. By the time Trindel joined, him. Byron was already in the cockpit.

"Don't let Surren get to you," his navigator offered.

"I'm not worried about Surren," Byron stated flatly, slipping on his helmet.

When the trainees were in place, the day's assignment was announced. It involved several flight patterns and brief engagement of targets, no live ammunition. Byron wondered at what point they would fire real weapons and decided to worry about it later. He had enough problems and concerns at the moment to occupy his time.

Trindel kept them on course for every flight pattern change. They maneuvered with precision, staying in line with the other ships. The squadron had practiced these movements many times and the teams knew the commands by heart.

The promise of an encounter crossed Byron's mind just as two drones appeared on the radar. His muscles tensed in anticipation of a chase.

"Flank right, 439T and 227T, engage," Officer Rellen instructed.

Byron maintained their position in the ranks, watching with envy as the two ships veered toward the targets. The drones changed course and the Cosbolts were off in pursuit. Forced to concentrate on the squadron's course, Byron was unable to watch the ensuing dogfight.

Incoming! cried Trindel, flashing the coordinates to Byron.

"291T and 479T, engage!"

Byron gritted his teeth and held his course. The squadron circled and flew between the two skirmishes. The first two Cosbolts had neutralized their targets and were returning to join the others. Today's encounter was to be brief, which meant four to six drones at best. Byron's team was unlikely to see action today.

Below us!

Spying two more drones on the radar, Byron caught his breath. The current position of their ship placed them in close proximity.

"192T and 715T, engage!"

Byron dove toward the targets. The drones changed course, and Byron relayed his intended target to the other team. Without waiting for an answer, he pursued the drone on the left.

The drones separated and Byron kept his sights on his selected target. The drone veered right and dropped. Byron followed, pushing the throttle forward. The drone altered course, but Byron would not be so easily shaken. Circling around, their quarry continued to avoid Byron's sights. Trindel suggested a new strategy and his pilot agreed. They began to gain ground on the drone.

Trindel suddenly flashed a visual of the other drone. Their target nosedived just as the second drone crossed their path. Byron could not pass up the opportunity and relayed his intensions to Trindel. He fired one shot and a green light flashed in the corner of his screen. One down!

Pull up! Trindel ordered.

Byron had failed to noticed the other Cosbolt in pursuit of the drone. The ship hadn't altered its position and they were on a collision course. Their trajectory provided more room to go over the approaching ship, but they would lose sight of their original target. Ignoring his navigator's suggestion, Byron projected an alternate course of action and sent the ship into a nosedive.

A brief flash of panic arose from Trindel and was quickly replaced by instructions for a safe crossover. Their ship shot underneath the other fighter. Byron sensed the close proximity, but they passed without incident.

Byron caught sight of the other drone. Lining his sights, he fired two shots. The second beam reached its mark. He grinned in triumph as the green light flashed a second time.

Byron! cried the other pilot, anger in his thoughts.

We conveyed our intensions, he replied. *Didn't we?* he privately asked Trindel.

Just barely, but yes, his navigator replied.

That was still too damn close! the pilot claimed.

Not as close as you think, Byron answered in exasperation as they returned to the squadron.

The ships joined the others and assumed formation. They completed the flight pattern with no further drone encounters and returned to base.

Byron felt proud of his team's first multiple kill. He sensed the other pilot's annoyance but chose to ignore the implication he'd done anything wrong. Two targets in one day was a rare occurrence and he intended to relish the moment.

The debriefing room meeting began with the analysis of each ship's flight pattern. The instructors discussed the target approaches of every pilot, making suggestions and corrections where necessary. Byron and Trindel's turn began with a compliment for the double kill. They had fired the fewest shots to achieve this goal, which also garnered praise. Officer Char offered a couple suggestions for their approach – a standard procedure. However, he paused when their final dive maneuver appeared on the screen and Bassa stepped forward.

"Why did you select that course?" he asked, his brows pulled together.

Sensing disapproval, Byron straightened his shoulders. "Going over the other Cosbolt meant we'd lose sight of our target and delay our pursuit. I knew we had enough clearance and seized the opportunity."

Bassa's expression did not alter and he turned to Trindel. "Did you share in his decision?"

"Well, yes," stammered Trindel. "And I did relay our intensions," he added, shifting in his seat.

Bassa's gaze returned to Byron. "Your maneuver assured acquirement of your target. However," he said in a firm voice, "I don't want to see another close call."

"We were within regulation distance …" began Byron.

" 'Within' being the key word! No more close crossovers, period," the senior officer admonished. "In fact, tomorrow's lesson will focus on crossovers until I am satisfied you can perform the maneuver precisely."

A scattering of moans were heard. Bassa's eyes were focused on Byron, who returned the man's stare with an equal amount of intensity. The senior officer's scowl deepened and Byron belatedly shielded his angry thoughts.

"That will be all for today," Bassa informed the young men. "Byron, I will see you in my office immediately."

Byron's body flushed with anger. Grasping his computer pad, he leapt to his feet and all but shoved Trindel out of the way. His navigator hastily stepped aside, his expression anxious. Providing Trindel with no opportunity to speak, Byron stormed out of the room. He reached the lifts ahead of the other trainees, but not before Surren's voice reached his ears.

"I told you those crazy antics would get you in trouble!" he exclaimed in triumph.

Shooting Surren a scathing glare, Byron stepped into the open lift.

"Level Two, now!" he growled, willing the doors to close.

None of the young men reached the lift in time and Byron rode in silence. The compartment was anything but still, though. He saw no need to shield his turbulent emotions, and the fury pounding between his ears was deafening. It overshadowed the hum of the lift and emanated unchecked from his body. Had Trindel joined him, Byron's navigator would've exited at the first available floor.

The doors sprang open, revealing an empty hallway. Byron strode out of the lift with a purpose, fury still pounding at his chest. The classrooms were on this level, but no sounds emanated from the rooms. He paused at a fork in the hallway, glancing in both directions. To his relief, no other personnel were present at this time of day. His passage would go unnoticed.

Turning to his left, Byron began the long walk to the officers' wing. He'd never been summoned to Bassa's office before, but every trainee knew the way. No man wanted to see the officers' wing, as doing so implied a disciplinary action, but everyone had to remember the exact location.

Byron turned the corner and proceeded down another long, white corridor. He wondered if Bassa's office resided on the far end of the complex just to make this walk more uncomfortable. If designed to give an errant pilot time to think, it was doing nothing for his state of mind.

Rounding yet another turn, he entered the officers' wing. Byron passed two sets of doors and paused at the double doors leading to Bassa's office. He eyed the doors with trepidation, reluctant to enter. Taking a deep breath, he attempted to quell the rising agitation and clear his thoughts. He could not afford a direct confrontation with the senior officer. Waving his hand over the panel, Byron was immediately told to enter.

The doors slid apart, revealing a large, well-lit room. Bassa was at his desk, his eyes on his computer screen. Byron stepped into the room and the doors silently closed. Bassa did not look up or give any indication that he was aware of a visitor.

"Sir?" Byron said, unsure what he was to do next.

"Have a seat," Bassa ordered, his eyes never leaving the screen.

Approaching the desk, Byron dropped heavily into the chair on the right. He felt like a disobedient boy, about to receive punishment for his unruly actions and attitude. He refrained from slumping in the chair and held a respectable stance with his hands in his lap.

Bassa was still staring at the screen, and Byron found his gaze wandering to the walls. The numerous plaques of recognition reflected Bassa's status as one of the best navigators ever to serve the fleet. The awards were many and Byron absently wondered why he would give it all up to be an instructor.

His eyes dropped to the desk. Byron noticed the picture frame, turned just enough for viewing, and frowned at the image. The young man in the photo could have been his twin. The eyes were closer together, but the shape of his face resembled his own, as did the jet black hair. The similarity was uncanny and Byron fidgeted in his seat. His movement caught Bassa's attention.

"So, you do not agree with my assessment of your flight today?" the senior officer inquired, leaning away from his desk.

Byron suspected the question to be a test, and his future on Guaard might depend on his answer. However, tact was not his strong suit. He was not about to back down from his convictions now.

"No, sir, I do not," he replied.

Cocking one eyebrow, Bassa regarded the young pilot with interest. "Elaborate."

"I was within regulation distance, sir," Byron stated with force. "At no time was either ship in danger. We relayed our intentions, performed the maneuver, and neutralized both targets!"

Bassa did not give any indication of his thoughts on the matter. Sensing he'd probably crossed the line, Byron prepared for the rebuttal.

Bassa raised one eyebrow. "Your past history," he said slowly, "indicates you have a problem with authority."

Clamping his jaws tight, lest he say something inappropriate, Byron struggled to shield his resentful thoughts. He was tired of his less-than-perfect record being thrust in his face. He managed to control his tongue and thoughts, but unfortunately he was not so quick to conceal his expression. Belatedly, Byron realized he was viewing the senior officer through slitted eyes.

"Well, that ends right here," Bassa proclaimed, his deep voice loud in the confines of the room. "Right now!"

Byron did not visibly flinch, but he knew that tone of voice all too well. He now stood at the brink, staring over the edge of a very deep chasm. One more step and he would cross the point of no return. Despite the anger coursing through his body, Byron did not want to lose his only opportunity.

"Yes, sir," he replied, conceding to the senior officer's authority.

Bassa stared hard at the young pilot, as if judging his sincerity. "Unless you want your records made public," he countered.

Byron's eyes widened in horror. Bassa possessed the authority, but he wouldn't dare throw open Byron's records for the entire world to view. Judging from the senior officer's stern expression, though, it was far from an empty threat.

"No, sir," Byron responded, his shoulders slumping in defeat.

Bassa took a deep breath and leaned back even further in his chair. "I expect total compliance and obedience from those residing here on Guaard. And I expect even more from you!"

Puzzled, Byron forced his gaze to remain steady. Bassa paused and cocked his head.

"Do you know why, Byron?"

"No, sir," Byron answered, confused.

"Because your skills in the cockpit far exceed that of the other pilots' abilities."

Byron paused. That was the last answer he expected to hear.

"I have two objectives with your training," continued Bassa. "First, to make sure you possess the necessary discipline to master and control those skills. Second, to prevent the other pilots from attempting maneuvers of which they do not possess the necessary skills to achieve."

Byron could scarcely believe his ears. "Yes, sir," he stammered.

"My comments today were meant to discourage the other pilots from trying your trick, as they would only meet with failure."

Nodding, Byron took a deep breath. "So, my maneuver was not wrong, sir?"

Bassa's eyes narrowed. "No."

His mind reeling, Byron grasped at the senior officer's assessment.

"I have seen many exceptional pilots come through Guaard. If we can properly develop your skills, you have the potential to be one of the best. However, I will not pass an undisciplined pilot. Understood?"

"Yes, sir!" Byron answered.

"Now, this conversation remains here, understood?"

"Yes, sir!"

Bassa leaned forward in his chair. "You are dismissed."

Byron leapt to his feet, eager to depart. A thought occurred to him.

"Sir?" he inquired. "How will I know when I make a real mistake?"

The senior officer met his eyes and Byron detected the fainted trace of a smile on his lips.

"You'll either be dead or on your way home!"

Chapter Four

Byron leaned away from his computer screen, pleased by the assessment of his previous day's flight. He and Trindel had performed well and without errors, and he looked forward to their afternoon session.

As ordered, Byron never mentioned the discussion in Bassa's office, not even to his navigator. He'd received several reprimands since that time, but not one resulted in a mark on his record. However, he'd endured numerous condemning comments and taunts from the other trainees. Byron had bit his tongue, fearful of Bassa's retribution should he reveal their conversation. Byron longed to tell the truth, as it would provide an opportunity to rub his superiority in their faces.

He suited up with the other trainees that afternoon and sensed the excitement in the room. Today's exercise involved an all-out dogfight that would require every ship to participate. After almost four months of training and individual encounters, they would at last face a real battle.

Trindel's enthusiasm was obvious, and Byron hoped he could control his navigator's nervous energy once they engaged the drones. Suppressing his own zeal, he kept his team in line during the basic maneuvers and necessary pre-encounter drills. Fortunately, they did not have long to wait.

"Incoming!" Officer Char's voice boomed over the com.

A large mass of drones appeared on the radar. Byron made visual contact with the approaching ships and realized they were a far greater force than the squadron. He felt his pulse quicken as they prepared to engage.

The instructor relayed orders and Byron turned his attention to their first target. Rolling to the right, he turned to face the enemy. The approaching drones opened fire at once and the squadron split as pilots took evasive action.

Dodging the incoming fire, Byron dove and then immediately climbed to meet his intended target. The drone banked
to the left, and he pursued with earnest, surprised the ship
would take the defensive position. The triumph was short-
lived, though. Trindel announced that another drone approached from the rear.

Without hesitation, Byron halted their forward progress.
He swung their Cosbolt around to face the attacker. Simu-
lated laser blasts flew over their ship as the drone opened
fire. Adjusting his sights, Byron returned the gesture. His
second shot struck the drone and neutralized the ship.

There was no time to gloat. Trindel updated him on their
current situation. Their original target had circled and was
preparing to engage. Byron turned his attention to the incoming drone and calculated their best plan of attack. Loath
to take the defensive position, he flew straight at the ship
and opened fire. Their target took evasive action and Byron
throttled forward in pursuit.

Their quarry led the team on a wild chase. Byron's navigator kept him informed of the position of the other ships, lest a
new drone engage in the chase. All fighters and enemy ships
appeared occupied at the moment, though. Byron remained
focused on their target, unwilling to be so easily shaken.

The drone pulled to the right as if to skirt around an inca-
pacitated ship. The movement seemed wrong to Byron,
though. Rather than follow the drone, he pulled back and sent
their Cosbolt on a steep climb. He sensed Trindel's mental
exclamation, although he uttered not a sound. Abruptly, he
forced the ship to dive. Trindel flashed him the location of the
drone and Byron grasped the throttle in anticipation.

Their target emerged from underneath the lifeless Cosbolt,
angled to climb. Before the drone had an opportunity, Byron
released one single shot. Without the need to fire another, he
neutralized their target.

Damn good! Trindel's exuberant thought echoed in his
mind.

Byron allowed himself a brief smile of satisfaction. *Get me
back in the action!*

Trindel guided him toward the heat of the battle. They
noted several disabled drones, and a couple Cosbolts dotted

the battlefield as well. Seeking another target, Byron had no time to contemplate the fate of those who'd failed so quickly today. Trindel scanned for the next drone and he indicated a possible opportunity to his pilot. Byron noted the Cosbolt approaching at a dangerous speed, a drone following close on its tail. An idea struck him.

Tell them when to yield, Byron instructed, flying the ship directly at their incoming comrades.

Trindel seemed to grasp the plan and relayed the information to the other ship's navigator. Byron throttled forward at top speed. The fleeing Cosbolt approached and collision appeared imminent. Byron held his breath, waiting for just the precise moment.

The incoming ship veered, providing Byron a clean shot. He fired, the blast neutralizing the drone, and initiated a jump at once to avoid impact with the disabled target. As he teleported, Trindel informed him of another drone in pursuit of a training vessel.

Their ship emerged on the fringes of the battle, and Byron felt relief that his navigator's sense of placement in space was so accurate. He did not pause to relish their success. Catching sight of Vitar's ship, his attention shifted to the drone on his tail. Byron at once set off in pursuit.

It's not giving us a clear shot, Trindel thought as they chased the vessels.

No, it's not, Byron replied, swinging wide. Their angle still did not provide a safe opportunity for engaging the drone, as it was too close to the Cosbolt.

Damn! he exclaimed. *Give me coordinates to jump in from the side.*

Can you do it?

Yes.

Trindel relayed the information. Byron acted upon it without hesitation. The teleporter vibrated in response and the view outside the cockpit altered. The drone ship was about to cross their path and Byron prepared to fire.

Another Cosbolt appeared just off their nose. The occupants of the ship echoed panic as they attempted evasive actions. Byron realized their forward progress meant that a collision was inevitable.

Without consulting Trindel, he jumped the ship. They reappeared a short distance away and facing the depths of space. His navigator expressed shock and Byron had to admit the abrupt jump surprised him as well. Gathering his wits, he requested their present location as he spun around the ship. Trindel's response was shaky but prompt.

Vitar and his pursuer are coming straight at us, he indicated.

Byron observed their comrade's ship and decided to follow through with his original intentions. *Tell them to yield at the last moment as well,* he ordered, throttling forward.

Holding his breath, Byron flew at Vitar's ship. He sensed Trindel's rising concern of a close encounter. Byron assured his navigator of their success, though.

Vitar exhibited nerves of steel and waited until the last possible moment to pull left. Receiving a clear shot, Byron fired at the drone. His aim was perfect, but their close proximity provided no opportunity for evasive action. Within that split moment, Byron made a decision. Before Trindel could respond, he teleported the ship.

Emerging at their previous jump location, Byron breathed a sigh of relief. His team had neutralized four targets today with no sustained damage. As the ship spun around, he realized that would be their final count. The battle was almost over and the last drone faced annihilation. After the intensity of the fight, Byron hoped his team had scored the most kills.

How did you do that? exclaimed Trindel in amazement.

Do what? The jump? Byron asked, contemplating the question. His answer was cut short, though.

"715T, return to formation at once!"

The voice over the com was Bassa's and he sounded furious. Byron felt his stomach sink. What had they done wrong now?

That didn't sound encouraging, Trindel noted, his solemn thought tinged with concern.

Irritation rising in his chest, Byron clenched his fists. "Damn!" he muttered under his breath.

Spirits dampened, his team returned to the squadron. The remaining drone was neutralized and the trainees assumed formation. Facing the scene of the battle, Byron noted three Cosbolts drifting among the lifeless drones. After a moment, power returned to the ships. The downed teams slowly joined the squadron while the drones proceeded toward the base. Byron hoped the three ships who'd failed to evade the drones would receive the brunt of Bassa's wrath. He still had no idea what error he and Trindel had committed.

Too many jumps? Trindel offered as they returned to base. *They were all successful, though!*

Trindel said no more. Byron's irritation continued to grow as they proceeded to land and taxi into the hanger. A couple of the men commented on his team's kills, but Byron's sullen mood discouraged further conversation. Retreating to the debriefing room, he dropped into his chair with incredible force and fumed in silence as the others joined him.

The officers did not enter until all of the trainees were present. One look at Bassa's angry expression and Byron's defenses rose in anticipation. This session would not be pleasant.

Officer Rellen gestured to Morden, and the instructor stepped forward. He glanced at his computer pad before scanning the room.

"Your first major battle was not without mistakes," began Morden, his tone grim, "including three downed ships. Fortunately, all drones were neutralized within an acceptable period of time. Several teams had multiple kills, and Byron and Trindel possessed the highest total with four ..."

"With a matching four jumps," interjected Bassa, his loud voice commanding everyone's attention. "And that is unacceptable!"

Byron felt his face flush with anger and embarrassment. "All four jumps were successful, sir," he protested.

"You were damned lucky!" the senior officer retorted. "We've repeatedly informed you of the dangers of multiple jumps, as your teleporter will fail with such misuse. Two successive jumps drain the element. You failed to give the teleporter time to recharge before jumping again. Those last two jumps were pure luck, and you never rely on luck!"

His words vibrated the walls of the room, punctuated by the fury emanating from the senior officer. Byron's jaw was tight as he held back the ugly words that rose to his lips. He could not lose his temper now. Beside him, Trindel shifted in his seat.

"Sir, if I may?" Byron's navigator offered.

"I don't want to hear it!" exclaimed Bassa, effectively silencing Trindel. "You are to report to my office the moment we finish here."

Consumed with fury, Byron paid little notice to the remainder of the debriefing. He had no doubt his team would receive their first mark today. While the successive jumps pushed the limit, not one had met with failure. It angered Byron that they would be punished despite their success. It annoyed him even more that their perfect record would now be tainted.

His attention returned when the instructor covered the incident that led to their third jump. It was but a small consolation that Byron and Trindel were not at fault, as Kernse's team was responsible for the ill-timed jump that placed both ships in danger. While this removed some of the blame for their third teleporting attempt, it did not excuse the fourth jump. The ensuing lecture from Officer Morden irritated Byron further, although it would pale in comparison to what awaited his team in Bassa's office.

The senior officer's gaze only strayed from the pair when he berated the three failed teams. His senses were not required to detect the growing fury in Byron, as the boy's expression revealed his emotions without question. Bassa did not allow the young man's resentment to alter his judgment, though. The pair would receive a berating that would occupy their thoughts for a long time.

When the debriefing drew to an end, Bassa exited without reiterating his instructions. Still furious with Byron's team for their blatant disregard for protocol and safety, he retreated to his office to await the young men. He'd been patient with Byron thus far, going out of his way to ensure the boy's skills were properly developed while ignoring his more daring antics. However, today's reckless stunt would not go unpunished.

When the chime announced his visitors, Bassa bellowed for Byron and Trindel to enter. The young men complied, and he noted their expressions at once. Trindel appeared pale, his eyes filled with apprehension, but Byron's face revealed indignation and defiance. This did not settle well with the senior officer and his fury was renewed.

"What do the regulations say about multiple jumps?" he demanded.

Byron took a deep breath. "Jumps should not be attempted closer than five minutes apart," he replied, his eyes cold.

"And how many jumps did you perform today in just under nine minutes?"

"Four, sir."

"How many?"

"Four, sir!" Byron and Trindel cried in unison.

Bassa stared hard at the men as he rose to his feet. Neither moved, but he sensed Trindel's mental flinch.

"You placed yourself and others at risk," he stated. "Jumping without allowing the teleporter to recharge is reckless and dangerous. Your third jump might be excused, but certainly not the final jump. That was sheer stupidity!"

Byron shifted his stance, but his face bore no traces of apology. Annoyed by the young man's continued defiance, Bassa realized there was only one way to reach the arrogant pilot.

"Not only will this result in a mark on your record, but I am considering dismissing you both from the program."

As if he'd just been slapped, Byron's eyes grew wide and his jaw dropped. For a brief moment, Bassa sensed fear in the young man. Byron's expression altered to one of indignation, his eyes narrowing to mere slits. Bassa wondered what foolish words the young man was about to spew and waited for the response.

"Sir?" came Trindel's timid voice. "If I may say something?"

Shifting his attention, Bassa scowled. "Out with it!"

Glancing at his pilot, Trindel swallowed hard. "Sir, Byron didn't use the teleporter's power on our last two jumps," he offered, the words tumbling out of his mouth in a rush.

"What do you mean?" demanded Bassa, assuming Trindel was searching for any excuse at this point.

"Our teleporter's power was at zero when he made those jumps, sir."

Confounded, Bassa stared at Trindel. Such a feat was preposterous. Pilots could not fold space without the teleporter. Unless by chance ...

Bassa turned to his computer and pulled up the transcript from their flight. Requesting the power level of the teleporter at the time of each jump, Bassa eyed the screen with skepticism. The first jump had required sixty percent of the unit's energy and the teleporter's power only recharged to fifty percent by the time they performed the second jump. It was the final two jumps that caused Bassa to pause in bewilderment. The teleporter's energy level rested at zero on both occasions, just as Trindel had claimed.

Bassa glanced up at the two men. Byron appeared confused and his angry thoughts had subsided. The senior officer stared at the young pilot as he digested the full implication of this new development.

Settling into his chair, Bassa retrieved Byron's records. Searching through the history, he attempted to locate the young man's last psyche evaluation. There had to be some mention of extraordinary powers that would explain jumps without using the teleporter's power. However, the most recent testing had occurred over ten years ago and was noted as just above normal.

Perplexed, Bassa began searching for any mention of additional powers. Byron's record was lengthy, but most of it covered physical skill or disciplinary measures. Frustrated by the lack of information, Bassa scrolled through the pages. The content provided no answers, though. Nothing in Byron's records indicated that he could teleport using his own power.

Bassa leaned away from the screen in frustration. He regarded the young men with annoyance, although the feeling was not directed at them. Byron and Trindel appeared quite confused and continued to wait in silence. Bassa decided there was only one way to discover the truth.

"I am ordering you both to remain silent on this matter, understood?"

"Yes, sir!" they replied.

Bassa nodded at the young navigator. "Trindel, you are dismissed."

He hesitated, glancing first at his pilot. With a nod, Trindel turned and beat a hasty retreat. Byron did not move, and Bassa thought he detected anxiety.

Leaning forward, he reached for the com. "Chief Toka?"

There was a pause before the flight chief responded. "Yes, sir?"

"How soon can you have 715T ready for launch?"

"I can have it ready in ten minutes, sir!"

"Make it happen, Toka."

Releasing the com button, Bassa retrieved his flight gloves and rose to his feet. "We're going to test this ability of yours," he announced to Byron. "Come with me."

Stepping around his desk, he gestured for the pilot to precede him out of the office. Byron complied, his apprehension at odds with his usual confident demeanor. Bassa wondered if he had at last found a means by which to break through Byron's cocky shell.

Upon entering the hallway, the young man hesitated. Bassa strode purposefully toward the teleportation pod, trusting Byron would follow. Determined to know the truth, he wanted to get Byron in the pilot's seat without further delay. The boy followed without question and joined Bassa in the pod.

Still dressed for flight, Bassa waited while the young man donned his suit. He sensed Byron's growing nervousness and wondered if he was aware of how strongly his feelings were projecting. Other than confidence and resentment, the pilot never allowed his emotions to show. Since Bassa was unsure what triggered the young man's extra powers, he let Byron remain on edge and tense. Perhaps emotion and adrenaline had fueled his ability.

They performed the necessary preflight check before departing. Byron appeared uncomfortable with the senior officer in the navigator's seat, but he settled once they entered space. Bassa relayed the coordinates and Byron set the proper course.

We'll perform two consecutive jumps and drain the teleporter's power first, understood? Bassa thought as he selected the locations of their jumps.

Yes, sir, Byron responded, his mental voice loud and clear.

Bassa focused on the young man's mind. *First jump!* he instructed.

A moment of darkness signified Byron's compliance and they emerged at the new location. Bassa confirmed their success before giving his pilot new coordinates.

Second jump!

The ship arrived without incident at the next location. Bassa checked the teleporter's power and discovered the two jumps had indeed drained the device. The next jump would rely solely on Byron's unique ability.

Teleporter's energy is at zero. Return to our original position, he instructed.

Sir, I don't even know how I did it, Byron protested. *I don't think...*

Don't think! I'm ordering you to jump, pilot. Now, jump!

The thought had barely left his mind when everything went black. The stars returned outside the cockpit and Bassa checked their location. Byron had performed a precise jump and with no energy in the teleporter. Bassa leaned his head against the seat and contemplated the facts.

Only one in 800,000 Cassans had extraordinary abilities. Of those possessing heightened powers, fewer still became pilots. In all his years of flying and instructing, Bassa had only once met such a fighter pilot. The man revealed his ability to just a select few, as it was feared those lacking such talent would try to emulate his multiple jumps and meet with failure. Now he was faced with a second pilot who could funnel his own power into the teleporter.

Bassa had worried that the other pilots might attempt some of Byron's more daring moves. Now the young man possessed yet another trick they could not hope to perform with any amount of success. The senior officer's efforts to suppress chaos would really be put to the test with this new development.

His thoughts shifted as he became aware of Byron's overflowing pride and elation. The young man sensed his great accomplishment and was making no attempt to hide his excitement. Bassa needed to regain control of the situation and fast.

New coordinates, he told Byron, selecting the location of their next jump.

Confirming the position, Byron jumped the ship once again. Bassa checked the teleporter's energy level and discovered his pilot hadn't even touched the five percent of restored power. The young man had jumped twice now using his own abilities.

Another jump, sir? Byron inquired, his eagerness obvious.

No, Bassa replied. *Return to base.*

Once in the hanger, Byron turned to face Bassa as they exited the cockpit.

"Sir, are we still receiving a mark on our record?" he asked, his demeanor humble.

Bassa straightened his shoulders. "I will make that decision tomorrow," he answered, dismissing Byron with a curt nod.

The young man retreated to the flight room to change. Bassa remained by the ship for a moment, lost in thought. He was in unchartered territory now and needed to contemplate his course of action. Byron would require guidance beyond standard Cosbolt training. Moreover, it would need to be performed in secret.

The boy's living up to his challenging reputation, Bassa thought.

The following day, squadron training focused on defensive combat maneuvers. Byron had anticipated teleporting regulations and procedures and felt relieved. The jabs he had received from the other trainees frustrated him, even more so because he couldn't reveal his unique ability.

He'd discussed the matter in private with Trindel. His navigator appeared in awe of the talent. Byron's own excitement was dampened by the thought of a mark on their record, though. It might even result in failure to pass the course, and that thought chilled him to the core.

Their afternoon flight was unmarred by incident and the instructor spent little time discussing their performance. Byron wondered when his team would learn of their fate. As the debriefing ended, though, he heard Bassa's voice in his head.

Report to my office.

Meeting the senior officer's gaze, Byron nodded in affirmation. He turned and realized Trindel was staring at his teammate, his eyes wide.

Let's go, he told Trindel, gesturing for his friend to move.

They rode the lift in silence. Trindel's anxiety filled the small compartment and Byron shifted uncomfortably. He wished his navigator could exhibit some control over his feelings. Whatever news they were about to receive, he didn't want to give Bassa the satisfaction of knowing it bothered them.

They exited the lift and walked toward Bassa's office. As the men approached the double doors, Byron turned to Trindel.

Relax. You're making me nervous!

I'll try, Trindel replied with a sigh. *I guess it can't be that bad. After all, he didn't call us out in front of everyone.*

Straightening his shoulders, Byron passed his hand over the press plate and announced their arrival. The doors slid aside and the young men entered, apprehensive but prepared to receive their fate.

Sitting at his desk, Bassa gestured for them to take a seat. Byron and Trindel sank into the large chairs, unable to read the senior officer's expression as he stared at the pair. Byron grasped the armrests and waited.

"You have presented me with a unique situation," Bassa announced, his eyes on Byron. "Exceptional abilities are incredibly rare, and for reasons beyond my understanding, yours were missed in earlier testing. However, you do possess the mental ability to jump even when the teleporter lacks energy by channeling your own into the unit."

Trindel shot Byron a quick glance, but his thoughts remained concealed. Byron kept his expression neutral and waited for Bassa to continue.

"First, I need to assess the extent of your ability. Tomorrow after the debriefing, you are to report to Officer Char for a full evaluation," instructed the senior officer.

"Yes, sir," Byron replied. Tomorrow's flight lesson was to be brief, giving the men a rare afternoon of freedom. However, if the psyche test meant he'd be free to jump more often, Byron was willing to sacrifice a few hours of down time.

"Once the extent of your ability has been assessed, you and I will practice every afternoon after the debriefing," Bassa announced. "When I've determined your skill level, Trindel will join you in the cockpit and I will supervise from my Darten. Understood?"

"Yes, sir," the men said in unison.

Bassa regarded them with cautious eyes. "During standard training, you are to refrain from performing more than one jump per exercise unless otherwise instructed."

"One jump, sir?" exclaimed Byron, the words tumbling out of his mouth before he could think.

"One jump! That is a direct order, pilot."

Byron felt his shoulders slump. "Yes, sir," he answered, disappointed by the turn of events. Many of his trademark maneuvers required jumps.

"I want you to focus on your skills during regular lessons. You will have ample opportunity to jump during our sessions. I don't want the other pilots getting it in their heads that they can make multiple jumps without consequence. Limiting your jumps is one way to accomplish that feat. Concealing your ability is another. Under no circumstances are you to reveal your ability to the other trainees or discuss our private sessions. Understood?"

"Yes, sir," Byron and Trindel replied.

"If you are fortunate enough to complete this course and join the fleet, your ability will remain concealed from all but your superiors. Once you have joined a real squadron, you will appreciate the need for secrecy.

"Any questions?"

"No, sir," Trindel answered without hesitation.

Byron sensed his navigator was eager to depart, but the issue of their record weighed on his mind.

"Sir?" he asked, feeling apprehensive. "Are we receiving a mark for yesterday's actions?"

Bassa appeared to contemplate his answer. Byron gripped the armrests even tighter and held his breath.

"After considering the conditions which lead to the reprimand," the senior officer announced, "I have decided not to include the incident in your permanent records."

A great weight fell from Byron's shoulders and he flashed his navigator a grin. Trindel sighed and smiled in return. Their record would remain unmarred.

"I will expect more from your team, though," Bassa warned, his deep voice commanding their attention. "Do not give me cause to reconsider my decision."

"No, sir!" they cried in unison.

"You are dismissed."

Neither required prodding, and the young men retreated from Bassa's office in haste. Once in the hallway and at a safe distance, Trindel let loose a loud exclamation of relief.

"No mark on our record!" he cried, patting Byron's shoulder.

"And we get specialized training, too," Byron added, eager to begin those lessons. It meant extra work and longer hours, but he suspected those flights would add value to his team.

"Hope it won't be long before I get to join you. Bassa's so thorough, he might hold you hostage for weeks," Trindel observed.

Byron rolled his eyes. "Don't even think such a thing!"

The thought of weeks trapped in the cockpit with the senior instructor sounded like torture. Byron hoped he could avoid such a scenario. He wanted to enjoy his special privileges, not dread the whole experience!

Chapter Five

Byron landed his ship with the utmost precision, pulling back on the throttle as the fighter glided down the runway. Easing into position, he felt his navigator's assistance. A second later, the runners locked into place and ship came to a halt.

Closing his eyes, Byron willed his muscles to relax. Today's session had exceeded intense. Bassa had run him through numerous scenarios and multiple jumps, pushing his limits to the extreme. Byron had performed the maneuvers without error, but it required every ounce of energy to maintain the necessary level of concentration. Adjusting to the nuances of Bassa's style of navigating had added to the challenge as well.

Once his initial solo sessions were complete, Byron had assumed all subsequent lessons would involve Trindel. To his dismay, Bassa insisted on one flight a week with his pupil. Byron found these flights uncomfortable. He was familiar with Trindel's subtle guidance and presence in his head. Bassa's navigation was more assertive and commanding. Byron didn't enjoy sharing his thoughts with the senior officer, either.

Their vessel taxied into the hanger and Byron shut off the engines. His emergence from the cockpit was slow, and his nerves were still on edge from the flight. Grasping the side of the ship to steady his trembling body, he realized Bassa was waiting for him at the foot of the ladder.

Your flight today was good! Bassa thought as Byron descended the steps with care. *I sensed fatigue after the final jump, though.*

I was still able to perform, sir, Byron replied, turning to face the senior officer.

You must understand your limits. That is the primary purpose of our solo flights.

Yes, sir, Byron answered, his thoughts guarded.

Bassa's brows came together, his eyes scrutinizing the young man's face. Byron could not hide his physical exhaustion, but he refused to divulge his mental state. He tolerated the invasion of his mind during their flights out of necessity. However, outside of the cockpit he preferred privacy.

I will be taking the evening meal in my office, Bassa announced. *You will join me.*

Dining with the senior officer held no appeal, but Byron sensed it was order rather than a request. *Yes, sir.*

With a nod, Bassa took his leave. Feeling apprehensive, Byron retreated to the flight room to change. Bassa had a purpose for their meeting tonight. Byron wondered what aspect of his attitude required adjustment this time.

Trindel visited his quarters just before the evening meal. Byron's navigator had enjoyed a couple hours of free time today and his high spirits reflected that liberty. His afternoon anything but relaxing, Byron resented his lack of opportunity to rejuvenate during the meal.

"How was the flight?" Trindel asked, leaning against the door.

"Exhausting," Byron conceded, rising from his chair. "I'd rather fly with you."

Trindel grinned, his eyes twinkling. "Appreciate that! So, it was really tough today?"

"Very!" exclaimed Byron, rubbing his eyes. His temples still throbbed from the multiple jumps and he contemplated taking a sedative for the pain. His headache would only increase during the evening meal.

"Just hate having him in my head," he growled.

His navigator shifted his feet. Byron sensed a quick suppression of emotion. Frowning, he gestured for Trindel to speak.

"Byron, you don't like anyone in your head," he bluntly stated.

"I don't object to your presence."

"Only because I'm your navigator," explained Trindel. "Otherwise, I doubt I'd enjoy that privilege."

Taken aback by his words, Byron stared at his navigator in disbelief. His friendship with Trindel wasn't just out of necessity. Their exchanges were genuine. Byron was open with his friend, and the trust ran beyond their professional relationship.

However, the validity of Trindel's statement struck Byron even as he tried to deny the possibility. He'd not allowed any individual to penetrate his thoughts until their pairing over a year ago. The years of impersonal instructors and specialists probing his young mind had caused Byron to develop an impenetrable mental shield. The sensation of another's presence in his head felt like an invasion of his privacy, and he'd gone through several navigators before discovering one whose thoughts didn't feel hostile. Trindel had become his last option at that point, which lent truth to his statement. Byron only allowed the navigator access to his mind because he had no other choice.

Stunned by this realization, Byron didn't know what to say. Closing his mouth, which had fallen open as he processed Trindel's observation, he stared helplessly at his friend.

"It's okay," Trindel offered, shrugging his shoulders. "Doesn't bother me. You've got your reasons for privacy."

Byron nodded, still searching for the right words to say. Trindel flashed him a smile and pushed away from the door.

"Ready for the evening meal?" he asked, quick to dismiss the whole conversation.

Shoulders slumping, Byron shook his head. "I'm to report to Bassa's office," he sighed.

"Oh? Why?"

"He probably wants to berate me. I'll find out soon enough," he added, glancing at the time.

"Maybe it's something good!" Trindel offered, touching the door panel. "I'll catch you later. Enjoy yourself!"

Enjoy myself, right, Byron thought. He did not relish the idea of sharing a meal with the man.

He did make an effort to adjust his attitude by the time he reached Bassa's office, though. The senior officer bade him to enter and Byron cleared his mind as the doors opened. He entered and noted two trays of food on the desk.

"Have a seat," Bassa instructed.

Byron sat down and edged his chair closer to the desk. The senior officer had not touched his food yet. Bassa waited until Byron was situated before lifting his fork.

"I think you will find this a more suitable meal," he offered, stabbing a slice of meat.

Byron had wondered if the officers ate better than the trainees. Judging from the generous portions and appetizing smells, his assumptions were correct.

Byron had not felt like eating when he arrived, but his appetite returned as the delicious aromas enveloped his nose. Selecting a piece of meat slathered in sauce, he lifted the fork to his mouth. The taste and texture rivaled the best meal he'd ever experienced on Cassa.

Raising his gaze, he realized Bassa was watching his reaction. He swallowed and nodded, reaching for his napkin. The senior officer smiled.

"More to your liking?"

"Yes, sir."

Bassa retrieved another piece of meat and Byron followed suit. The strips were fresh and bore none of the processed flavor predominant in the dining hall's fare. He tried the vegetables next and was surprised by the crispness. The bread tasted fresh as well.

"Today was our last session," Bassa suddenly announced. "You and Trindel must be sharp for your final two weeks of training."

"We're finished, sir?"

"Yes, I believe we established your limit today. A dozen jumps is still ten above average," he reminded Byron when the young man's mouth opened. "You comprehend the parameters of your ability and can transfer your own energy to the teleporter without error. You and Trindel have performed to my satisfaction as navigator and pilot. If you complete the course, you will receive my recommendation."

"If, sir?" Byron asked.

Bassa cocked one eyebrow. "There are still two weeks remaining," he reminded him.

"Yes, sir," replied Byron, his gaze returning to his food.

They ate in silence for several minutes. Byron sensed the senior officer was watching, but he refrained from making eye contact with Bassa. His mental shields were locked in place, protecting his private thoughts. Byron felt the instructor was gathering information by observation alone, though. The intense scrutiny further rattled his nerves.

As he finished his meal, Byron heard Bassa shift in his chair. The noise caused him to look up and the senior officer met his eyes.

"Why did you want to be a Cosbolt pilot?"

Bassa's question caught him off-guard, and Byron searched for a suitable reply. "For the prestige, sir," he answered, affecting a nonchalant pose. "For the chance at a life beyond Cassa."

The senior officer did not respond and continued to gaze at Byron. Sensing Bassa was waiting for more, he nervously swirled the remainder of his food with his fork. Contemplating the real reason behind his motives, Byron pressed his lips together and frowned.

"And because it was the only profession for which I possessed any aptitude," he admitted with reluctance. "Sir," he added, aware he had responded without properly addressing the senior officer.

"Piloting a fighter was your only option?" inquired Bassa.

Byron nodded, his eyes still on his plate.

"The next two weeks will decide your fate then."

Byron set down his fork, no longer interested in his food. The thought of failing as a Cosbolt pilot after almost a year and a half of intense training made him feel ill. If he did not pass the course, Byron had no idea what else he'd do with his life. There were few other options.

"Has my fate already been decided, sir?" he asked, his voice bold despite the gnawing fear in his stomach.

Bassa reclined in his chair and crossed his hands in his lap. "No, it has not. It's still up to you."

Puzzled by the response, Byron stared at the senior officer. Something told him there was more to the senior officer's statement than the obvious, though.

"Is there something you wish to say?" Bassa inquired, breaking into his thoughts.

Shifting in his seat, Byron realized that while his mind was shielded, his expression was not so easily concealed. Frustrated by Bassa's powers of observation, he decided to take a bold approach.

"Do I have what it takes to successfully complete this course, sir?" he asked.

"As far as your skills as a pilot, yes," Bassa announced. "It's your mental state that concerns me. All that talent and ability requires discipline and responsibility. Overconfidence leads to mistakes. I need to be certain that when I send you out to the fleet, you are capable of making the right choices. If I haven't properly prepared you on all levels, then not only have I failed, I've cost the life of a valuable young man and pilot. And your death would be a terrible waste, Byron."

The senior officer's words perplexed Byron. "A waste, sir? I'm not sure I understand."

Bassa's expression turned solemn. "Before I became an instructor, another talented young pilot trained here on Guaard. He did not possess your talent for multiple jumps, but he was just as skilled. He entered the fleet determined to prove his worth and gain the attention of his fellow officers. His career was cut short less than two months later when a bold maneuver and jump resulted in a collision with an asteroid."

Leaning forward in his seat, Bassa regarded Byron with a stern look. "I do not want you to suffer a similar fate, and I will do everything in my power to ensure you have a long and successful career. Understood?"

Byron could only nod in agreement, caught off-guard by the rare hint of emotion in Bassa's voice. His concern was genuine, although Byron could not imagine why. His previous instructors had no need for a troublesome young man, and he was sure the senior officer despised him as well.

"That is why I have gone to great lengths to ensure you are properly prepared," Bassa added. "It is now up to you, Byron."

"Yes, sir," he replied, still confused.

Bassa moved his tray aside and leaned back in his chair. "That was all I wanted to discuss with you, pilot. Unless you have another question, you are dismissed."

"Yes, sir," said Byron, pushing back his chair.

His gaze fell on the photo adorning Bassa's desk. Feeling brave, he decided to satisfy his curiosity.

"Sir?" he asked, rising to his feet. "If I may ask, who is that in the photo?"

Bassa's gaze flicked briefly to the frame. "That was my younger brother, Tal."

"Was, sir?"

"He died many years ago."

"I'm sorry, sir," Byron answered, feeling awkward. "Thank you for the meal."

Retreating from the room, he emitted a sigh of relief. He'd survived the experience, which in fact was not as agonizing as he'd anticipated. Bassa had given him much to ponder.

His future was in his hands. Byron's performance had to be perfect the next two weeks. He could not fail now.

The men dressed in silence, the weight of today's exercise suppressing the normal chatter. Byron's thoughts were somber as he pulled on his flight suit and even Trindel was quiet. The instructors had placed a great deal of emphasis on the success of their flight, proclaiming it the trainees' greatest test. Considering it was only the first day of their weeklong assessment, Byron felt wary.

Upon entering the hanger, he noticed a transport shuttle near the drones. A single officer waited by the open hatch, and even from that distance, he could see the man's security badge. Byron assembled with the other men, he eyes still on the visiting ship. The last trainee fell into place and Bassa began to speak, diverting Byron's attention.

"The next few days are critical. They will determine your success or failure," he stated, his expression grave. "We begin the testing process today with what will be your most difficult task. Shooting drones is easy, as they are but mere machines. Once you have joined the fleet, the ships you destroy will contain living beings.

"That is why today's exercise is so vital."

Pivoting to face the shuttle, he signaled to the officer standing guard. The man nodded and entered the ship. A moment later, he and another officer emerged, leading a group of men bound by security cuffs. The procession moved toward the waiting drone ships.

"Those men," Bassa announced, "are prisoners slated for execution. One man will be placed in each drone ship, all of which have been programmed for battle."

He placed his hands behind his back and stared at the young men. "This will be your ultimate test. Today, you will each destroy a live target."

Beside him, Byron heard Trindel's sharp intake of breath. Suppressing his own surprise, he kept his eyes on the senior officer.

"Now, to your ships!"

No one spoke as the men moved to their Cosbolts. Byron sensed Trindel's anxiety pulsating like a beacon and one glance revealed his navigator's ashen complexion. He kept his own emotions in control as they performed the preflight check. Occasionally his gaze wandered to the group of prisoners. The first man was being placed in a drone as their fighter wheeled into position.

Once every Cosbolt had launched, the squadron assembled and set a course away from the base. On his radar, Byron noted the drones emerging from the launch tubes. He caught his breath, a moment of doubt grasping at his throat. They were about to shoot down real people. Prisoners or not, his first live kill would be a fellow Cassan.

They're still the enemy, he told himself. They were scheduled for execution because they'd committed a crime.

Satisfied with his reasoning, Byron wiped all thought of the drone's passengers from his mind and prepared for battle. He would not fail this first test.

Aware that Trindel had not uttered a word, he reached out to his navigator. *You okay?*

Yes, came the hesitant reply.

Don't fade on me now! Byron ordered. *We can do this.*

He sensed Trindel's reluctant compliance and decided not to pursue the issue. As long as his navigator maintained awareness of their position, Byron would ensure their success today.

They did not have long to wait, for which he was grateful. The drones assembled and began to bear down on the squadron. Defensive orders were quickly relayed and the ships turned to meet the enemy.

The drones fanned out and split into two groups. Byron's team was ordered to pursue the smaller cluster. Six Cosbolts followed the instructor's ship as it veered off in pursuit. The drones took evasive action and broke formation, sending each vessel on an individual course.

"715T, Drone Five!"

Byron locked on his assigned target. They rolled to the right and followed the drone.

Keep an eye on the others! he ordered, glancing at the screen. Several drones had already changed direction. Soon their sector of space would grow congested. So far, none of the drones had issued a shot. Byron assumed confusion rather than actual engagement would be their defensive.

An alert from Trindel forced him to dive as a drone passed overhead. Annoyed by the distraction, Byron increased their speed in an attempt to catch their target. He veered left and then right, dodging a Cosbolt in the process. The drone continued to elude them, though.

I need to get in front of him! he exclaimed, frustrated by the pursuit.

His flight pattern's too erratic, his navigator protested. *And they're not even firing back.*

A flash of red above them told Byron a different story. Without need for a visual confirmation, he sensed the ensuing dogfight over their craft. If they did not escape the confusion soon, they'd be caught in the crossfire.

Damn it, Trindel, give me an option!

Their target descended and almost collided with another drone. Byron exclaimed aloud as he was forced to take evasive action.

There's too much confusion …

Trindel! Byron screamed.

His navigator hesitated for only a second before suggesting coordinates. Taking immediate action, Byron jumped the ship to the new position. They emerged on the edge of the fracas and discovered the drone bearing down on them. Byron fired a shot just as the drone opened fire. Without waiting for coordinates, he jumped the ship again.

Trindel gasped as they emerged just below the previous location. A flash of light informed Byron of the drone's demise. It was closer than he preferred, but his team had completed their assignment.

Head on? he demanded.

You wanted options, his navigator offered.

"715T, retreat to a secure position and do not engage unless absolutely necessary," Officer Rellen's voice echoed from the com.

"Yes, sir!" Byron replied, veering the ship away from the fight.

As their ship circled the perimeter, another drone exploded. The men did not get to blow up drones often due to the cost, but it provided a greater sense of accomplishment when they were permitted that luxury. It was far more satisfying than mere laser tagging. Considering the live occupant of the drone, this particular exercise seemed hollow, but Byron felt no regret. Oddly enough, he felt neither remorse nor elation over his first live kill.

When the final drone was destroyed, the fighters resumed formation and returned to base. Byron sensed Trindel's heavy mood and did not converse with his navigator as they taxied into the hanger. If the situation bothered Trindel, then there was little Byron could say to ease his friend's mind.

The flight apparently weighed heavy on everyone's thoughts, as little was said in the changing room. The overall mood was somber. Byron wondered if any of the teams had failed their objective, but he did not ponder long on that thought. He and Trindel had succeeded, and that was all that mattered.

As they crossed the hanger to the briefing room, Byron glanced in the direction of the visiting transport. The security officers were in evidence and speaking with two hanger crew personnel. They appeared relaxed and he thought he detected laughter drifting across the hanger.

The young men filed into the room and took their seats in silence. Trindel dropped like a stone into the chair beside Byron, his expression solemn. Frowning at his navigator's demeanor, Byron was about to speak when Bassa called for attention.

"Men, this will be brief," he announced. "With the exception of team 143T, who is to remain here, you are to return to your quarters. Team 479T, you are to report to my office immediately."

Byron glanced at Surren and noticed his cocky smile was absent. He and his navigator were slumped in their seats, faces drawn and complexions ashen. They failed, Byron thought.

"If anyone else now realizes he doesn't have what it takes to fulfill his role as a pilot or navigator, he is to see me in my office before the midday meal," Bassa instructed. He scanned the faces of those present, his eyes briefly pausing on Byron's team.

"This exercise separates the men from the boys. Be damned sure of your decision!"

A couple young men fidgeted, but no one spoke. Bassa simply nodded.

"After the midday meal, each team will receive a debriefing in my office. Until then, you are dismissed!"

The instructors exited the room right away, but the trainees moved slower in their departure. Byron followed Trindel into the hallway and caught his navigator's elbow.

You okay? he asked, concerned by his friend's despondency.

Trindel nodded, his lips pressed in a thin line. His gaze quickly dropped to the floor.

We did it! Byron thought, his eager tone causing Trindel to raise his eyes. *And that's probably the worst thing we'll ever face.*

Grasping Byron's forearm, Trindel nodded again. *You're right.*

Smiling, Byron slapped his friend's back and propelled him toward the lift. They had just faced their greatest challenge and returned triumphant.

Byron remained in his quarters until the midday meal as instructed. Gathering a generous portion of food on his plate, he joined Trindel at an open table. Spirits rejuvenated, Byron dove into his meal. His navigator said little, his mood still somber, so Byron sought conversation with the others seated at the table. It appeared that most of the men had recovered from the shock of the exercise, but no one seemed inclined to discuss the morning's session.

It wasn't until Byron rose from the table that he considered Surren and Arenth's absence. If they had indeed failed the exercise, then that meant two marks on their record. He knew he shouldn't revel in their apparent dismissal, but Surren had taunted Byron at every opportunity, and he felt vindicated.

"We're not scheduled to sit down with Bassa until late afternoon," he informed Trindel as they departed the dining hall. "Guess our team's last. But, since you've told me to expect the best, I'm taking it as a good sign!"

Trindel lowered his chin. "Byron, you'll be meeting with Bassa alone."

"Why?" asked Byron, his step faltering.

"I met with him this morning after the exercise."

"What?" he demanded. Coming to an abrupt halt, Byron grabbed his navigator's shoulder and forced Trindel to look him in the eye. "What for?"

Trindel met his gaze, his expression troubled. "Because, I can't do it," he admitted in a meek voice.

"Do what?"

"I can't kill another living being!"

Releasing Trindel's shoulder as if he'd been stung, Byron stared open-mouthed at his friend. He could not believe what he was hearing.

"Byron, I'm sorry, but I can't do it," stammered Trindel, his eyes wide and pleading. "I thought I could handle it, but I can't. And it's not just because those men were Cassans. I don't want to kill anyone!"

Feeling his insides sink, Byron clenched his fists at his sides. "Damn it, we're a team! What am I supposed to do without a navigator?"

"I intend to finish the course with you," Trindel offered. "I know how important piloting is to you. But once we're finished here on Guaard, I'm pursuing another career field."

Anger rose in Byron's chest. He held his sharp retort as Vitar and Hansen strolled past the pair in the hallway. Frustrated but unwilling to create a scene, Byron turned away from Trindel.

He'd worked so hard to get this far, pouring everything into his training. Piloting a Cosbolt was Byron's dream and his only option. Now those hopes lay shattered alongside the other failed aspirations in his life. How could Trindel abandon him when he was so close to achieving this goal? Byron felt betrayed by the one person he'd trusted.

"How am I supposed to join the fleet without a navigator?" he snapped, now furious with Trindel.

"They'll assign you another one," the young man replied with a nervous quaver.

"Who knows how long that will take! Or how much training will be involved," Byron exclaimed, whirling on Trindel. "Damn it, we are so close! How can you give up on me now?"

Holding out his hands, Trindel stepped forward. "Byron, I'm really sorry," he offered, his entire body trembling.

Byron brushed aside his hand as Trindel reached for his shoulder. He didn't want sympathy. Realizing he was about to spew some very ugly words, Byron turned and retreated from the unpleasant scene, moving as fast as his long legs would carry him.

Byron, please! Trindel entreated.

Ignoring his friend's desperate plea, Byron entered the first available lift. He requested the hanger level and the doors closed before Trindel could join him. The unit descended and the doors opened to an empty corridor. Grateful to find seclusion, Byron proceeded to the main hanger.

His stride was full of anger, and his heavy steps echoed in the empty corridor. Byron's mind continued to reel with the news. How could Trindel desert him now? They were within days of completing their training. He'd hoped that his team's record would secure a good first assignment. Now he'd have to wait for a replacement and endure more training with a new navigator.

Rounding a corner, the hanger came into view. Few of the station's personnel lingered and the visiting transporter was no longer in evidence. The expanse appeared even greater than usual and the cavernous maw felt cold and foreboding. Immersed in dejection, the sight caused Byron to feel even more insignificant and without hope.

His gaze fell on the fighters neatly arranged on the flight deck in rows of five. Those vessels represented his only chance of a decent future. Their streamlined shape carried a sense of purpose, a quality lacking in Byron's life until recently.

Trindel's decision now cast doubt on his resolution to pilot a Cosbolt.

The anger ebbed from his body, hastened by his rapid retreat, and Byron felt his shoulders slump. Entering the hanger, he approached the resting ships. The emanations of the teleporters reached his senses and vibrated in his chest. Byron wandered among the vessels until he located his fighter situated at the end of the last row.

Stretching out with tentative fingers, he placed his hand over the compartment that housed the teleporter. The unit's power pulsated through his mind and body and he closed his eyes, enjoying the sensation. If only he could use that energy to correct his situation! To come so far, only to have his hopes dashed yet again.

Rejected by family and friends and thwarted in his attempts to achieve any level of success, Byron felt as if he'd never escape his past.

Retrieving Byron's profile, Bassa stared at the screen, lost in thought. He'd saved the pilot for last, aware this review would prove the most challenging. Byron would be difficult to handle this afternoon and Bassa needed to proceed with caution.

The young man arrived at his appointed time and Bassa gestured for him to take a seat. He noted Byron's sluggish movements and solemn express and surmised Trindel had revealed his session with the senior officer as requested. Once the pilot rested in a chair, his sagging posture reflecting defeat, Bassa leaned forward.

"Your team performed well this morning," he stated, diving right into the evaluation. "The placement of your first jump was questionable, but Trindel admitted the coordinates were to give the drone a chance."

"He set us up?" demanded Byron, straightening his back and grasping the armrests. "Sir?" he added.

"Trindel couldn't stomach killing another man. He was trying to give the drone a fighting chance," Bassa informed the angry pilot, holding up his hand. "Regardless of his motives, you still managed to destroy the target and avoid a direct hit.

Your team was the first to complete its assignment, I might add."

Byron slouched in his seat, and Bassa realized that fact was of small consolation now. He would receive little response from Byron on the subject of their flight. Bassa opted to turn to more pressing matters.

"I assume Trindel discussed his resignation with you?" he asked.

Eyes narrowing, Byron nodded.

"Since Trindel has agreed to complete the program, his decision will not affect the outcome of this week's tests, nor will it alter my assessment of your skill level."

Byron took a deep breath and nodded again. His posture remained defensive and withdrawn, and the coldness of his eyes revealed a deep displeasure that bordered on agony. Clasping his hands together, Bassa selected his next words with care.

"This exercise eliminates more men than any other test," he admitted, watching Byron's reaction. "I lost two teams and a navigator today. It's a tough test, but I need to know if each man possesses the ability to destroy an enemy without hesitation. It's better to eliminate them now than to place those teams in the fleet where their inability to act endangers the lives of others."

Byron's gaze had dropped while Bassa spoke, and he sensed the young pilot was about to shut down mentally as well. Leaning on his desk, Bassa made one last attempt to reach Byron.

"I do not want to lose three complete teams today," he stated with conviction.

His voice sounded loud in the room's silence, but his words caught Byron's attention. The young man raised his head and met Bassa's gaze. The senior officer noted a spark of determination in his steel blue eyes.

"I refuse to quit now, sir," Byron replied.

Bassa nodded. "Then you and Trindel will complete your training as originally planned. If you are successful, you'll receive a new navigator when a suitable match becomes available."

Byron opened his mouth to speak and Bassa caught a hint of desperation in his thoughts. The young man's brows came together and he at once shielded his mind. Bassa frowned, perplexed by Byron's refusal to divulge his thoughts or appear vulnerable. Gazing at the pilot, Bassa decided he genuinely wanted to help the young man. If he ever hoped to reach the person trapped behind that protective shield, Bassa needed to do so now.

Leaning back in his chair, he assumed a receptive pose, allowing his hands to drop to his lap. Byron watched with apparent curiosity, but did not speak. Bassa selected his next words with care.

"I suggest," he began in a non-threatening voice, "that you take advantage of this opportunity to speak candidly."

Byron eyed his superior with skepticism. Shifting in his seat, he leaned heavily on the armrests.

"Sir, how long will I have to wait for a new navigator?" he asked, the words tumbling from his lips.

"The process could take a month or more," Bassa explained. "You will require a navigator of exceptional skill."

"Will I have to go through training again, sir?"

"A minimum of twenty hours in the cockpit is required before a team is certified, sometimes more if warranted," he conceded. "Occasionally this is done on location, but more often than not, a new team trains together at a facility on Cassa."

Byron's gaze dropped to the floor. For a brief moment, his dejection penetrated his mental shields.

"Then it will be months before I join the fleet," he murmured.

His guard dropped even further, and Bassa sensed a deep fear of failure and rejection in Byron. The young man's desperate need for accomplishment and acceptance rang clear in his mind. Bassa was surprised when his own emotions stirred at the memory of another young pilot's desire for confirmation of his worth. Before his thoughts revealed themselves, he cleared his mind.

"If you successfully complete your training," Bassa said with authority, causing Byron to meet his gaze. "Not only will I give you the highest recommendation possible, but I promise I will do everything in my power to locate a quality navigator and assignment for you."

Byron's eyes widened and he sat up straight in his seat. "Really, sir?"

"If you complete your training to my satisfaction," the senior officer reminded him.

"Yes, sir, that's a promise!"

Bassa had to suppress a smile. The young man's spirit had returned with a vengeance.

"Then I suggest you settle your differences with your current navigator and concentrate on giving your best performance."

"Yes, sir," Byron promised.

"Good! You are dismissed, Byron," ordered Bassa, leaning forward in his chair.

"Yes, sir!" the young man exclaimed, rising to his feet. "And thank you, sir."

Byron retreated from his office with a bounce to his step. When the doors closed, Bassa chuckled at the young man's reaction before turning to his computer screen. He added final notes to the pilot's file, pleased with their session. As he completed his task, his eyes strayed to the photo on his desk.

A chime signified a visitor. Leaning away from his computer, Bassa gave permission to enter. Officer Rellen sauntered into the room, his customary smile in place.

"Finished with the trainees?" he inquired.

"Yes, the last session just ended," Bassa replied, cocking his head. "Did you speak to Security Officer Solate before his departure?"

Rellen nodded and dropped into the chair vacated by Byron. "And his team thanked us again. They enjoyed the opportunity to play prisoners."

Bassa chuckled at his instructor's observation. "I think they enjoy the charade as much as than the bonus in pay."

"If the trainees only knew they were shooting down empty drones ..."

"If they knew, the test would not be effective!"

Rellen nodded in agreement. "Any surprises this afternoon?" he asked, eyebrows raised in anticipation.

"No one else was eliminated. 715T's navigator will remain long enough to ensure his pilot completes the course," Bassa announced.

"You intend to pass Byron, then?"

Noting the skepticism in Rellen's voice, Bassa fixed him with an authoritative stare. "If he successfully completes the final sessions, yes, I do!"

Rellen did not appear threatened by Bassa's tone, but he did offer a polite nod of acceptance.

"The fleet will have a difficult time locating a suitable navigator for that young buck," he said, shaking his head. "He'll require a man with experience, not to mention a strong will. I don't envy the navigator who aligns himself with Byron!"

Sliding back his chair, Bassa rose to his feet. "A suitable replacement will be located."

Rellen leapt from his seat. "Well, that is not our concern! If you're ready to dine?"

"I am."

He reached for his computer and hesitated before clearing the screen. Byron's dilemma promised to occupy his thoughts for the remainder of the evening. Rellen's assessment was correct, though. The fleet would be hard-pressed to match Byron with a navigator of equal skill and ability. Those with experience would balk at an alliance with a rookie pilot, and those who might be willing would lack the skill and fortitude to keep the young man in line. And that worried Bassa.

He won't stand a chance in the fleet, he thought to himself as the screen's image vanished.

Chapter Six

The small, formal ceremony came to a close, concluding with the joyous shouts of twenty young men. Thirty-six started the program six months ago, but of those gathered today, Byron doubted any thought about the ones who'd failed. They were officially Cosbolt pilots and navigators now.

Byron returned to his quarters to retrieve his gear. The men were departing at once for Cassa and three days of much needed leave. He couldn't even remember his last free day. Byron intended to live it up until he reported for his first official assignment as a pilot. He still needed a navigator, which might require another month or two on Cassa, but that problem could wait. He had three days to revel in his success.

Slinging his bag over his shoulder, he surveyed his quarters one more time before departing. Byron jumped when the door panel opened and he discovered Trindel waiting. His friend appeared just as surprised.

"Sorry!" Trindel exclaimed, adjusting the bag in his hand. "Thought we could go down to the shuttle together."

"Sure," Byron replied with a shrug.

Trindel fell in step beside him as they moved toward the lift. Neither seemed inclined to speak; a testimony to the unease between pilot and navigator. Byron still resented his friend's decision to pursue another career, although he'd suppressed his hostile feelings while they completed the program. Trindel had apologized repeatedly and almost to the point of annoyance. Byron knew he was acting childish by ignoring his navigator's attempts to make peace, but he still felt betrayed. They had managed to set aside their differences during their flights, but the rift in their friendship continued to separate the two men.

Another team joined them in the lift, and the men's eager banter regarding their trip to Cassa elicited a smile from Trindel. The young man's amusement bubbled forth from his thoughts and Byron felt a twinge of guilt for acting so harsh the past few days. Despite his mixed feelings, he would miss Trindel's sense of humor and overzealous spirit. If not for his navigator, Byron's smile would've remained hidden during their training.

The officers awaited the men at the transport. Each instructor offered his congratulations to the new junior officers as they boarded the ship. Byron accepted the handshakes and salutes with a grin, proud of his new title and rank.

The senior officer was the last to speak to the men before they entered the ship. Bassa wished Trindel well in his next career as the young man stepped on the ramp. Byron moved forward and offered the senior instructor a proper salute.

"Thank you, sir, for all of your assistance," he said. *And for believing in me,* he added privately.

"As you will soon discover, I have total faith in your abilities and skills, Byron," the senior officer stated, the hint of a smile on his lips.

Byron was puzzled by his choice of words. Before he could speak again, Bassa held out his hand.

"Safe flying, pilot."

Byron returned his handshake and offered a rare smile. "Thank you, sir."

He proceeded up the ramp and into the ship. Stowing his bag with the others, he glanced around for Trindel. Most of the men had spread out across the cabin in pairs. Byron located his friend sitting by himself. Another wave of guilt struck him. Trindel had tried so hard to seek forgiveness, and Byron had returned his gestures with cold indifference. The return flight to Cassa might be their last opportunity to spend time together. Indeed, it might be the last time he ever saw his friend. Straightening his shoulders, Byron decided to bury his resentment and just enjoy Trindel's company.

He paused by the open seat and his friend looked up in surprise. "Can I sit here?" Byron asked.

"Sure," replied Trindel, straightening his posture.

Byron dropped into the seat and stretched his long legs. He did not know what to say to Trindel, and battled with his reluctance to speak. Discussing his thoughts and feelings was not Byron's strength, and admitting he was wrong was even more difficult. However, he possessed precious few friends. Byron did not want this friendship to end on a sour note.

Still struggling with his words, Byron cleared his throat. "You do realize," he said, his eyes on the hands in his lap, "that my next navigator won't be half as good as you."

Without raising his chin, Byron cast a sideways glance at his friend. With only a moment's hesitation, Trindel flashed a broad smile.

"I appreciate that," he said, his gratitude reflected in his eyes.

"You were there when I needed you," Byron admitted. "We made a damned good team, too."

Trindel nodded, his eyes dropping. "Byron, I'm really sorry …" he began, fingers nervously plucking at the armrest.

"You've apologized enough!" Byron cried, holding up his hand to forestall Trindel's words.

His friend flashed a pitiful look, his eyes wide. Byron leaned his head against the seat and felt the final twinges of anger leave his body.

"I just wish you the best," he concluded, offering his friend a faint smile.

Trindel did not speak, but Byron felt relief pour from his friend like cascading water. Nodding, Trindel returned his smile.

"Thanks," he said.

The exchange lifted a great weight from Byron's shoulders. His mind at once shifted to a new subject.

"So, what are you going to do for three days?" he inquired.

"I'm not sure," Trindel admitted. "I'll probably go see my family. I guess I have a whole week to decide my next career path. I'll stay with navigation, but not sure in which field."

He paused and stared at Byron. "What are you going to do?"

Byron shrugged. "I really don't know."

"Maybe we can spend a day or two together before I go see my family?" Trindel offered, his voice tinged with hope.

Meeting his friend's gaze, Byron smiled. "That would be great!" he exclaimed, pleased with the offer.

Trindel's grin grew to enormous proportions and Byron discovered he mirrored his friend's expression.

The transport began to move and the men prepared for takeoff. As the ship taxied out of the hanger, Byron felt a renewed sense of hope. His future partner might be uncertain, but at least his friendship with Trindel remained intact.

Bag slung over his shoulder, Byron maneuvered through the heavy foot traffic. The military terminal was busy today, as evidenced by the crowds wandering the facility. He darted around the slower moving men, determined to catch his ship before it departed.

Locating the correct terminal and launch bay at last, Byron hesitated just inside the massive opening. His gaze fell on his ship and he realized it was no ordinary transport. A massive, deep space vessel filled the hanger, dwarfing the two smaller ships nearby. He gasped and stared in awe at the ship. Just where was the fleet sending him?

Noting cargo and equipment waiting at the loading dock, Byron realized he had a few minutes to spare. Glancing over his shoulder, he spied an open computer station in the hallway. His assignment had been unavailable earlier, and Byron was eager to discover his destination. He slipped over to the computer station and punched in his security code.

Holding his breath, he watched his profile information scroll across the screen. He hoped the fleet wasn't sending him to a remote base on a desolate moon. Without a navigator, though, his options were limited.

Noting his profile had just received an update, he scanned the new information. Reading the notification under 'Current Assignment,' his mouth fell open in disbelief. He reread the first line again, afraid it was a mistake. Byron could not hide his foolish grin as he realized his incredible good fortune. His first assignment was the flagship Sorenthia!

His mind reeled at the news. The deep space cruiser was legendary. The ship had participated in numerous battles and her captain was one of the top commanders in the fleet. The Sorenthia possessed an elite reputation, and men earned the right and honor to serve with her crew. Byron hadn't even considered this assignment a possibility. Commander Kernen never accepted pilots fresh out of training. Experience and a high recommendation were required to serve on the Sorenthia.

Bassa had promised high marks, but Byron didn't possess combat experience.

Byron scanned the information once more, but discovered no mention of a navigator other than 'pending.' He'd have to wait until he arrived on board the Sorenthia to satisfy that curiosity.

Even with multiple jumps, which required more energy but carried the ship a greater distance, the journey to reach the Sorenthia consumed most of the day. The deep space transport carried predominantly cargo and supplies. The only passengers besides Byron were three medical personnel. He conversed with the men during the first hour of flight, but after that, he kept to himself. The rhythmic pulses of the teleporter were far more inviting, and Byron's mind focused on the unique sensation. Soon he would take his first flight as an official Cosbolt pilot.

It was past time for the evening meal when the transport arrived at the Sorenthia's location. Byron regretted the lack of view from the shuttle, as the sight was surely spectacular. Adrenaline surged through his system as the transport landed and he could scarcely wait to disembark. After almost two years of training, he was about to begin his first official assignment!

Retrieving his bag, Byron exited the vessel behind the three medical technicians. The men were greeted by a fellow medical officer who welcomed them aboard the Sorenthia. As they stepped aside, Byron realized someone awaited his arrival as well.

"Officer Byron?" the ensign inquired.

"Yes," he replied.

"Welcome to the Sorenthia. Would you come with me please?"

Byron followed the young man as he led him out of the hanger. He did not want to appear unseasoned, but his gaze travelled across the hanger, absorbing his new surroundings. Once they entered the hallway, Byron kept his eyes on his escort. The ensign navigated two hallways before stepping into a lift, his gaze averted. Byron was curious, but refrained from asking questions.

From that point, they traversed another long hallway, passing several men as they walked. Byron observed their curious stares and maintained a neutral expression, his thoughts shielded. The scrutiny unnerved him, and it was with great relief when his escort paused by a closed door.

"These are your quarters, sir," he announced, gesturing to the press plate.

Byron waved his hand over the panel and the door slid aside. He stepped into a room larger than his quarters on Guaard, although just as sterile. In addition to a bed, workstation, and storage area, a small table and two chairs occupied the room. Another door opened to a bathroom, which also appeared more spacious than his previous quarters.

"Sir, you just missed the evening meal, so someone will bring you food shortly," the young man informed him, his high-pitched voiced almost squeaking from the effort. "Further instructions are located in your file. You are to report to Officer Larnth this evening. You can access the ship's layout for the location of his office on your computer."

Byron nodded, and without another word, the ensign departed. The door closed, leaving Byron in the silence of his quarters.

Dropping his bag on the bed, he decided a shower was in order before anything else. The cold water felt good on his face, but he did not linger in the bathroom. He still needed to eat and locate Officer Larnth's office before his appointed meeting with the man.

An ensign arrived with his meal and Byron consumed his food in front of the computer, studying the floor plan of the ship. Locating the appropriate section, he calculated the quickest route. He smiled as he realized the teleporter pods were now available for use. No longer would he be forced to rely on slow and cumbersome lifts!

Departing early, he located the nearest teleporter pod. Once again, local personnel noted his presence. Byron felt curious eyes as he passed each man, questioning his right to be in that area. He pretended not to notice and acted as if he was at complete ease with his surroundings. One aspect he could not ignore, though; every man he encountered was several years his senior.

Teleporting to the appropriate corridor, Byron emerged just a few steps from Officer Larnth's door. Hearing sounds in the distance, he glanced down the hallway. Satisfied his passage would go unobserved, he approached the office. Pausing at the closed door, he adjusted his uniform and took a deep breath. Unable to delay any longer, he reached for the panel.

"Enter!" a voice commanded over the com link.

The door slid aside and Byron lifted his chin as he entered. He took three steps and came to an abrupt halt. He'd grown accustomed to Bassa's immense office, but this room was not even a third of the size. Byron regained his composure and waited by the chair opposite of Larnth's desk. He stood at attention, his eyes facing forward, and waited for the officer to speak first.

The man behind the desk leaned away from his computer screen. "At least you're punctual," he commented.

"Yes, sir," Byron responded.

Out of the corner of his eye, Byron noticed Officer Larnth's skeptical expression. The man's dark, thick hair carried over to his eyebrows, which were pulled together in a scowl. Byron's thoughts were already guarded, but the sight of Larnth caused his defenses to lock into place. They had just met, but already Byron could sense the man didn't like him.

"You have been assigned to my squadron, Officer Byron," he announced in a voice as cold as death. "Under normal circumstances, I'd protest the inclusion of a rookie pilot fresh from Guaard."

Byron met his gaze, but did not speak. He'd not expected a warm welcome, but the resentment in Larnth's words did not set him at ease.

"However, I've been informed your navigator is one of the best in the fleet. I will expect your performance to match his excellence, understood?"

"Yes, sir," Byron replied with as much respect and enthusiasm as he could muster.

Officer Larnth glanced at his screen. "I understand you're a jumper," he stated, his tone less severe.

"Yes, sir."

"You are to maintain a low profile of the ability. I'll not have my pilots performing reckless multiple jumps."

"Understood, sir."

Leaning back in his chair, Larnth stared hard at Byron. "Your navigator arrives tomorrow morning. You will both report to briefing room nine at 700 hours for squadron assignments.

"Commander Kernen is expecting you as well. His private office is on level fourteen, section two. Dismissed."

With a nod, Byron turned on his heels and beat a hasty retreat from Larnth's office. Nerves still quivering, he entered the teleporter pod and visualized his destination.

The prospect of an assignment on the Sorenthia, once so inviting, now felt soured. Byron questioned his own desire to remain at this post, despite the honor. The resistance toward his presence was unsettling. Bassa's glowing recommendation had placed Byron in yet another awkward situation.

Emerging from the telepod, he glanced in both directions before proceeding. Byron stood at attention as two senior officers passed, but they scarcely noticed his presence. Annoyed by his failure to study the ship's layout in depth, Byron elected to move away from the officers and try his luck at that end of the corridor first.

Fortunately, the commander's office was clearly marked. He paused at the door and reached for the press plate.

One moment, echoed a voice in his mind.

Startled by the non-verbal response, Byron stepped aside to wait. A moment later, the doors slid open. Two officers emerged, and he was told to enter.

The layout of the commander's office was inviting and a sharp contrast to Larnth's. Byron had only a split second to observe the numerous personal effects, photos, and awards before a deep voice commanded his attention.

"Officer Byron?"

He turned to face the commander, who was retrieving a bottle from an ornate cabinet. "Yes, sir" he responded, standing at attention.

"Take a seat," Kernen offered, gesturing with a glass in his hand.

Byron slid into one of large chairs opposite the desk. He watched the commander pour two drinks before returning the bottle to the cabinet. Retrieving the glasses, he approached Byron.

"I trust you've seen your quarters and met with your squadron leader?" he asked, handing Byron a drink.

"Yes, sir," he replied, accepting the glass. "Thank you, sir."

The commander nodded and took a seat at his desk. Byron estimated Kernen was the same age as Guaard's senior officer. He sported a similar weathered and seasoned appearance, and his eyes were filled with a wisdom that only came from age and experience. The commander possessed a persona of complete authority, which was certainly due an officer of his rank, but an air of openness exuded from him as well. Byron hoped this meeting would be more pleasant than the previous one.

"I can't recall the last time I accepted a pilot fresh from Guaard," Commander Kernen admitted, taking a sip of his drink.

Byron felt resentment rise in his chest and he quickly reinforced his mental shields. Fingers tightening around the glass in his hands, he prepared for another unsettling encounter. Kernen's next words surprised him, though.

"However, Officer Bassa assured me it would be beneficial to bring you on board," the commander stated, regarding Byron with a thoughtful expression. "He said you were one of the best; precise in your flying and aim, and able to respond to crisis situations without hesitation. I also understand you have a rare ability."

"Yes, sir," answered Byron, adjusting his hold on the glass.

Kernen raised his drink and cocked one eyebrow. "Take a drink before you spill it, son," he suggested.

Embarassed, Byron lifted the glass to his lips and took a sip. The liquid slid down this throat without so much as a tickle. Good alcohol was not to be wasted on low ranking officers, and he felt honored Kernen would share his private stock with him.

The commander finished his drink and set the glass on his desk with a flourish. "I've been over your file. There are a couple questionable issues, but Officer Bassa assured me none were of great concern. I trust his assessment will prove correct?"

"Yes, sir!" Byron said quickly. He had no intention of causing trouble during his first assignment.

Leaning back in his chair, the commander's eyes narrowed.
However, Byron thought he detected a smile playing at the
corner of the man's lips.

"I don't imagine you'll have the opportunity to cause problems, either," Kernen observed.

"Sir?" Byron inquired, uncertain of the commander's implication. "I'm not here to cause problems, sir."

"What are your intentions, pilot?"

Byron hesitated, his brain analyzing Kernen's question.
Searching for a suitable response, he decided to be bold.

"I intend to be the best damn Cosbolt pilot in the fleet,
sir!"

This time Kernen's smile was obvious. "Bassa said you had
spirit, among many other qualities," he said, fingers drum-
ming the armrest of his chair. "He spoke very highly of you,
young man."

"Of my abilities, sir?"

The commander nodded. "Your abilities as well."

Byron felt puzzled and wondered what Bassa had told the
commander. He shifted in his seat and the movement reminded him of the half-empty glass in his hand. Without further hesitation, he downed the contents and set the glass on
the edge of the commander's desk.

"I suggest you take the remainder of the evening to study
your squadron's flight drills," the commander instructed, leaning forward in his chair. "You will be expected to fly tomorrow."

That news surprised Byron. He'd have no time to train
with his new navigator.

Realizing he was being dismissed, Byron rose to his feet.
He felt relieved the commander did not share Larnth's resentment that an inexperienced pilot now resided on board
the Sorenthia, He was now twice as determined to prove his
worth. The identity of his navigator still eluded him, though.

"Sir, if I may?" he inquired, waiting for Kernen's signal to
continue. "Who is my navigator?"

"You will meet him tomorrow at your squadron's briefing."

With those words, the commander turned his attention to the computer screen, ending all further discussion on the matter. Reluctant to press further, lest he lose favor with Kernen, Byron retreated from the man's office.

I'm in way over my head, he thought.

Chapter Seven

Arising early, Byron dressed in his new flight suit. Personal computer pad in hand, he went in search of the dining hall. He expected an assortment of personnel, but on this level, only officers were in evidence. He received a few stares while retrieving his food but chose to ignore the curious onlookers. Securing one end of a table to himself, he used the time to scan the drills once more. Byron would not allow himself to break pattern or fail to perform a maneuver during his very first official flight.

The other pilots and navigators were just beginning to arrive when he entered the briefing room. Feeling uneasy after the earlier scrutiny, Byron elected to postpone social interaction and selected a seat on the far edge of the room. He tried to tune out the conversation and laughter of his fellow officers as they filled the room and waited for the meeting to begin.

Soon, only a couple seats remained unoccupied, including the chair beside Byron. He finally dared to glance around the room, curious as to which of the men would become his navigator. Those present appeared familiar with one another and he suspected his new partner had yet to arrive.

The squadron leader entered the room and the men's chatter subsided. Larnth surveyed those gathered, his gaze falling for a moment on Byron, before addressing the men.

"Today we will be patrolling sectors 74-107 and 73-107. There's been no report of activity in this area, but that does not render today's patrol routine. We're still at the edge of Cassan boundaries, so be prepared for anything. Understood?"

His question was met with a round of affirmation from the men. Officer Larnth turned to the large monitor on the wall behind him and pulled up the sector of space they would patrol today. The visual clearly showed their proximity to uncontrolled space, and Byron understood the severity of his warning.

Larnth turned to face the men and paused, his gaze traveling to the back of the room. Byron sensed a wave of astonishment from the far side of the room. Curious, he peered in the direction of the doorway. Over the top of the heads of those seated, he caught sight of a late arrival, and his heart missed a beat.

It was Bassa.

"Glad you could join us," Larnth said, a smile playing at the corners of his mouth.

Byron could only stare, his mouth open in shock. He sensed the awe and excitement of the officers around him but did not share in their elation. Why was Bassa on board the Sorenthia? Was he here to oversee special training? After six months of the man's presence on Guaard, Byron shuddered to think he'd be forced to endure more instruction from the senior officer.

"Now that both men are present, I'd like to introduce our newest team members," Larnth announced.

Bassa was now searching for an empty seat, and Byron's eyes widened in horror as he realized the man was moving in his direction. His progress was hindered, as the other officers eagerly greeted the senior officer in passing.

"Most of you already know Officer Bassa, as I'm sure he trained a good portion of those present," the squadron leader stated with pride. "He's regarded as one of the most decorated and accomplished navigators in the fleet."

Larnth paused. "We are also joined by Officer Byron, who will act as his pilot."

The news fell on Byron with a resounding thud and his stomach sank to his toes. Bassa finally reached the empty seat beside him and slid into the chair. Byron simply stared at his former instructor, mind reeling with this latest development and scarcely bothering to hide his indignation. Bassa met his eyes, his expression wary. If he expected a greeting, Byron was too stunned to respond.

Distracted by a comment, Bassa turned to the man behind him. Feeling dejected, not to mention frustrated by at the turn of events, Byron slumped in his seat and stared straight ahead. Life was beyond his control once again.

"Now, to continue going over today's flight," Larnth said with authority, silencing the excited murmurs.

Byron made every effort to focus on the squadron leader's instructions. He didn't want to commit an error during his first flight. Bassa's presence was distracting, though. Several times, his attention drifted to the man at his right, and he had to suppress the indignation that threatened to consume his mind. His first experience as a pilot would be marred by Bassa's presence.

Larnth concluded the meeting by wishing the men a safe flight and everyone began to rise to his feet. Byron arose and realized he was trapped. Several officers now congregated around Bassa, creating a traffic jam. By the time he exited the briefing room, Byron was at the rear of the procession. He followed the group to the hanger, his irritation growing with every step as he listened to the men around Bassa. The senior officer might be a veteran, which entitled him to some respect, but the others acted as if he was a hero bigger than life.

Byron located their ship and began the preflight check. Bassa joined him a moment later, a smile on his face. Staring hard at his navigator, he projected an angry thought.

Why are you here? he demanded.

Bassa's smile faded and he returned Byron's cold expression. *You needed a qualified navigator and we possessed the necessary training time.*

Was there no one else available? Byron replied.

A few, Bassa stated, *and your first assignment would've been patrolling a dead moon!*

Annoyed that it was probably the truth, Byron dug in even deeper. *I'm supposed to thank you then?* he retorted

Bassa scowled, his displeasure with Byron's attitude obvious. He stepped in front of his pilot and assumed an intimidating pose.

I sacrificed a high-ranking position, not only to ensure a decent first assignment but to give you a chance to survive out here. You may not agree with my decision right now, but I do expect some measure of respect.

His tone left no room for argument. Byron shook his head, but did not pursue the discussion. With no further exchange of words, they completed the preflight check and prepared for launch.

His spirit subdued, Byron waited while Bassa navigated their vessel to the launch tubes. His muscles tightened as they wheeled into position and the second door closed behind them. At the end of the tunnel, he could see a starry expanse and felt a twinge of excitement. Aware his navigator could detect his feelings, Byron suppressed his enthusiasm.

I've been here a thousand times, Bassa's voice echoed in his head. *This is your moment, Byron. Do not forget to enjoy it!*

Taking a deep breath, Byron forced the tension from his body and cleared his mind. The countdown commenced and he braced his head in preparation. The final number sounded and the ship shot through the tube and out into open space.

Five other ships emerged with their vessel. Byron maneuvered into position and the Cosbolts joined those already waiting. The squadron assumed full formation and set off for the coordinates of their patrol.

The three-hour flight was routine and uneventful. Once Byron recovered from his initial dismay, he did indeed enjoy the experience. At least he was familiar with Bassa's style of navigating and adjusted to his directions. During their training flights, Byron had been at the mercy of the senior officer's commands. He expected a similar experience here as well, but during their first flight as a team, Bassa's navigation felt more like guidance. Aware that could change without notice, Byron filed that thought away for future reference.

Tired but elated, he returned to the Sorenthia. Byron landed the ship with precision and Bassa locked their runners in place. As the vessel taxied into the hanger, Byron felt intense relief. Not only had he completed his first flight as a Cosbolt pilot, but he'd also survived Bassa's presence as his navigator. Both were monumental achievements.

Emerging from the ship, Byron turned to face his navigator. Resentment continued to linger in his heart, but regardless of his feelings toward their pairing, they had flown well together. He did not know what to say to his new partner, but Bassa possessed no such inhibitions.

"You did well today," he offered, slapping together his gloves.

Byron shrugged. "It was a routine mission," he replied.

Bassa regarded him with a steady gaze. "Sometimes those can be the most telling," he explained. "You flew well for your first mission."

Byron managed a brief nod of appreciation. He was not ready to display acceptance of his new navigator, though. Grasping the ladder, Byron retreated from Bassa's presence.

The men reconvened in the debriefing room, and listened to the squadron leader's assessment of the morning's mission. When Larnth finished, those around Bassa came to life and began to ask questions.

"What prompted you to come out of retirement?"

"Why were you assigned to the Sorenthia?"

"Is this assignment permanent?"

Annoyed with the enthusiasm of the other officers, Byron sidestepped the group surrounding Bassa. He escaped their notice and exited the room. Unprepared for intense scrutiny, Byron felt relief as he reached the safety of the teleporter pod. However, it irritated him that Bassa commanded such attention. It seemed to go beyond the senior officer's accomplishments, and Byron found himself caught in a rare moment of envy. No one was ever happy to see him.

Returning to his quarters, Byron showered and changed. He intended to complete his very first flight report before exploring the ship. If time permitted, he'd end the day with a solitary game of gravball. His first priority was food, though.

Emerging from his quarters, Byron proceeded toward the dining hall. As he passed the quarters beside his own, the door slid open, and he was surprised to see Bassa. He faltered as their eyes met. His inclination was to acknowledge the senior officer with a nod and continue on his way. It occurred to Byron that might not be the appropriate way to treat his new navigator, though. Fighting the urge to run, he paused for a moment.

"On your way to the dining hall?" Bassa asked as he joined him in the corridor.

Byron nodded, aware that he was about to acquire a dining partner.

"Mind if I join you?"

"No," Byron said quickly before his true answer could surface.

The men walked the short distance to the dining hall in silence. Once they'd retrieved their food, Byron and Bassa turned to face the crowded hall. Almost immediately, another officer flagged down the men, and Bassa moved to join him. Reluctantly, Byron followed his navigator.

"Officer Bassa, please join us," the man enticed.

Those present shifted their position, providing the newcomers room at the end of the table. Bassa sat next to the man and Byron took the seat across from his partner. The man at his elbow nodded at Byron and turned at once to Bassa.

"It's an honor to have you join our squadron," he stated with pride. "Your service record and achievements are legendary."

Bassa flashed a patient smile. "Legend implies I'm dead," he said, lifting his drink. "And I am very much alive!"

The man beside Bassa chuckled. "Well, only a few of us remember your days of active service."

"But the rest of us recall your training!" an officer further down the table offered.

That elicited laughter from those present. The man beside Bassa offered his hand.

"Don't know if you remember, but we served on the Masenna together," he said.

Bassa exchanged handclasps, a wry smile on his face. "Deacer, how could I forget you? Even if that was many years ago."

"More than I care to count!" Deacer exclaimed, the deep lines around his eyes and mouth reflecting the years. "Guess you remember my pilot, too."

The officer beside Byron exchanged greetings with Bassa. Hannar's deep voice resonated with experience, and while neither man appeared as old as Bassa, they were both many years Byron's senior. The men at the table were all older by a decade or more, and he felt very conspicuous in his youth. Compared to the other officers, he was just a boy.

Bassa smiled at Byron. "And this is my pilot, Byron," he announced with pride.

Byron looked up from his food and realized everyone at that end of the table now stared at him. Swallowing his food in haste, he offered a curt nod.

"Good to meet you, son," said Hannar, roughly patting his shoulder.

Unaccustomed to physical touch, Byron flinched ever so slightly before regaining his composure. He could prevent the mental invasion of his privacy, but not the physical, and had learned to endure such gestures.

Deacer shook his hand, his eyes studying the young pilot. Byron returned to his meal, content just to listen to the discussions around him. The men continued to ask many questions of Bassa, and Byron wondered if they'd permit his navigator to eat. Bassa knew how to control a conversation, though, and enticed the others to speak. Byron listened with interest as they spoke of past assignments and alien encounters.

"Most recent problems have been with the Vindicarn," Deacer announced, brushing the straggly locks from his square forehead. "Damned fighters are fast, too."

"Yes, I've been monitoring the encounters," Bassa replied. "They seem to be increasing."

Hannar nodded and leaned forward on the table. "Mostly skirmishes, but the Vindicarn have been patrolling the edge of Cassan space for the past month. And occasionally crossing that border, I might add."

"Peaceful negotiations not effective?" inquired Bassa, reaching for his drink.

"Hardly!" scoffed Hannar. "The Arellens have dealt with them for years, but it's an uneasy truce at best. At the moment, they show no interest in talking with the Cassan fleet."

"They send out raiding parties to secure new territories. Guess they've decided to venture into our part of the galaxy," Deacer offered. "Now that they've developed new technology, they're looking to expand their domain."

"The disrupters?"

Bassa's query perked Byron's interest. Secluded on Guaard for the past six months, he'd heard only bits and pieces from the outside world. However, news of the Vindicarn's disrupters had penetrated that protective bubble and created quite a stir among the trainees.

"Haven't seen them in action yet," Hannar admitted. "I understand the weapon not only knocks out teleporters, it fries a man's senses. Couple that with the Vindicarn's bold aggression and it makes them a dangerous enemy."

"Well, they better not consider us an easy target," Deacer declared, placing his fist on the table. "Just let them try to take any of our planets by force!"

Byron mulled this information over in his mind as the discussion shifted to lighter topics. Finishing his meal, he set down his fork and reached for his drink. Upon lowering the empty glass, he realized the officer beside Deacer was staring at him.

"So, where was your last post?" the man asked, his brows drawn together.

The suspicious tone alerted Byron at once. Stalling for time, he licked his lips and returned the glass to the table. His answer would not please those gathered.

"Guaard," he replied.

Deacer frowned. "You're too young to be an instructor," he observed.

The man beside the navigator gasped. "You just finished training?" he exclaimed in a loud voice. "A wet-behind-the-ears rookie?"

The rest of the table grew still. Byron felt his defenses rise as shock and indignation rippled through the group. He was about to offer a sharp retort when Bassa intervened.

"Yes, and he's one of the best damn pilots to ever complete the program!" he stated.

Byron knew that tone all too well and wondered if any would dare challenge his navigator's assessment. Despite Bassa's words, he sensed the mood of the table had changed. The men resented the presence of an unproven pilot in their squadron. He struggled to contain the anger that rose in his chest and clenched his fists under the table. They had passed judgment without allowing him the opportunity to prove himself.

"That's a first," someone muttered.

Deacer shifted his position but no one else spoke.

Don't let it bother you, Bassa's voice echoed in his head. *You will prove your worth in time.*

Byron lifted his chin and met Bassa's eyes. *In time?*

Rising from the table, he cast an icy glare at those seated before departing. There were things Byron wanted to accomplish today.

Byron completed his report and then set out to explore the ship. For the most part, he enjoyed the opportunity to be alone with his thoughts. Those he passed were busy with duties and paid the young pilot little heed. Ending his investigation of the Sorenthia with the ship's workout facility, Byron spent the remainder of his afternoon taking out his frustrations on one of the gravball courts.

Arriving late in the dining hall on purpose, he discovered the room less than half occupied. Bassa was present and surrounded by other officers. Byron didn't want to endure another unpleasant scene and selected an unoccupied table in the corner. The hall continued to empty as men departed in small groups, but Byron's presence failed to attract attention.

He noticed Bassa as the man rose to his feet. Several other officers followed suit and Byron assumed his navigator would remain with friendly company. To his surprise, the senior officer broke away from the group and approached Byron's table. Straightening his posture, he waited while Bassa took the seat opposite him at the table.

"I wondered if you were skipping the evening meal," Bassa observed, assuming a relaxed pose.

Byron regarded his partner with suspicion, contemplating his response. "Just skipping the company," he answered, his eyes scanning the room.

"I told you not to worry about the others. You'll earn their respect from the cockpit." Bassa leaned against the table, his hands clasped together. "At any rate, you can't let it affect your attitude or become a distraction. Just ignore the negative comments."

"Ignore the fact they don't want me here?" Byron growled.

"They don't know your capabilities, yet," explained Bassa. He pointed a finger at Byron. "You can only control your attitude, not theirs. Take the high road and let it slide. The men will trust and like you when they know you better."

Lowering his gaze, Byron stabbed at the remains of his meal. "I don't exactly excel at making friends, you know," he stated.

Stunned by the bluntness of his own words, Byron brought his fork down with great force on a chunk of meat. He tossed it into his mouth, hoping to prevent further thoughts from tumbling unchecked from his lips. On the other side of the table, he heard Bassa sigh.

"Yes, of that I am well aware," his navigator said in a low voice.

Lifting his head, Byron flashed Bassa an angry look, but there was neither malice nor condemnation in the man's eyes. The senior officer was quite capable of appearing cold and indifferent, but his expression lacked harsh judgment. To his surprise, Byron detected regret in his partner's thoughts.

Feeling exposed and self-conscious, he shifted his position. "Fine, I'll try to work with them," he offered.

Bassa slapped his hands on the table and rose to his feet. "Appreciate it. Well, the commander requested my presence this evening, so I'll leave you to your meal," he said briskly. "Evening, Byron."

Byron nodded. "Evening."

He stabbed at his food for a moment before rising to deposit his tray on the counter and return to his quarters. The shock of Bassa's appearance had worn off but not Byron's resistance to the man's presence on the Sorenthia. Bassa's navigational style felt awkward and Byron missed Trindel's gentle guidance. He felt inhibited, as if every move now fell under the scrutiny of the senior officer.

The status of Cosbolt pilot implied freedom, but not while Byron lay chained to the one person he'd hoped to escape.

Chapter Eight

Patrols filled the next three days and their squadron pulled double duty. Officer Larnth sent the men through an exhaustive training exercise on the fourth day, focusing on intricate tactics and maneuvers. Byron felt as if he were on Guaard again, especially with Bassa occupying the navigator seat in his cockpit. To his credit, the senior officer was quite familiar with the drills. Bassa prevented Byron from committing errors during the more complex maneuvers. He still felt uneasy with his new navigator, but Bassa did bring skill and experience to their team.

Byron tried to ignore the prevailing sense of displeasure from the other officers. No one voiced his opinion in Bassa's presence, but that did not prevent stray bitter thoughts from drifting in Byron's direction. He was aware of the mental conversations and suspected the others were trying to rattle him on purpose. That did not curb his annoyance, though, and Byron kept to himself whenever possible.

Outside of their flights together, the only time he saw Bassa was during meals. Aware that it was vital he connect with his navigator, Byron did not protest Bassa's presence or his attempts at conversation. However, his thoughts were conflicted between developing at least one friend on the Sorenthia and a deep desire to avoid contact with his former instructor. Their discussions were awkward at best, but if not for Bassa, Byron wouldn't be on speaking terms with anyone.

A week after their arrival, the ship was placed on alert. The men were in the dining hall when ordered to the briefing room. Already dressed in flight suits, the men leapt to their feet. Bassa saw Byron reach for his tray and he signaled for him to leave it.

No time! he thought, one hand on Byron's shoulder.

Eyes wide, Byron moved toward the exit and Bassa followed his pilot. Every telepod boasted a line and Bassa guided

his partner past the crowds. Rounding a corner, they discovered the lines were much shorter and secured a telepod within
seconds.

Once in the briefing room, the squadron leader wasted no
time. The last officers to arrive scrambled for their seats as
Larnth began to speak.

"Several minutes ago, we detected a small squadron of
Vindicarn fighters in sector 67-146," he announced.

The screen behind Larnth flashed the coordinates. A dozen
ships were visible in the corner and moving in the same direction as the Sorenthia.

"Yesterday, the Islanta endured a heavy Vindicarn attack,
so they are to be treated as hostiles. We will approach from
this direction," he stated, indicating the position on the screen.

Bassa listened attentively. Many years had passed since
his last real dogfight and he'd never encountered the
Vindicarn. He'd followed every report since the first engagement with this enemy, though. They were aggressive and not
interested in peace talks or negotiations. Bassa suspected it
was only a matter of time before open war was declared.

"Remember to watch for disruptor fire!" Larnth instructed,
his expression grim. "If your teleporter is hit, it drains all
power, and you'll be unable to jump. If you are hit, it scrambles
your senses. And the effects can be permanent!"

Larnth dismissed the squadron and the men moved quickly.

We'll have to guard against disrupter fire, Bassa warned
his pilot as they entered the hanger. *I understand a direct hit
is quite painful.*

Byron nodded, his stride rapid as they moved across the
hanger. Bassa sensed his pilot was anxious for this flight.
His thoughts were shielded as usual, but the young man
couldn't suppress all emotion and his pensive expression revealed his nervousness. Bassa was determined to keep his
inexperienced pilot from committing any serious mistakes.

They burst into space and joined the squadron. Bassa
reached out mentally. As always, he met with resistance. After a moment's hesitation, his pilot lowered his shields just
enough to allow a connection. Bassa suppressed his annoyance with his pilot's inhibitions. They might be a new team,

but at some point, Byron would have to show him a measure of trust.

Four squadrons assembled and prepared to jump to the enemy's position. Bassa conveyed the proper coordinates to Byron and they waited for the signal. Two squadrons vanished, and a moment later, they were instructed to jump. Byron performed the maneuver, and Bassa glanced at the teleporter's power level. As expected, he detected no drain on the device. He sent a brief thought of praise for the conservation, and his pilot acknowledged his approval before his attention shifted to their current situation.

The first two squadrons now approached the enemy fighters. The thin, silver ships were horribly outnumbered, but the Vindicarn held their ground as the Cosbolts drew near. Their squadron was ordered to hold position and Byron assumed a hovering thrust. Bassa kept one eye on his navigational equipment and the other on their fellow comrades as the first two squadrons drew closer to the target. An unexpected surge of memories flooded his mind as he watched the situation unfold. The enemy was different, but their predicament was the same.

Flying in tight formation, the squadrons closed the gap. The enemy ships had yet to respond and remained motionless in space. Their actions carried a menacing tone as sharp as their narrow vessels. Bassa held his breath as he waited.

Suddenly the Vindicarn ships came to life. With an enormous burst of speed, the fighters shot into the ranks of the waiting squadrons, lasers blasting. The Cassans were not caught unaware, though, and returned fire at once. Several enemy ships were neutralized, but a flash of light told Bassa the Cassans had not escaped injury.

"Intercept!" commanded Larnth as the Vindicarn ships passed through the first two squadrons.

Byron reacted without hesitation, and Bassa sensed his eagerness to engage the enemy. Selecting a Vindicarn ship bearing down on their location, he directed his pilot toward the target. Byron complied and prepared to engage.

The Cosbolt beside them announced intensions to fire. Bassa relayed the information to Byron, concerned he'd continue his pursuit regardless. He sensed reluctance in the young man's mind, but Byron conceded to the other ship's request. With one shot, their comrades eliminated the approaching vessel.

I had him! Byron thought even as he sought another target.

Menth called his shot first, Bassa reminded him.

They circled around, hoping to pursue the enemy ships that had escaped initial fire. Bassa felt the pull as Byron performed a tight curve at full speed. He located several Vindicarn ships, but before they had time to engage, the fighters vanished from sight.

Byron's disappointed exclamation rang loud in his head. The Vindicarn's reaction did not surprise Bassa, though.

They knew they were outnumbered, he explained, guiding his pilot back into formation.

Why did they wait to jump? asked Byron. *Shooting through our squadron – that was suicide!*

They're testing us.

Bassa listened for the damage report. They had suffered no loss of life, but three ships were damaged. A request was issued to the Sorenthia for a transport, as two of the ships were completely out of commission. One had lost its teleporter due to a disrupter blast, but the crew was all right.

That wouldn't be a problem for us! Byron thought.

Let's just avoid getting hit, Bassa cautioned.

They spent an additional four hours patrolling the sector, but there were no further encounters. When other squadrons appeared to assume their position, the fighters returned to the Sorenthia. The men were hungry, but they had to undergo debriefing first. It was well past the midday meal and Bassa suggested food as the first priority.

"Sounds good," agreed Byron as they entered the telepod. "I'm starving!"

"Get used to it," Bassa warned. "You'll miss a lot of meals out here."

The dining hall filled rapidly with others who shared their sentiments. Most of the conversations centered on the morning's brief battle and included speculation on the next Vindicarn encounter. Bassa preferred to avoid second-guessing the enemy's moves, though. One had to be prepared for anything.

He tried to include Byron in the discussion, but his pilot said little. He'd hoped to penetrate Byron's defenses and gain his trust, but so far, Bassa's attempts were unsuccessful. He understood the young man's frustrations with the other officers, but Byron made no effort to fit in with the squadron. It was challenging enough to entice the young man to speak when they were alone, but the boy refused to talk in mixed company.

Finishing his meal, Bassa leaned away from the table and stretched his back. Hunger sated, he felt ready for a long, hot shower. His ears caught a conversation at the table behind him and Bassa's attention shifted.

"Didn't think you'd get that kill, Menth."

"I wasn't about to let that rookie claim it," Menth growled in a low voice. "Boy has no business in our squadron."

"He certainly doesn't deserve to be on the Sorenthia," someone else muttered.

Bassa suddenly detected resentment in Byron's thoughts and realized he'd overheard the exchange as well. Meeting his pilot's gaze, Bassa noted anger and hurt in the young man's eyes. He reached out to comfort Byron but met only resistance as his pilot's mental shields locked into place. Byron grabbed his tray and rose to his feet.

Byron, Bassa entreated.

Don't worry about it, his pilot answered and turned from the table.

I don't envy you, Bassa, Deacer thought, his tone solemn.

He just needs time to adjust, Bassa offered, hoping his explanation sounded convincing.

Bassa did not linger in the dining hall and returned to his quarters. He enjoyed a long shower before tackling his report. Once his task was completed, he decided to have a word with Byron. Bassa doubted his pilot would be receptive, but he had to make the attempt. Byron could not remain in mental seclusion forever.

Byron was not in his quarters. Bassa contemplated other options for privacy on the ship. His pilot often retreated to the courts to take out his frustrations and Bassa decided to try that location first.

His missing partner was not in the workout facility. Bassa could not touch his mind, either. Growing impatient, he resorted to the ship's computer to locate Byron, and discovered him in the hanger.

Well, at least that narrows my search, Bassa thought as he entered the nearest telepod.

Several squadrons were currently on patrol but activity in the hanger was light. Glancing at the rows of fighters, Bassa decided to seek Byron among the Cosbolts. He wondered why the young man would select the company of the ships and assumed it was simply a good place to hide.

Weaving in among the fighters, Bassa detected angry voices. Concerned, he quickened his pace. Stepping around the tail of a Cosbolt, he caught Byron and another pilot exchanging words. A small group of officers encircled the antagonists, watching the verbal battle. The men were laughing at the pilot's words, which Bassa had missed. Byron's eyes narrowed and he clenched his fists.

"I've seen your flying and you've got no business operating a garbage shuttle, let alone a Cosbolt," Byron replied in his most arrogant tone of voice.

Infuriated, the pilot took a swing at him. Byron leaned back and the man's fist passed through empty air. His arm already cocked and ready, Byron delivered a quick blow. His fist connected with the side of the pilot's face. The man staggered off balance and Bassa's partner followed up with another blow to the stomach.

The others reacted immediately. Three men charged Byron and pinned him against a Cosbolt. He fought to break free, but there were too many. Yanking him forward, they restrained Byron, their hands wrapped around his arms. The downed man approached, absently wiping blood from his nose. He hesitated before striking Byron in the face. Before Bassa's pilot could recover, another blow struck his stomach. Byron doubled over in pain and Bassa decided it was time to intervene.

"That's enough!" exclaimed Bassa in his most authoritative voice.

Startled, the men holding Byron released him. Bassa's pilot dropped to his knees and clutched at his midsection. The antagonists stared at the senior officer, their panicked thoughts echoing in his head.

Damn, we've been discovered!

It's Bassa!

The rookie called for help!

"No, I didn't!" gasped Byron. "I don't need his help."

Bassa stared at the offenders, seething with indignation. "What is the meaning of this?" he interjected over the clamor.

The voices ceased. Byron's attackers stared at the senior officer, their eyes wide. No one appeared inclined to explain the situation. Still on his knees, Byron emitted another gasp.

"Six against one?" exclaimed Bassa, stepping forward. "That is unbecoming of an officer in this fleet. I could have all of you thrown off the ship for such behavior!"

The men cringed at his threat. Bassa no longer had the authority to carry out such punishment, but he doubted these men realized that fact. Regardless, his status as a senior officer still carried weight. Their squadron leader would value his opinion above all others.

"Sorry, sir," one of the men offered, still cowering in fear.

"If you've a problem with my pilot, you can take it up with me," Bassa ordered, still appalled by their unruly conduct.

A fleeting thought of resentment escaped one of the men before he could suppress his feelings. Bassa decided to address that issue once and for all.

"And if you doubt Byron's skills as a pilot, then you doubt my abilities as well! Not to mention my capacity to select a quality partner. If you have anything intelligent to say on the matter, then speak up now!"

The men nervously glanced at one another, but no one spoke. Bassa shook his head in disgust.

"I suggest you return to your quarters for the remainder of the day," he growled. "Now!"

"Yes, sir," the men mumbled as they beat a hasty retreat from the senior officer. Bassa confirmed their compliance with his order before moving to Byron's side.

"You all right?" he asked, extending his hand.

Brushing the back of his hand across his bleeding nose, Byron growled in disgust. "Yes."

Grasping Bassa's outstretched arm with his other hand, Byron rose to his feet. Bassa ensured the young man was steady on his feet before gently patting his back.

"Come on, let's get you cleaned up."

He escorted Byron to his quarters without further incident. The young man retreated to his bathroom and Bassa eased into a chair. Glancing around the room, he noted few possessions of significance. His partner was either very neat or lacked an affinity for material items.

"Want to tell me what happened?" he asked when Byron returned to the room.

Still dabbing his nose with a wet washcloth, Byron sank into the other chair. He shook his head, his eyes on the floor.

"Not much to tell," he growled.

Bassa frowned, annoyed by his pilot's reluctance to speak. "What started the fracas?" he asked.

Byron at last met his gaze. Bassa allowed his scowl to fade and presented a patient expression to his pilot. Emitting an exasperated sigh, Byron slumped in his chair.

"They told me I hadn't earned the right to be here," he admitted in a low voice. "That inexperienced rookies don't belong on the Sorenthia."

"How did you respond?"

Byron guffawed. "How do you think?"

Bassa shook his head. "Six against one?"

"I've faced worse."

Byron wiped his nose again and tossed the washcloth on the table. Bassa leaned forward, determined to reassure his pilot.

"You wouldn't be here if you weren't qualified," he stated.

"No, I wouldn't be here if it weren't for you!" Byron exclaimed.

There was no mistaking the accusation in his voice or Byron's emphasis on the final word. Bassa stared at his young protégée, stung by his resentful attitude. He fought the urge to call Byron to task for such insolence, as he'd done on Guaard. However, he wanted to avoid the role of senior instructor here on the Sorenthia. They were supposed to be teammates now.

His disapproving thoughts were obviously revealed in his expression, as Byron's gaze once again dropped to the floor. He took a deep breath, his shoulders sagging even further.

"Damn Trindel for giving up on me," he murmured.

Sensing Byron's dejection in a rare moment of unshielded thought, Bassa adjusted his own attitude with haste. It was imperative that he reach the young man. Byron did not need instruction or a reprimand. He needed a friend.

"That is why I am not giving up on you," Bassa said in a quiet but convicted voice.

Raising his eyes, Byron's doubt of that fact was apparent. Bassa held his gaze steady, hoping to convince the troubled young man of his sincerity. He had to restore Byron's confidence if they hoped to survive as a team.

"You have the talent and ability," assured Bassa, "regardless of what the others believe. I have total confidence in your skills as a pilot. Given time and opportunity, you will prove your worth to those who doubt."

He leaned back in his chair and flashed Byron a wry expression. "You may think you wouldn't be here if not for me, but I promise, I wouldn't be here if it weren't for you!"

Byron managed a faint smile. "Thanks," he offered.

"Now, are you going to be all right?" Bassa asked.

"I'll recover," Byron answered, rubbing his midsection.

Bassa rose to his feet. "I'll see you at the evening meal, then."

Byron nodded and Bassa left the young man's quarters with a trace of hope. Perhaps he was finally reaching his pilot.

Chapter Nine

You hesitated during that last maneuver, Bassa thought as they entered the telepod.

Byron sighed and leaned against the wall. He'd paused before making the jump but only because he saw a better location for their reemergence.

We should've approached from below, he offered.

That would've placed us too close to Wentar's ship.

I could've done it.

Not safely! Bassa replied, his tone stern.

The telepod's doors opened. Disgusted, Byron pushed off the wall and exited the compartment. He retreated to his quarters, hoping a shower would cool his temper.

I could've done it safely enough, he thought, dropping his computer pad on the table. Besides, hasn't he noticed? It's not very safe out there!

During the past few flights, Bassa had corrected him several times. Byron had worried the senior officer's dominance as a former instructor would resurface. His navigator now chastised every perceived mistake. It annoyed Byron to find himself on the receiving end of a lesson once again.

He felt better after a shower. Retrieving a glass of water, Byron sat at his desk to complete his report. His irritation flared again as he analyzed today's flight, but he manage to finish his task before anger got the better of him.

An hour remained before the midday meal. Byron wanted to take his frustrations out on the court and changed into appropriate clothing for such an activity. He'd need another shower, but the exertions would clear his mind.

Pleased to discover an empty court, he commenced to striking the ball with his racket. The slightly lower gravity of the room felt liberating. The sound of the ball hitting the wall reverberated throughout the court, creating an almost rhythmic noise. The plain, white walls were mesmerizing, and only the faint odor of stale sweat disrupted the sterile atmosphere. Byron concentrated on the ball, but eventually the banality of the room caused his mind to wander.

Why had Bassa followed him into active duty? Did the man enjoy torturing him? After six months of the senior officer's overbearing presence, Byron had been happy to escape. He assumed that Bassa had entertained similar thoughts and was glad to see the pilot leave Guaard. Instead, the man chose to follow him and continue exerting his dominance at every opportunity.

Picking up the pace, Byron struck the ball even harder, channeling his annoyance into each swing. He resented the fact that Bassa criticized his every move. It felt as if his navigator doubted Byron's abilities as a pilot. Why the glowing recommendation if Bassa continued to find fault? How was he to advance as a pilot with the senior officer inhibiting his actions?

With renewed fury, he struck the ball with all his might. The blow sent the ball flying with such velocity that he'd no hopes of following its trajectory. Exhausted by his efforts, Byron crouched on the court and watched as the wild bounces dwindled to a roll. Wiping the sweat from his brow, he stared at the now motionless ball.

How am I going to survive this assignment? he thought.

That evening, the men were informed that the Sorenthia was proceeding to new coordinates. She would join another deep space cruiser whose recent encounters with the Vindicarn fleet required reinforcement. Rumors of the declaration of war circled the dining hall, and Byron listened to the conversations with interest. He was not afraid, but his nerves tingled with excitement at the thought of another enemy encounter. He would not fail to make a kill the next time, either.

"I hear the Jentra suffered casualties," Hannar informed the others.

"First in the fleet," added Deacer, shoving aside his tray.

The man's pilot nodded. "It's about to get ugly. Hope you're ready for this, Bassa."

"Don't enjoy it, but I'm ready," the navigator proclaimed, his gaze falling on Byron. *You're ready, too,* he said privately.

Byron nodded. Finished with his meal, he stood to his feet. His navigator also arose.

"We won't be flying while the ship is teleporting," Bassa warned as they exited the dining hall. "Be prepared for intense simulator drills tomorrow."

"Will do," Byron answered.

And hopefully I'll go without your criticism tomorrow as well, he thought.

Banking to the right, Byron pursued the enemy vessel. The Vindicarn ship dove in an attempt to shake him, but he adjusted course and continued to close the distance. Receiving assurance from Bassa that the area was clear, Byron lined his sights and fired one shot. The enemy ship exploded in a cloud of debris.

Byron emitted a triumphant cry and veered away from the wreckage. He'd just completed his first kill as a Cosbolt pilot.

That's how it's done! exclaimed Bassa, seconding his pilot's exuberance.

Elated, Byron changed course as Bassa relayed new headings. The battle continued and there were still many enemy ships in the vicinity.

He did not get another opportunity, though. The Vindicarn broke off their attack and vanished a moment later. Byron rejoined the squadron and continued patrolling the sector for another hour. He felt proud of his victory today, although he doubted one kill would garner respect from the other officers. Perhaps it would curtail Bassa's endless criticisms, though.

Two ships were damaged during the fight, but there was no loss of life. The men were in good spirits when they returned to the Sorenthia. Byron tried to conceal his smugness, but he smiled when he heard another pilot comment that the rookie had downed an enemy fighter. Bassa again extended thoughts of praise, but they were followed by a word of caution.

Don't let it go to your head.

Byron frowned at the implication and chose to ignore his navigator's comment. This was his moment of glory and he'd not permit Bassa to dampen his spirits.

After the debriefing, one of the pilots approached Byron as he exited the room.

"Congratulations," he said, his eyes bright. "First kill?"

Byron stared at the man, contemplating his response. He was one of the younger officers, although still several years Byron's senior. The pilot's blue eyes reflected genuine interest and sincerity.

"Yes," Byron admitted, still wary.

The man nodded, his dark, curly locks bobbing across his forehead. "You stay aboard the Sorenthia for long, it won't be your last one. I've seen more action on this ship that my previous two assignments put together."

"That so?" asked Byron.

The pilot smiled and offered his hand. "I'm Ernx."

"Byron," he replied, returning the pilot's gesture.

They arrived at the telepods and Ernx flashed another grin. "See you in the dining hall."

Presenting what he hoped was a smile, Byron nodded as the man stepped into the unit. Their brief exchange surprised him. No one in his squadron had spoken to him since his first day aboard ship. The prospect of companionship outside of Bassa's company pleased him. Perhaps he'd even make a friend.

The following few days saw no action from the Vindicarn, and the squadron concentrated on drills. While his attempts to forge a friendship with Ernx were succeeding, his interaction in the cockpit with Bassa was rapidly deteriorating. His navigator corrected numerous maneuvers, questioning Byron's every decision, and their flights reflected this uneven exchange of opinion.

His patience came to an end during an engagement exercise. In pursuit of a drone, their path was set to coincide with another Cosbolt. Making a quick calculation, Byron sensed the drone would veer right and provide a clear shot. He conveyed his intensions to Bassa as the other fighter pulled alongside their ship and prepared to accelerate.

No, dive, came the response.

I have this!

Rorth's closer. Dive!

Infuriated, Byron dove. As he'd suspected, the drone veered right and Rorth missed the target. Without waiting for instruction from his navigator, Byron announced coordinates and jumped their ship to a new position. Emerging just above the drone, he pulled back on the throttle, placing their target in a direct line of sight. Firing the laser once, Byron neutralized the drone.

Rorth's ship veered away from the drone and Byron adjusted their position as well. Despite his success, Byron sensed Bassa's disapproval.

That jump was unnecessary, his navigator charged. *Rorth had that drone.*

I had the better angle initially. You need to trust my judgment!

And you need to listen to my instruction!

Annoyed with the whole situation, Byron closed his mind, silencing any further conversation. He was tired of the limitations placed upon him by Bassa. Unless he was permitted to achieve his full potential, his assignment to the Sorenthia was a waste of time. He might as well transfer to a remote moon base than squander his talent here.

"We cannot work as a team if you refuse to hear me!" exclaimed Bassa over the com system.

Gritting his teeth, Byron contemplated ignoring his navigator's words. Banking to the left, he channeled his frustration into a very tight turn that would annoy his navigator. The sudden burst drained some of his anger and with reluctance, he lowered the barrier around his mind.

Rejoin the squadron. Now! Bassa ordered, his thoughts burning with fury.

Gripping the throttle even tighter, Byron steered toward the formation. The remaining drones hung lifeless in space as a testimony to the squadron's success. Byron had been responsible for two of those drones, but the victory felt hollow. He wanted nothing more than to return to the Sorenthia and escape the confines of the cockpit.

Their ship was the last to enter the hanger. Byron burst from his seat the moment the canopy opened. Leaping onto the platform before the flight crew had even secured it to their ship, he grabbed the outside rung of the ladder and slid to the floor.

Byron!

He glanced up at the platform and scowled. Unwilling to engage in further conversation with Bassa, he closed his mind and turned to join the others in the debriefing room.

"Byron!"

The fury in his navigator's voice was unmistakable and it caused a passing member of the hanger crew to jump. The man's gaze fell on Byron and he stared at the pilot in surprise. Feeling foolish, Byron stopped dead in his tracks, his fists clenched to his sides. He heard Bassa's boots strike the floor of the hanger and he turned to face his navigator.

"You do not close your mind while we are in that ship!" Bassa exclaimed, squaring his shoulders as he approached. "We're ineffective as a team and vulnerable without mental communication."

Byron's frown deepened. "We are ineffective regardless," he growled.

"We are when you defy my instructions!" Bassa countered, coming to a halt in front of his pilot.

"You don't trust my judgment!" Byron retorted, no longer concerned their heated exchange would attract attention. "You tell me I'm one of the best damned pilots you've ever seen and yet you hold me back at every opportunity."

"I am trying to instill some caution in you."

"Why? You think I'm going to make some reckless mistake?"

"I'd like to prevent that," Bassa countered, leaning closer.

"Is that why you're here?"

"Yes! I'm here so you don't get yourself killed," Bassa replied, brandishing his gloves to emphasize his point.

Byron stared at his navigator. Bassa's solemn expression was at odds with his anger. The memory of a photo on Bassa's desk and the story of the young pilot killed fresh out of training crossed Byron's mind. Suddenly he understood the real reason why Bassa had followed him into space. However, despite the senior officer's intentions, it infuriated Byron.

"I'm sorry you couldn't prevent your brother from a tragic death," Byron offered, his eyes narrowing, "But damn it, I am not your brother!"

His cold words caused Bassa to lean away, his eyes full of doubt. Sensing he'd struck a nerve, Byron abandoned all pretense of remorse or tact.

"I didn't ask you to follow me and I don't need your protection," he growled, standing up to his full height. "I certainly don't need someone riding my tail every damn day. I don't need or want your help! Got it?"

Bassa's stern expression dissolved, replace by stunned disbelief. Byron's words were meant to hurt and he realized he'd achieved the desired result. The bitterness he felt inside was now apparent in the older man's eyes. Byron had successfully transferred his pain, and he was prepared to revel in that minor victory. To his surprise, Bassa did not speak. His navigator stared at him as if mortally injured, and Byron's moment of satisfaction was suddenly marred by regret.

Desperate to escape the unpleasant scene, Byron turned on his heels and strode from the hanger. He retreated to the back of the debriefing room and not even an encouraging word from Ernx could elicit more than a curt nod. He didn't want to connect with anyone, himself included. Slipping into survival mode, Byron turned off all thoughts and feelings.

If only I could turn them off forever, he thought.

Byron and Bassa avoided each other that evening in the dining hall. The young pilot sat at the far end of the table with Ernx and his navigator, Nintal. Despite Byron's solemn expression upon entering the hall, his new friend enticed him to talk, and in no time, they were bantering back and forth. Bassa could only watch with a heavy heart, aware that he would never share such a jovial moment with his pilot. Byron had made his feelings very clear in the hanger.

After the meal, Bassa retreated to his quarters to read. Unable to concentrate, his thoughts continued to drift to the exchange with Byron. Not since Tal's death had Bassa's heart felt so heavy. Any hopes of connecting with Byron now lay shattered on the hanger floor. He'd failed to reach the boy.

The words on his computer pad appeared to blur and Bassa leaned away from the screen. Arching his stiff back, he glanced around the room. His gaze fell on the picture of Tal, nestled beside his main computer on the desk. His brother's image reminded Bassa of the young man who was now his pilot, but he realized their looks and skills no longer seemed so similar. The only common thread was the fact that he'd lost both men.

Rising to his feet, Bassa slipped on his boots and stepped into the hallway. He proceeded to Byron's quarters and paused at the door. After their earlier exchange, he wondered if the young man would even grant him access. Straightening his shoulders, Bassa passed his hand over the press plate and announced his presence.

There was no response. He was about to turn and leave when the door slid aside. Bassa peered into the room and caught sight of Byron stretched out on his bed. The young man did not acknowledge Bassa's presence in any fashion and his eyes remained fixed on the ceiling. Sensing resistance, Bassa grasped the edge of the doorframe.

"May I enter?" he asked, hoping courtesy might break the ice.

Byron's gaze briefly flicked his direction before returning to the ceiling. He nodded and crossed his arms, assuming a defensive posture.

Entering his pilot's quarters, Bassa stared at the unresponsive and withdrawn young man. How am I supposed to reach him? he thought. Pulling out a chair, Bassa took a seat and leaned against the table. He had to find the right words tonight.

"When I first saw your profile," he began, "your similarity to my brother was striking, from your appearance to your skills. And in dealing with you that first month, Tal crossed my mind more than once. I'll always regret denying my brother's request to be his navigator."

Leaning forward, Bassa placed both elbows on his knees. Clasping his hands together, he stared at the rough texture of his skin as he pieced together his next sentence.

"Despite my feelings, though, you're right, Byron. You are not my brother. And the more I got to know you, the more I realized you were very much your own person. Your qualities go beyond your skills in the cockpit or your unique ability to jump. You possess a quiet strength. You're focused, determined, and more capable than most men twice your age, and I admire those traits in you."

He paused, hoping for a sign that his words were registering with Byron. The young man had not changed his position and his mind remained closed. However, resentment no longer dominated his expression.

"I didn't come out here because of my brother or to harass you," said Bassa, his voice as heavy as his heart. "I'm here because I care about a young man named Byron."

Confusion rolled across Byron's face and he shifted his position. Bassa leaned back in his chair and assumed a relaxed stance. His next words were the most difficult, as he was about to reveal his most personal feelings. Byron was not the only one accustomed to privacy and Bassa struggled with his thoughts.

"During those brief moments when you've permitted me past that barrier of yours, I've liked what I've seen. Even the darker aspects haven't scared me. In truth, I can relate. I don't have anyone either, Byron. No mate, no family." Bassa admitted. "I'd hoped that once we got to know each other better, we might even be friends."

Arms dropping to his sides, Byron finally turned to face Bassa. His eyes were no longer filled with spite.

"I want the best for you, Byron, I really do," Bassa stated, mustering every ounce of conviction to convey his sincerity. "I know how much piloting a Cosbolt means to you. I want you to be successful.

"But if that success cannot be achieved with me, I will relinquish that privilege to another officer."

Those words dropped from his lips as if made of lead. Bassa could not discern if Byron's wide-eyed expression stemmed from dismay or joy. The young man rolled onto his side, propping his body on one elbow.

"Don't make a decision tonight," Bassa instructed before Byron could speak. He might only be delaying the inevitable, but it was important that the young man consider all of his options first. "Give it until tomorrow. If you request a new navigator, I will do everything in my power to secure the best man for the position.

"And if you want me to remain, I promise I will trust your judgment in the cockpit. Do those terms sound fair to you?"

Byron nodded. His mind remained guarded, but Bassa sensed the young man was deep in thought. With any luck, Byron would deliberate his decision with care.

Bassa rose to his feet, weary from the emotional exertion tonight's one-sided conversation had required. "Give me your decision tomorrow," he announced, clearing his throat.

Bassa moved to the exit and the door slid aside. Pausing in the doorframe, he noticed Byron had slid his feet to the floor and sat upright, his troubled gaze on his navigator. Bassa flashed a faint smile even as he felt his heart sinking.

"I care about you, Byron, and I really want the best for your life."

Bassa stepped into the hallway and the door closed. Clenching his fists, he lowered his chin to his chest. Tomorrow would likely lead to disappointment. It wouldn't be the first time a pilot had let him down, but it would hurt the most.

He'd done everything within his power. It was all up to Byron now.

Rising with a headache after a restless night, Byron could not seem to get moving the next morning. He arrived late for the morning meal and received the last scraps of food in the pans. Eyeing his cold and overdone meal with disdain, he staggered toward the tables. Scanning the remaining occupants of the room, Byron noticed Ernx and Nintal at the far end of the hall. Bassa was nowhere to be seen, so Byron sought the company of his new friends.

"Morning!" Ernx cried, greeting him with an enthusiastic but sleepy grin.

"Morning," Byron replied, dropping into his seat. Dumping his tray on the table, he reached for his fork.

Nintal leaned away from the table and stretched. "Glad we have the day off. I couldn't have flown today to save my life."

"Me neither," admitted Byron, poking at his food. "Seen Bassa this morning?" he asked in a nonchalant tone.

"No, but we arrived late," replied Ernx.

Byron managed to choke down half his food before the smell became too nauseating. The camaraderie of his friends as they chatted unsettled him, as he did not share a similar relationship with his partner. Excusing himself at the first opportune moment, Byron retreated from the dining hall. He hesitated as he passed Bassa's quarters, aware that his navigator awaited his response. That conversation required a clear head, though, and Byron continued to his quarters.

He straightened his living space before checking for new messages. Trindel was the only person who ever sent messages and the last note from his friend had arrived two days ago. Feeling cut off from the outside world and yearning for a word of encouragement, he reread Trindel's previous messages. His friend sounded so content with his transporter training, passing along several amusing stories regarding the differences between shuttle and fighter ship. Byron could hear his friend's jovial tone as he read and missed Trindel's lighthearted outlook on life.

Reading in reverse order, he soon found himself scanning the very first message. Byron had informed Trindel of his new navigator, and Trindel's reply was quite amusing. The final line caught his eye and he read it twice, pondering the implication. Trindel had ended his message with a comment that Bassa must've seen something special in him. Byron stared at those words for several moments.

As if a switch were thrown, his mind reached a decision. Rising from his desk, Byron exited his quarters. He came to an abrupt halt outside Bassa's door and eyed the press plate with trepidation. Straightening his shoulders, he waved his hand over the sensor. There was no reply.

Perplexed, it dawned on Byron that he'd no idea what Bassa did with his free time. He couldn't begin to imagine where to search first. Returning to his quarters, he requested the whereabouts of Bassa. The ship's computer indicated his navigator currently occupied the hydroponics bay.

That's an odd place to hang out, he thought.

His curiosity overrode anxiety and he plotted a path to reach the hydroponics bay. He recalled seeing the ship's eco-terrarium during his exploration of the Sorenthia when he'd first arrived, but never felt a desire to return. Using the telepod, he traveled to the appropriate level and approached the hydroponics bay. The double glass doors slid open and he entered the facility.

A large percentage of the eco-terrarium was devoted to food crops. Those areas were restricted and required an escort. It was the other portion of the facility, a garden created for both oxygen production and recreation, that Byron focused his attention. At some point along the winding trails, he hoped to locate his missing navigator.

The air was ripe with a thousand exotic scents, all vying for his attention. Byron tried to ignore the overwhelming aroma of plants and flowers as he traversed the path, but it tickled his nose. The sensation wasn't unpleasant, but it was a sharp contrast to the ship's customary smells. He wondered why Bassa would seek the company of foliage when he obviously possessed many friends and admirers on the Sorenthia. Once again, he was reminded how little he knew about his navigator.

Rounding a corner, Byron caught sight of Bassa sitting on a bench, his computer pad in his lap. He slowed his rapid pace, now hesitant to approach the man. Bassa looked up from his screen and noticed Byron's presence. He nodded and gestured for the pilot to approach.

"Morning," he offered as Byron took a seat at the other end of the bench.

"Morning. I've been trying to locate you."

"I'm sorry," said Bassa, stretching his arm across the back of the bench. "I come here sometimes to work."

Byron glanced at the colorful foliage, most of which appeared foreign. "You like exotic plants?"

"It's peaceful," Bassa explained. "I like this part of the garden, with its alien flowers and vines. I'd originally wanted to navigate an exploration vessel and view this type of scenery in its natural habitat."

"Really?" exclaimed Byron, surprised by the divergent vocation. "You didn't want to navigate a Cosbolt?"

"Exploring space was my first love. I scored so well in initial tests that a different path was suggested, though."

"Oh," Byron answered, at a loss for words. He couldn't imagine Bassa navigating an exploration vessel.

"I believe you once told me that piloting a Cosbolt was not your first choice, either."

"No," he admitted. "I guess the aptitude tests affected my decision as well."

Byron shifted his position on the bench. Dropping his gaze to the path at his feet, he attempted to quell his growing anxiety. Bassa knew why he was there. If Byron didn't speak soon, he'd lose the nerve.

"I thought about what you said last night, and I've made my decision."

He'd tried to sound calm and collected, but his voice faltered. Out of the corner of his eye, he saw Bassa raise his eyebrows. Feeling vulnerable, he clenched his fists and took a deep breath.

"I want us to remain a team," he announced.

His thoughts out in the open, Byron glanced at Bassa. His navigator appeared skeptical of his decision, but Byron sensed relief in the man's thoughts.

"If that's what you really want," Bassa offered, his voice gentle.

Byron nodded. "Yes."

Setting his computer pad on the bench, Bassa leaned forward and rested his elbows on his knees. "I'd prefer to stay here as well," he stated.

Bassa's serious expression caused Byron to look away. He nodded again, his gaze fixed firmly on the ground.

"Can I ask why?" inquired Bassa.

Suppressing the thoughts and emotions that arose in his mind, Byron clenched his fists even tighter. "Well, I'd be an idiot to discard a navigator of your caliber," he explained, hoping that answer would suffice.

Sensing his navigator's touch on his mind, Byron tightened his shields out of habit. Opening his mind always felt uncomfortable; a result of invasive probes from analysts and instructors when he was a child.

You need to trust me, Byron.

Bassa's sincere entreaty caused Byron to relax his shields. If they were to work together as a team, a certain level of confidence and trust was required. He might resist, but Byron needed that bond to fly the ship.

"I'm not very good at making friends, either," he conceded. "I could probably use one."

"I am your friend, Byron."

Mustering courage he did not feel, Byron turned to his navigator. Bassa's smile was genuine, as was the feeling of acceptance that drifted into Byron's senses. It still puzzled him that the man wanted to be his friend. Byron didn't feel likeable in any sense of the word. He'd resisted Bassa's attempts to foster a friendship outside of the cockpit almost to the point of open hostility. His opposition stemmed from more than a reluctance to connect. Byron feared he would fail miserably as a friend.

Bassa's expression softened and his thoughts revealed compassion. Byron suddenly noticed the transparency of his own feelings. Alarmed, he closed his mind.

With a sigh, Bassa leaned back. "It's okay to open up every now and then. That's what friends are for."

Byron couldn't think of a suitable reply, but Bassa didn't seem to expect one. Stretching his back, the senior officer picked up his computer pad.

"So, what are your plans for your day off?" he asked.

"I was going to hit the courts before the midday meal." An idea occurred to Byron. "Do you play gravball?"

Bassa arched one eyebrow. "Feel like losing?"

"Do you?"

"You're on then!"

Byron rose to his feet, a genuine grin on his face. However, his elation went beyond the chance to play against an opponent. The prospect of a real friend held more meaning and satisfaction.

Chapter Ten

30.75 degrees!

Byron altered his course as instructed, his eye on the drone. Another fighter flew over their ship in pursuit of a separate drone, but he paid it no heed. Their target had begun to dive and he followed with all intensity.

Quadrant 749, incoming!

The drone continued on its path, but Byron was forced to pull up as a Cosbolt emerged from a jump. The split second was all the drone required and it accelerated to top speed.

Jumping, Quadrant 681! Byron announced.

Bassa relayed their intentions. The announcement consumed less than a second and Byron jumped before the thought vanished from his mind. Reappearing a few lengths behind the drone, he reduced speed and fired. The green light registered another direct hit.

That's three today! he cried, banking left.

We're on a roll, observed Bassa, calculating their next course of action.

Ever since Byron's complete acceptance of Bassa's place as his navigator, their performance in the cockpit had shown vast improvement. As promised, Bassa now trusted his judgment, permitting Byron the freedom to exercise his ability as a pilot. In return, Byron no longer balked when his navigator suggested a different tactic or approach. It was still a struggle to permit Bassa full access to his mind, but Byron felt he was making progress in that area as well. He couldn't deny the results when they did connect and wanted the trend to continue.

One drone remaining, Bassa announced. *Hannar's on it.*

Damn! I was hoping for one more.

Share the glory, Bassa answered, a hint of humor in his tone.

Once the final drone was neutralized, they returned to the Sorenthia and joined their squadron in the debriefing room. When every man was present, Larnth began to cover the day's exercise.

"Good flying, everyone. All drones neutralized within reasonable time and no Cosbolt losses. The squadron has adapted well to the changes in programming, which seem to simulate the Vindicarn's flight patterns with a bit more accuracy. There were numerous multiple kills today, including three by Byron and Bassa's team. Good job, men.

"Now, a couple items we need to work on ..."

Byron listened, but it was difficult to focus on Larnth's words. That was the third time this week he and Bassa had scored the most kills. The other officers might still resent a rookie in their squadron, but they couldn't deny the figures his team was posting. Those stats did not lie.

"For the last bit of news," Larnth announced, his words cutting into Byron's thoughts. "We are proceeding to a new location this afternoon, so tomorrow's drills will take place in the simulator."

There were scattered groans throughout the room. One look from the squadron leader silenced the protests.

"Perhaps I shouldn't tell you that we'll be stopping at Spaceport 89 en route," he chastised.

That announcement brought a round of cheers. Larnth permitted a reserved smile to cross his face as he viewed the men's reaction.

"You are dismissed!" he ordered.

The room erupted with chatter. Byron smiled at his navigator, excited by the news.

"Do I sense trouble?" Bassa inquired as they rose to their feet.

"Me?" cried Byron, eyes wide to feign innocence. "No trouble here! Just ready for some fun. You do remember fun, don't you?"

"Yes, it was something I had before I met you!"

Bassa's sarcastic reply was offset by a hint of mischief in his eyes. The older man had likely enjoyed adventurous exploits with reckless abandon when he was younger. Byron doubted his partner would repeat any of those escapades on

Spaceport 89, but perhaps he could coax some of the stories from Bassa.

The Sorenthia docked at the spaceport two days later. The officers were given a ten-hour pass with implicit instructions to behave in a manner worthy of their position. Judging from the exchanges as the men walked down the ramp to freedom, that command was open to interpretation. Byron wondered how far Bassa would be willing to push the limit today.

The enclosed ramp spilled out into a secure hanger. Several minutes passed before they cleared the various checkpoints, and Byron grew restless. He sensed his navigator's amusement regarding his eagerness to view his first spaceport. Unashamed of his feelings, he made no effort to contain or hide his enthusiasm.

Trust me, ten hours will be more than enough time to see everything, Bassa informed him as they followed Ernx and Nintal toward the exit.

Yes, but will it be enough time to do everything?

The women here are pretty fast, so I guess that depends on you.

Byron shot his partner a startled look. Bassa's comments were always proper and reserved. His navigator winked, and Byron smiled knowingly. That thought was lost as he stepped through the oversized doorway at the end of the tunnel and viewed his very first spaceport.

An artificial sun shone from the vaulted ceiling, lighting the wide walkway that led to another tunnel at the far end. Rows of businesses and shops lined either side of the foot corridor, their designs unique and varied, and many boasted colorful signs and marquees. The glowing emblems and lights would undoubtedly take on a new life when the main lights dimmed at night, casting strange shadows across the crowds. Benches and computer terminals dotted the center of the walkway, and two large glass lifts were moving up the far wall, their compartments full.

From his vantage point on the wide balcony, Byron noted several species in evidence. He'd encountered most of the alien races at one point or another on Cassa, but not in such vast quantities. The sea of beings moved like an ever-changing kaleidoscope, as colorful as the glowing shop signs. The spaceport boasted a wide variety of people and creatures, which meant the establishments would match the diversity represented. As promised, the men would not lack for entertainment while on Spaceport 89.

Someone brushed his arm in passing, and the sensation returned Byron to reality. He glanced at Bassa and noticed his navigator was grinning. Aware that his mouth hung open, Byron straightened his shoulders and regained his composure. Hopefully no one else observed his foolish expression.

"Come on, Byron!" Ernx cried.

Without further delay, he and Bassa followed their friends down the short ramp. Joining the throngs of people on the main walkway, they began navigating the obstacle course. The Sorenthia's arrival had coincided with the midday meal and various aromas permeated the air. The enticing smell of food caused his stomach to growl.

"First thing, I want some real food!" he announced.

"Real spicy food!" Ernx exclaimed, flashing a grin Byron's direction. His eager expression altered when his gaze shifted to Bassa. "If that's all right with you, sir?"

Bassa exhibited a patient smile. "Sure."

The young man glanced at Byron, who offered a sly wink. Ernx's smile returned.

Riding a lift to the next level, the men found an establishment to their liking. The small dining area was well lit, offsetting the dark red tapestries on the walls, and the atmosphere felt comfortable. Several other officers were already present and indulging in the foreign cuisine. Hannar and Deacer occupied a large table in the corner and gestured for the newcomers to join them.

"A decent meal's always the first order of business," Deacer observed with a smirk.

"Some things never change," said Bassa, taking the seat next to the man.

Byron dropped into the chair beside Bassa, unsure of the present company. Hannar and Deacer rarely spoke to him on board the Sorenthia. However, in this casual setting they were a little more congenial. Byron's two friends were not at a loss for words and discussed their plans for the day in detail.

Among good company and food, Byron discovered that he enjoyed sharing a meal with the other officers.

"I think it's time," Ernx announced, glancing at his navigator, "to do some gambling."

Nintal grinned and rose to his feet. "Anyone care to join us?" he enticed, scanning the table.

Deacer waved the men away. "That's an evening activity for me," he declared, his smile suggesting amusement at their haste. "You young ones go waste your credits early."

Ernx glanced at Byron, and he toyed with the idea of spending the day with his friends. He sensed Bassa held no interest in gambling, although he didn't seem opposed to the idea. Byron decided to trust the wisdom of his partner and declined Ernx's offer.

You could've joined them, Bassa commented as the young men departed.

Well, if I'm going to get into trouble, I'd probably fare better in your company, Byron explained.

Deacer and Hannar accompanied them when Bassa and Byron set out to explore the spaceport. The experience was new to Byron and he struggled to control his eager naiveté. Viewing the vast array of shops, shows and people, he realized that it would be easy for a young officer to run astray. Paired with Ernx and Nintal, Byron would've felt tempted to flirt with danger. Under normal circumstances, he resented supervision and authoritative control, but the company of seasoned veterans was a wiser choice.

Entering a new section, the men hadn't gone far when Hannar paused at the entryway of a small shop. The others stopped as the pilot let out an exclamation of surprise.

"They carry Torbethian artifacts," he observed, nodding at Deacer. "Sorry, I've got to go inside. My mate, she collects those things."

Deacer gestured for his pilot to enter. Hannar stepped into the shop and Deacer glanced at Bassa.

"We'll wait," Bassa offered. *Unless you want to go inside,* he asked Byron.

No thanks! Byron answered, his response punctuated by a mental chuckle.

Turning to face the mingling crowd, he scanned the other businesses. This level boasted predominantly independent vendors from across the galaxy and the collage of cultures and planets was almost overwhelming. Byron entertained little desire for material possessions, and none of the displays presented items of interest. He was eager to continue exploring and hoped Hannar wouldn't delay his selection longer than necessary.

"Damn, look who we have here!"

The sarcastic tone caught Byron's attention and caused a ripple of annoyance in his thoughts. He turned to face the speaker and observed two officers bearing down on his and Bassa's location. They were not members of the Sorenthia, and their appearance was scraggly and unkempt. The man in the lead smiled at Bassa, but there was nothing friendly in his evil grin. His tall, wiry frame and uneven gait suggested a rough life coupled with an even more difficult attitude. Sensing trouble, Byron braced himself as the officer came to an abrupt halt in front of Bassa, his shoulders back and chest forward in defiance.

"Cerenth," Byron's navigator said by way of acknowledgement, his voice calm but cold.

"Bassa," the man replied, drawling the name on purpose.

Animosity sparked between the two men, as evidenced in their defensive postures and narrowed eyes. Despite the man's toughness as an instructor, others tended to like and respect Bassa. Byron wondered what circumstances could've invoked such resentment in Cerenth and regarded the stranger with caution.

"So what brings an instructor from Guaard all the way to Spaceport 89?" Cerenth demanded, crossing his arms.

Bassa's expression tightened. "I am assigned to the Sorenthia now, and we are here on leave."

The man's eyes widened and anger exuded from his thoughts. "You're flying again?" Cerenth demanded, his lips pulled back in a snarl.

"Yes," Bassa replied with resignation.

Cerenth's gaze shifted to Byron, who stood just behind and to one side of his navigator. "With him?"

"Yes, this is my pilot, Byron."

That answer did not seem to please Cerenth. He stared at Byron with hostile eyes and an indignant sneer.

"A boy?" he cried. "You swore you'd never navigate again and you return to the fleet with an inexperienced child?"

Anger stirred in Byron and he clenched his fists. Those thoughts were demeaning enough coming from the officers of his squadron but intolerable from a complete stranger. It was but a small consolation when he sensed Bassa's enraged feelings toward Cerenth as well.

"This young man is one of the best damn pilots I've ever encountered," Bassa countered. "And the reasons for my return to active duty are none of your business, Cerenth."

"Do you plan to abandon this boy, too?"

"No, I don't!" replied Bassa, fury pouring from his thoughts like water. "And I didn't abandon you. Cerenth. You knew the reason why I couldn't continue as your navigator."

The man took a step back and rolled his eyes. "Oh, I remember!" he announced, his arms dropping to his sides. "You and your guilty conscience turned tail and ran, leaving me without a navigator. Do you know how many years it took me to find a decent replacement? How many degenerate, low-ranking assignments I endured due to incompetent navigators? By the time I acquired Durn, I no longer qualified for the better posts – and all thanks to you!"

The hostility in Cerenth's voice rose with each syllable. Sensing the man's fury, Byron realized the exchange might turn physical. He edged closer to Bassa, his gaze locked on Cerenth and the man accompanying the irate pilot.

My fight, not yours, Bassa told Byron.

We're a team, remember?

"I am not responsible for your uneven career," Bassa said aloud, still focused on his antagonist. "You had every opportunity after my departure."

"Opportunity?" Cerenth demanded, his fists clenched. "You left me with no options!"

"Your lack of leadership qualities left you with no options."

Enraged by Bassa's words, Cerenth swung his right fist, moving with incredible agility. Bassa reacted with equal speed, jostling Byron out of position, and avoiding a direct hit. This only infuriated the man and he pressed forward, fist raised again. Hannar and Deacer appeared in the shop's doorway as the two men braced and Bassa appeared to hesitate. Cerenth swung his fist, which Bassa avoided, but it was the man's left jab coming in low that he missed. Before Byron or the others could intervene, Cerenth slammed his fist into Bassa's mid-section. Uttering an expletive, Deacer moved forward to seize Bassa's attacker.

Seeing his friend double over in pain, Byron reacted first. Without any thought for his own safety, he charged Cerenth and buried his shoulder into the man's exposed side. Throwing all of his weight into the maneuver, Byron knocked Bassa's attacker into Deacer's outstretched hands. Grasping the man's shoulders, the navigator pulled Cerenth away from his intended target, and in one fluid, twisting motion, shoved the antagonist into Durn.

"I see you still can't control that temper, Cerenth!" observed Deacer.

Regaining his footing, Cerenth appeared ready to attack Deacer as well. Hannar moved to his navigator's side, their shoulders just touching. Byron held his position on the other side of the senior officer, and together, they formed an impenetrable barrier. Eyeing the living wall before him, Cerenth hesitated in a crouch. He face appeared flushed from his exertions, but he showed no signs of yielding.

"This isn't your fight!" he exclaimed, staring at the others with hate-filled eyes. Cerenth shook off the restraining hand of his navigator, who seemed more concerned than his pilot with the situation.

"If you want a fight," began Bassa, his voice strained, "let's take it from the streets to the circle, Cerenth."

Byron glanced at his navigator, his body still prepared to react should Cerenth charge again. Bassa's posture remained stooped, but Byron knew that threatening tone all too well. The senior officer might appear shaken, but his threat was not empty. He intended to make good on the promise to fight Cerenth in a legitimate fight.

"Come on, Cerenth, we're creating a scene," his navigator admonished, seizing the man's forearm.

Shoving aside his partner's hand in obvious disgust, Cerenth scowled. He glanced at the mingling crowd, and Byron sensed reluctance in the man's thoughts. Flashing another angry glare at Bassa, he lowered his head and set his lips in a thin line. Byron felt sure private words were exchanged between the men, although he couldn't hear the conversation. Prepared for another attack, he squared his shoulders.

To his surprise, Cerenth decided not to pursue the issue any further. Surrendering to Durn's insistent prodding, he retreated from the scene, and his angry footsteps were as loud as his resentful thoughts.

Feeling his muscles unknot, Byron turned at once to his navigator. "Are you all right?" he asked.

Straightening his posture, Bassa nodded. "Just winded," he replied, one hand over his stomach.

Sensing the man's discomfort, Byron wondered if he shouldn't offer assistance. Deacer responded first and moved to Bassa's side.

"Cerenth hasn't changed one damn bit!" he growled, grasping Bassa's elbow.

"Wish he'd taken you up on the offer of a fair fight in the circle," Hannar added. "I would've enjoyed seeing you put him in his place."

Bassa offered a weak smile. Hannar turned to Byron and nodded.

"You showed some gumption young man, taking on Cerenth like that. He didn't expect it, that's for sure!" Hannar proclaimed, a wicked smile spreading across his face.

Byron inclined his head in appreciation. Those were the first encouraging words ever offered by Hannar. Ironic that his comment had nothing to do with Byron's flying ability, though, but it was a step in the right direction.

"Let's get out of here," asserted Deacer, grasping Bassa's shoulder. "Traders always attract a rough crowd."

Byron and Hannar followed behind the two men. They rode a lift to the next level and discovered the crowds were thinner in this section of the spaceport. Most of the establishments in the area seemed geared toward entertainment and spirits. At this time of day, patronage appeared light, but the glow of the evening probably attracted the multitudes.

An ornate set of double doors attracted his attention and Byron glanced up at the marquee as they passed. He frowned at the strange words. He detected the Cassan words for virtual and simulation, but the remainder of the phrase lay beyond his understanding.

Bassa paused and glanced at his pilot. "Have you ever viewed a Fesellan light display?" he asked, inclining his head toward the double doors.

Byron recalled reading about the incredible feature of light and sound created by the Fesell. The display was designed to immerse the viewer and he would enter a state more complete than any simulator. The involvement of the audience's emotions supposedly invoked an intense and realistic response. That aspect unnerved him, as it invaded his privacy. The concept intrigued him, though, and Byron realized his curiosity outweighed his caution.

His gaze shifted from the front of the building to his navigator. Judging from his partner's smile, Byron's thoughts on the matter were already apparent.

"You need to experience it at least once," Bassa proclaimed.

"I think I'll skip this adventure," Deacer announced. "Makes me dizzy."

Hannar chuckled. "And my flying doesn't?"

The two men elected to pass on the light show and they parted company. Feeling uncertain of his decision, Byron followed his navigator inside. If the experience proved too intense or intrusive, he could always leave.

Entering the main room, he was surprised by the simplicity of the set. The theater-styled facility was lit by low light, revealing a round stage situated prominently in the center. Otherworldly music floated on the air, although not loud enough to overwhelm. Thin tables with oversized, padded chairs circled the stage in a spiraling pattern, rising in altitude and providing every patron with a clear view of the action. Byron noted that many of the seats were already occupied. He suspected that the prospect of an afternoon drink drew in many of the men, but the Fesellan display was clearly a popular attraction.

Bassa gestured to an open table in the back row. A server appeared and Byron permitted his navigator the honor of ordering drinks. His thoughts were on the empty stage and the show that would soon ensue. From his vantage point, the stage appeared liquid, although there were no ripples across the surface to confirm his suspicions. Perplexed, Byron continued to stare at the apparatus until the server returned with their drinks.

"So this show will really amaze me, then?" he asked, reaching for his drink.

Bassa had already raised his glass to his lips. "You won't be disappointed," he promised, setting his drink on the table. "At any rate, I needed a moment to sit and collect myself."

His admission caught Byron's attention. "Are you all right?" he inquired, concerned for his older partner.

Taking another drink, Bassa nodded. "I will be."

Byron did not have time to ponder his navigator's words. The lights dimmed and the room plunged into darkness. The surface of the stage now glowed with flowing swirls of color, proof that his earlier assumptions were correct. The glow from the spectrum rose above the stage, and Byron followed the trails of light to the ceiling, where he noticed the pattern was repeated on an inverted stage. Fascinated and yet still cautious, he leaned back in his chair and prepared for the spectacle.

A burst of light erupted, filling the space between the mirrored stages with color. The flash of luminance was accompanied by music, and the sound filled the room with a physical presence. Byron felt it vibrate in his chest although it did not hurt his ears. The colorful lights began to twist and spiral, presenting a kaleidoscope of shifting images and shapes. His senses enveloped in a manner more consuming than reality, Byron felt mesmerized by the display and did not fight the sensation.

At some point, he realized that his emotions were captivated as well. The sights and sounds were inviting, prompting the release of his mental shields. He sensed Bassa's mental surrender, but balked at the revelation of his own feelings. Fighting the exposure and reckless inhibition, not to mention panic rising in his chest, Byron struggled to close his mind.

Don't fight it, echoed Bassa's voice within his head. *There's nothing to fear. No one else can hear you.*

His steady tone appealed to Byron's thoughts, as did Bassa's reasoning. Forcing his mind to relax, he realized the sights and sounds held no real threat. Byron at once felt foolish. His greatest fear did not stem from the possibility of death every time he climbed into the cockpit. It resided in his inability to open his mind.

The churning lights began to fade. The music dwindled to a few soft notes, punctuating the last flashes of color. Within seconds, the room plunged into darkness. The sudden lack of input startled him, and Byron reached out with his hands for a tangible object. His fingers grasped the edge of the table, providing a physical connection. Byron's eyes caught the lights as they returned to full illumination, and the eager voices of the other participants reached his ears. His heart continued to race from the emotional charge of the show. Still grasping the edge of the table, Byron shot his navigator an accusing glare.

"You didn't tell me it would invade my mind!" he hissed.

Bassa chuckled and reached for his drink. "No, because you would've refused and missed out on an incredible spectacle."

Annoyed by the violation of his privacy, not to mention his childish fear of such an occurrence, Byron reached for his glass. To his chagrin, his hand trembled as he raised the drink to his lips. He downed the contents in one gulp, hoping to settle his agitated nerves. The Fesellan light display had penetrated his mind further than he preferred. In such close proximity, Bassa had obviously heard his exposed thoughts.

I did.

Startled, Byron almost dropped his glass. He didn't realize his thoughts were continuing to project.

"You need to learn to relax," Bassa continued aloud, stretching his legs under the table. "Fesellan lights are supposed to still a troubled mind. I think you needed it. I know I did."

Byron caught the emotional charge of his friend's voice. He did not need to read Bassa's thoughts to know the incident with Cerenth troubled his navigator. Leaning back in his seat, Byron regarded his partner with concerned interest.

"Cerenth was your pilot," he said, stating the obvious.

144

"Before I became an instructor on Guaard, yes," Bassa replied, eyeing the empty glass in his hands. "And we obviously did not part on friendly terms."

The server appeared once again, bringing two more drinks. Byron waited until the man had moved to the next table before speaking again.

"I really can't picture Cerenth as your pilot," he declared in a firm voice.

A smile tugged at Bassa's lips. "He was my pilot for over ten years. I'd flown with two other pilots prior to Cerenth. By the time we joined forces, my skills were at their peak. Cerenth was a talented and daring pilot and together we made a decent team. It did not take long before we were the talk of the fleet. No one else could match our talent and ability in the cockpit."

Byron frowned. "But you gave it all up?"

The senior officer nodded, his thoughts and expression solemn. "After Tal was killed, I didn't have the heart to continue. I couldn't change his fate, but I wanted to prevent other young men from meeting a similar demise. I resigned my position as squadron leader and transferred to Guaard. Cerenth did not follow."

"Is that why he's so damn bitter?"

"He thinks I let him down and ruined his career." Bassa turned to meet Byron's anxious gaze. "But Cerenth had already sealed his own fate. He was very volatile and difficult to work with under the best of circumstances. We functioned well in the cockpit, but it was a strain. At the time, our esteemed reputation outweighed the challenges and aggravation of dealing with Cerenth.

"After my departure, no one wanted to be his partner. It was months before a navigator accepted the position. Cerenth's attitude grew worse and he was demoted. For years, he sought a suitable replacement, never realizing the real problem resided with the pilot of his ship, not the navigator."

Byron shifted in his seat. "Hope I'm not as difficult as Cerenth," he murmured, his eyes on his glass.

Feeling a wave of acceptance, he turned and noticed Bassa's genuine smile.

"You're not," he stated with conviction.

"I'm sure I have my moments," Byron countered, dismissing the compliment with a shrug.

"Oh, you still have your moments."

That elicited a smile from Byron. He possessed no false assumptions when it came to his attitude and behavior. He was far from the perfect teammate. However, he was trying to change.

"And thanks for coming to my assistance back there," Bassa added, finishing his drink.

"You could've taken him without my help."

"Ah, but then I wouldn't be setting the right example."

Byron cocked his eyebrows in exasperation. "Damn, forget about impressing me. Just hit him next time!"

Bassa laughed at his pilot's words. In a rare moment of friendship, he patted Byron's shoulder.

"Are you ready to explore again?" he enticed, a glint of mischief in his eyes.

"You bet!" Byron cried, eager to continue.

"Then let's go," Bassa answered, rising to his feet. "And hopefully we'll have no more surprises!"

Chapter Eleven

Scurrying up the ladder, Byron hastened to his seat. Bassa joined him in the cockpit and they ran through the emergency checklist in record time. The moment the ship's canopy sealed, their ship began moving into position.

"Seven squadrons of Vindicarn ships confirmed," Larnth announced over the com. "Engage immediately. Repeat, engage immediately!"

Seven? Guess they're serious this time, Byron observed.

They're making an attack run on the ship, Bassa replied. *We're going to be shot out into the thick of it, so be prepared.*

Damn, they're not giving us much chance.

Welcome to war.

Byron checked the weapons again as they slid into the launch tube. The outer door opened and even at that distance, he could see enemy fighters against the stars. The moment they left the safety of the Sorenthia, Vindicarns would be upon them.

"Three ... two ... one ..."

Byron kept his eyes on the section of space they were about to occupy and hoped their ship wouldn't collide with enemy craft. A Vindicarn ship flew past just as they emerged and Byron pulled a hard left to avoid impact. Before he could acquire his bearings, laser fire streaked over their canopy.

Jump! Bassa cried, the coordinates flashing in Byron's mind.

Without hesitation, he teleported to the new position. Bassa's calculations placed them on the trail of an enemy ship and Byron fired. In the blink of an eye, they went from potential casualty to victor.

"Defend that launch tube!" Larnth ordered.

Give the others a fighting chance, commented Bassa as Byron maneuvered their ship through the ensuing confusion.

They returned to the launch tubes. Vindicarn ships swarmed the area, waiting like scavengers for an easy kill. Byron brought the ship in at an angle and engaged the first enemy vessel that crossed his path. Before the ship had time to evade, he dispatched the Vindicarn with one shot.

Five more Cosbolts about to launch! Bassa forewarned.

Hannar's ship joined them and the teams flew cross patterns across the launch tubes, determined to prevent the slaughter of their fellow pilots. Byron focused solely on the ships in front of him and Bassa's voice in his head. This was their fifth encounter since the declaration of war, and he'd learned to rely on his navigator's guidance. If they were to remain alive, Byron and Bassa had to trust each other implicitly.

Once their squadron was in the air and other ships assumed defense of the launch tubes, they moved away from the Sorenthia and engaged the enemy one-on-one. Byron ignored the flashes of light around their ship. If the explosions were their own ships, he couldn't help those teams now.

Caught up in the fight, he wasn't sure at what point the enemy's numbers began to dwindle. Adrenaline continued to course through his body, but not at the same frantic pace as earlier. Byron pursued every new target and Bassa guided his pilot. If the older officer preferred they rein in their attack, he did not voice his thoughts to Byron.

Without warning, the enemy fighters closest to the Sorenthia turned and headed for deep space. Byron followed the Vindicarn ships, hoping for one more kill.

Pull back, ordered Bassa.

With great reluctance, Byron eased back on the throttle. He watched as the enemy vessels convened, and in a flash of light, vanished from view.

Good thing they only do longs jumps, Bassa growled.

Byron sagged in his seat. His shoulders ached from the intensity of the battle. As he brought the ship around, he caught sight of a Cosbolt motionless in space, and recognized his friend's vessel at once. He could discern no visible damage, but Byron sensed something was very wrong.

Ernx? he called. *Ernx, talk to me!*

Nintal's been hit by a disrupter! came the desperate reply.

Bring your ship around, commanded Bassa. *You've got to get him back to the Sorenthia immediately.*

He's not answering me!

Hearing the panic in Ernx's voice, Byron pulled up beside their ship. *Ernx, follow me,* he instructed, hoping he could entice the frantic pilot to safety. *Come on, Nintal needs help!*

Slowly, Ernx's ship altered position. Byron throttled forward a few lengths and waited. His friend's ship began to move, and the fighters glided toward the landing bay. Bassa informed the hanger medics of the incoming injured navigator. Judging from the exchange, Byron sensed Nintal was not the only casualty today.

The ships landed without incident and taxied into the hanger together. The moment Ernx's canopy retracted, he leapt out of the cockpit and turned to assist his navigator. Byron yanked off his helmet, his eyes on the pair as medical technicians rushed up the ladder. He scrambled to his feet and was down the service ladder before Bassa even exited the craft.

Racing to Ernx's ship, he paused as the medics brought Nintal down to the waiting gurney. His face was twisted with agony and Byron winced. Ernx grasped his friend's hand as the navigator was stretched out on the gurney, his thoughts in turmoil. Aghast at the sight, Byron gently touched Ernx's shoulder, hoping he could offer a measure of comfort. Ernx glanced up, his eyes wide with fear.

"I couldn't dive fast enough!" he exclaimed. "He took a direct hit."

"He'll be all right," assured Byron, feeling Ernx's fear in the pit of his stomach

The medics indicated they were ready to move Nintal. Byron glanced over his shoulder, seeking Bassa's reassurance. His navigator had remained by their ship, and he met Byron's gaze.

Go with Ernx, he instructed.

Byron nodded, although he felt uncomfortable with the situation. He followed the procession out of the hanger, his eyes on his friends. Ernx still held his navigator's hand, talking to Nintal as they entered the telepod. The young man was too far gone in pain to hear the encouraging words, but his white-knuckled grip on Ernx's hand revealed his aware-ness. No agony echoed in Nintal's mind, as his senses were numb from the disrupter blast, but Ernx's thoughts projected loud and clear. The ripples of fear and anger were overwhelm-ing. If not for Bassa's orders, Byron would've run from the unpleasant scene.

Once they reached the medical facility, Ernx was forced to relinquish his friend's hand. The technicians continued through the double doors, leaving Byron and Ernx behind. Unable to follow, Ernx stared in frustration at the doors, his mind a jumble of anxious emotions.

Byron grasped his shoulder. Ernx gave no indication that he was aware of Byron's presence and continued to stare ahead.

"He took that hit full force," he mumbled.

Desperation emanated unchecked from Ernx. Unnerved by the emotional outpouring from his otherwise stable friend, Byron stared helplessly at the pilot. Beneath his fingertips, Ernx trembled.

"I can't even hear him ..."

Byron wished he knew how to comfort his friend. Fighting the urge to flee, as Ernx's agony pounded at his senses, Byron scanned the waiting room. A bench sat unoccupied near the main entrance.

"Come on," he enticed, pulling on Ernx's shoulder. "All you can do now is wait."

The distraught pilot allowed Byron to guide him to the bench and he dropped like a stone onto its surface. Ernx leaned forward, elbows on his knees and shoulders hunched, and grasped his hands together. He continued to stare at the double doors, and Byron sensed his deep longing to be with Nintal.

"If he loses his senses," Ernx murmured, "I'm not flying with another navigator."

"He won't," assured Byron. "And you can't even think about that right now."

Ernx glanced at Byron, his eyes wide. "You don't under-stand! We've been together since the beginning. Nintal's my best friend and I refuse to fly with anyone else!"

Stunned by the conviction in his friend's voice, Byron stared at Ernx, at a total loss for words. Shaking his head, Ernx's gaze dropped to the floor. Byron felt annoyed by his inability to comfort his friend and realized he lacked the skill. In the past, no one had ever comforted him, and he didn't know how to reach out to another person.

Unable to offer support in the manner he desired, Byron resorted to the only remaining option. He grasped Ernx's shoulder, hoping his physical presence would suffice. His friend glanced in his direction and nodded before returning his gaze to the floor. With no further exchange, they awaited word of Nintal's condition.

An hour passed before a technician emerged to retrieve Ernx. His navigator was currently sleeping off the effects of the disrupter blast, but Ernx was free to wait by his side. Shooting Byron an anxious but thankful look, the pilot followed the medic into the main facility.

Relieved his presence was no longer required, Byron retreated to his quarters. He felt exhausted on every level and his stomach rumbled from a lack of food. Grabbing a shower and a change of clothes, Byron went in search of a decent meal.

The dining hall was still serving and he retrieved a tray of food. He'd felt the heavy mood of the room upon entering and few men remained. Byron toyed with the idea of returning to his quarters, but a light touch on his mind alerted him to Bassa's presence. Locating his navigator with a small group of officers, Byron joined his friend. Bassa's stable and wise nature was exactly what he needed right now.

A couple men nodded as he joined them, sitting across from his partner. The older man's expression was solemn but resigned as he regarded his pilot.

"How's Nintal?" he inquired.

"Sleeping right now," Byron replied, poking at his food with his fork. "I stayed with Ernx until he was allowed to see him."

"Sleep's the kindest thing right now," commented Wentar. "Especially when it feels as if your mind's on fire."

Byron met his navigator's eyes. "No wonder he was in so much pain," he murmured.

"Takes a day for the senses to return. Although sometimes they don't," Bassa added.

Byron frowned, disturbed by that possibility. Recalling the sounds originating from behind the double doors in the medical facility, unnerving to those waiting in the main room, Byron suspected Nintal wasn't the only injured man.

There were several casualties today, Bassa answered in private. *Three injuries in our squadron and ... we lost Menth's team.*

That news settled on Byron's thoughts like a lead ball. He swallowed his half-chewed mouthful of food and reached for his water. Death was a very real possibility for those who flew fighters, but up to this point, their squadron had sustained no losses. Despite his feelings toward Menth and his navigator, their death was disconcerting.

Reluctant to hear more on the matter, Byron instead concentrated on his food. The conversations around the table soon subsided as the men departed. By the time he finished eating, only Bassa remained to keep him company. Shoving aside his tray, Byron noticed that only four other officers remained in the hall. Leaning his elbows on the table, he met Bassa's gaze.

Are you all right? his navigator asked.

Byron nodded, his eyes dropping to the table. *Just really tired.*

How's Ernx holding up?

That question bothered Byron. *He's really worried about Nintal. Says he won't fly without him.*

They're a close team. I'm sure he appreciated your presence.

Bassa's comment sent a surge of emotion through Byron's mind. He raised his shields in an effort to hide his feelings and inability to comfort Ernx. His ineptness as a friend continued to trouble him. Bassa's comment regarding the team's tight bond also bothered Byron. He doubted any man on the Sorenthia entertained similar thoughts about his bond with Bassa.

Byron ...

Bassa's prodding was light and not intended to feel intrusive. Relaxing his mental shields, he raised his head and met Bassa's gaze. He sensed understanding in his navigator's patient expression.

"Don't think I did any good," Byron mumbled. "I didn't know what to say, so I just sat with him."

"Sometimes that is enough."

His navigator's words were accompanied by thoughts of reassurance. Byron suspected the comment carried a double meaning and applied to him as well. After all, he'd sought Bassa's company knowing his friend's presence would provide comfort.

"Well, I may excel in the cockpit, but I sure lack everywhere else," Byron grumbled, crossing his arms.

"You don't give yourself enough credit," Bassa countered, leaning back in his seat.

Byron shook his head. "I'm better with machines than I am with people."

"At one time, that may have been true. But not now. You are a far greater friend than you realize."

Raising his gaze, Byron stared at his navigator in disbelief. Why Bassa continued to see anything of value in him was beyond Byron. His navigator provided encouragement beyond his role in the cockpit, while Byron felt he contributed little to their friendship. Comforting Ernx was difficult enough. He doubted he'd even know how to respond if Bassa were injured.

Bassa's curious expression alerted Byron that his thoughts were completely exposed. Alarmed, he silenced his mental voice and shifted in his seat. His unguarded moments were occurring too often for his tastes and he couldn't understand the reason for such frequent lapses.

Offering a reassuring smile, Bassa sat up straight. "You are far more capable than you realize, Byron," he stated, grasping his tray as he rose to his feet. "One day you will see that."

Unwilling to sit alone in the hall, Byron departed with his navigator. He felt drained by the day's events, especially those that occurred after the fight with the Vindicarn. Byron hoped he could retire early this evening.

Emerging from the telepod, Byron felt Bassa's hand on his shoulder.

"Don't spend all night on your report," he cautioned. "Get some rest. Tomorrow may be more of the same."

"Hope you follow your own advice," Byron countered. Bassa's fatigue was just as apparent.

His navigator offered a smile. "I promise I will sleep hard tonight!"

The morning held only drills for their squadron. The mood was subdued, but no one faltered in his flight pattern. The men were dismissed from the debriefing with a reminder that they were still on alert. After the previous day's long morning patrol and afternoon battle, Byron hoped the remainder of his day was a little less eventful.

Inquiring on his friends, he discovered they were now in Nintal's quarters. The navigator's senses were returning and Ernx seemed delighted his friend would soon return to full capacity.

"I started hearing Nintal about two hours ago," Ernx stated with pride, beaming at his partner. "We've been connecting and exchanging thoughts ever since!"

His navigator returned his eager grin. Seated at his table, Nintal's posture sagged, but his eyes sparkled with energy. The man's thoughts were loud and echoed throughout the room, and Byron couldn't miss the gratitude Nintal felt toward his pilot.

"I'm wondering at what point he'll tell me to shut up, too," he teased.

"Considering the alternative, you can chatter in my head all day long!" exclaimed Ernx.

Byron smiled at their banter. It reminded him of Trindel and his comical monologue. He doubted his former navigator's endless chatter in his head would be a pleasant experience, though.

Ernx grasped the chair opposite Nintal with one hand. "The medics instructed me how to connect with Nintal and entice his senses to function again. My thoughts provided a path to follow. Now it's just a matter of keeping the mental exchanges going while his mind grows strong again."

"You can't imagine the lack of feeling," Nintal said in a grave voice. "It was just nothingness until I heard Ernx's voice in my head. I grabbed on to that sound as if my life depended on it. Ernx led me out of the darkest place I've ever known."

The depth of conviction and feelings of gratitude broadcast strongly from Nintal. Ernx ducked his head, as if embarrassed by his friend's assessment of the situation. However, the exchange that passed between the men spoke of great friendship and trust.

Shifting his position, Byron cleared his throat. "I'll leave you to continue the healing process," he offered, nodding at Nintal. "Glad you'll recover."

The man smiled and Byron felt a hand on his shoulder.

"Thanks for waiting with me yesterday," Ernx said in earnest, his gratitude transparent and obvious with his mental shields lowered. "That really meant a lot to me."

"Least I could do," Byron countered, eager to leave the room.

Once out in the hallway, he breathed a sigh of relief. The lack of mental inhibitions had almost overwhelmed his senses. Byron was relieved Nintal would regain his mental abilities, as navigators needed to communicate telepathically with their pilots. Ernx would not be forced to make a career-changing decision. Judging from their commitment level, neither man would've continued without the other.

Byron wondered if he was that devoted to Bassa and decided not to dwell on that thought.

Bassa poked at the remaining food on his plate, contemplating his next bite. Constant dogfights for four days straight had taken its toll on his body and he found he possessed no appetite. Giving up the effort, he dropped his fork on the tray.

Byron glanced up from his meal. "Nothing tastes good tonight," he observed, hunching further over his plate.

Rubbing his forehead, Bassa leaned away from the table. He glanced around the room, which was rather quiet considering the amount of officers present. Everyone seemed too tired to waste precious energy on verbal conversation. Bassa felt his shoulders sag at the thought of another day of battle. He was growing too old to maintain such a pace.

"Are you going to make it?" asked Byron.

His gaze returning to his pilot, Bassa nodded. "I'm as able as you."

"That's not saying much right now," the young man mumbled.

Byron stabbed at his food, as if searching for an edible piece. Uttering a growl of disgust, he shoved aside the tray. Crossing his arms, Byron leaned against the table.

"At least they could serve food with flavor," he charged. Byron frowned as he scanned the room. "I didn't see Hannar tonight. He wasn't injured, was he?"

"His mate went into labor," Bassa explained, resting his arm on the chair beside him. "He remained in his quarters so he can concentrate on the experience with her."

Byron's expression turned to one of disbelief. "He can hear her all the way out here?"

"Yes. Bonded mates can hear one another at all times."

"Oh," the young man said, his thoughts still confused. "Didn't realize bonding was that strong."

"It's the most powerful connection between two people. And it's permanent."

That fact obviously bothered Byron. "Not sure I'd like that," he declared, scrunching further into his seat.

"You may one day," said Bassa, amused by his friend's reluctance.

"You've never had a mate."

"No, I haven't."

"Why not?"

Byron's directness caused him to pause as he pondered his response. "I got close once, but it didn't work out," he finally admitted.

"Any regrets?"

"I often wonder," Bassa mused, contemplating that thought. "My life would've been different."

"You wouldn't be out here risking your neck for me?" Byron teased.

Bassa offered a weak smile. "Probably not. But I've no regrets being your navigator."

Byron emitted a short bark of laughter. "I'd like to think I'm a poor replacement for a real mate."

That triggered a sense of the ridiculous in Bassa. "Well, you do lack in certain areas," he observed, one eyebrow cocked.

"Can't help you there!"

Bassa chuckled. "At least you're good company."

His pilot smiled. It occurred to Bassa that Byron's mental shields were down and his mind unguarded. Under normal circumstances, the young man was protective of his privacy. He was not actively blocking now, though. Bassa considered testing his partner's open stance, but decided to save that experience for another time.

Byron glanced at the other tables and Bassa sensed unease. Byron turned to his navigator with troubled eyes.

"Is it true Corten lost his senses?" he asked in a wary voice.

Bassa emitted a heavy sigh. Corten had received a direct hit from a Vindicarn disrupter as well as physical injuries to both he and his navigator. Their wounds would heal, but Corten's senses had failed to return. Unable to communicate telepathically, he could no longer function as a Cosbolt pilot.

"Unfortunately, yes," Bassa replied.

"What's he going to do now?"

Bassa shook his head. "I think he's still in shock. His navigator hasn't decided if he'll continue without Corten, either."

Byron sighed, his gaze dropping to the table's surface. Bassa sensed discomfort and indecision as his pilot's mind processed the information. The possibility that either of them could lose their senses bothered Byron on multiple levels. The conflicting emotions flit through his mind at a rapid pace before the young man settled on anger.

"Need to blast every damn one of the Vindicarn out of existence," Byron growled.

Bassa pushed his chair back and stretched his legs. "Tomorrow! Right now, let's go get some sleep."

"That's the best idea I've heard all day," answered Byron, pulling himself to his feet.

Despite his exhaustion, sleep did not come easy to Bassa that night. He'd faced many enemies in his career, but none as frightening as the Vindicarn. Casualties were bad enough without the threat of losing one's senses forever. He'd survived hundreds of battles in his long career, but his pilot was still just a boy. Bassa worried Byron would not enjoy a similar tenure in the fleet. Despite his guidance, his greatest fear resided in the thought that the young man still wouldn't escape tragedy. Bassa was now more determined than ever to ensure that Byron survived.

Chapter Twelve

Byron fired two shots, determined to hit the elusive target. The second blast sheared off a wing, sending the ship into a violent tailspin.

Jump! commanded Bassa, the coordinates flashing into Byron's mind.

He felt a slight impact as they teleported to safety. Upon re-entry, he scanned for damage.

Just nicked the hull, Bassa announced. *We can still fly.*

That was too close, Byron replied, turning the ship to rejoin the fight.

Incoming!

Byron noted the enemy fighter bearing down on their position and went on the defensive. Their ship dove, spiraling downward. The Vindicarn followed, taking the bait. Laser blasts shot past their nose, the flashes almost blinding. Byron caught his breath as he conveyed his intentions. Bassa's reply was instant affirmation.

In the blink of an eye, they were behind the enemy fighter and bearing down at full speed. Byron's thumb pressed hard on the trigger and a single bolt emanated from their vessel. In a brilliant flash of light, the Vindicarn ship exploded.

Gotcha! exclaimed Byron, soaring past the scraps of debris.

Watch your jump count, cautioned Bassa.

Only seven! Byron protested. He still had several jumps remaining.

Rorth's in trouble!

Following his navigator's direction, Byron located Rorth's team amidst the confusion. Their weapons damaged and jump capabilities exhausted, the ship was defenseless against the Vindicarn. They were trying to outrun the enemy in a desperate attempt to return to the Sorenthia.

Don't know if I can catch him, he thought, contemplating another jump.

Full thrusters. You can!

Byron saw two other enemy fighters join the pursuit. *Damn them!*

Almost in range …

Pushing the Cosbolt as hard as it would fly, Byron gritted his teeth. He couldn't allow those vessels to reach their mark. Bassa informed him that another Cassan ship had joined the chase, which tipped the odds in their favor.

Coming into range at the same time, Byron and the other pilot fired. One enemy ship exploded while another's flight pattern turned erratic from tail damage. The other Cosbolt pursued the struggling craft and Byron set his sights on the third Vindicarn vessel.

Tell Rorth to dive! he cried.

Bassa relayed the request. The crippled Cosbolt altered course and the enemy ship followed, firing two shots that grazed Rorth's wing. However, the new route reduced the distance between ships. Byron fired the instant he was in range and emitted a triumphant cry as the Vindicarn ship exploded.

"Much obliged!" Rorth exclaimed over the com as he resumed course to the Sorenthia.

Byron did not have the opportunity to respond as Bassa announced the arrival of another wave of enemy fighters.

Do they have a replicator that just keeps spitting out ships? he gasped.

Let's go ask!

Upon hearing his navigator's dry but witty response, Byron felt his enthusiasm return. Coordinating with other Cosbolts in their squadron, they approached the new Vindicarn fleet. The enemy showed no signs of slowing and Byron prepared to meet the newcomers head on.

He dodged the initial fire and even took out one vessel before diving under the enemy's wing. A beam of blue light crossed their nose and he veered left. Suddenly, multiple shots streaked past their ship. Bassa guided Byron through the obstacle course of destruction. He had no time to think as they avoided numerous disrupter beams before their ship pulled out of range.

What was that? he exclaimed, his heart pounding in his chest.

Multiple direction disrupter shots, Bassa answered. His mental voice was calm but strained, and Byron sensed genuine alarm.

They can shoot in every direction now? he gasped, bringing the ship around for another attack.

It would seem so!

The new Vindicarn ships hadn't paused to engage their squadron and were continuing toward the center of the main battle. Multiple disrupter blasts emanated from the enemy vessels. The centralized weapons atop the Vindicarn ships were firing laterally at Cosbolts as they passed, creating confusion.

Damn, it's about to get crazy, Byron warned as they rejoined the fight.

Larnth issued a caution to all ships, warning of the new technology. Byron could foresee only one course of action.

We've got to stay below them, he told Bassa.

If we can!

Several other pilots shared their idea. A dozen Cosbolts dove in an attempt to get below the enemy fleet. However, the Vindicarn refused to cooperate and provide the Cassans with an easy target. Once the enemy reached the edge of the battle, which now resided dangerously close to the Sorenthia, the vessels scattered like leaves on a blustery day.

Hang on!

Selecting a suitable target, Byron spun the ship to the right. The Vindicarn returned his fire with several disrupter blasts. Avoiding a direct hit, Byron managed to clip the ship's wing. Another enemy craft approached from the left and he realized they were caught in the crossfire.

Jump!

Their new position provided Byron only a second to collect his thoughts. Two enemy ships bore down on them, placing their team on the defensive once more. The Vindicarn fired lasers and disrupters, sending their ship scurrying. It required several maniacal maneuvers before Byron could eliminate one target and level the odds again.

Every time he felt they were making progress, they were forced to take evasive action. The endless stream of random disrupter shots kept them on the run. Byron's hands trembled as he struggled to navigate the incoming blasts and he relied heavily on Bassa's guidance. They eliminated three more ships, but he was forced to jump three times as well. His nerves tingled from the repeated teleportation and he wondered if he'd last until the end of the fight.

Dive! cried Bassa.

Byron obeyed his navigator's order. Laser blasts flew over the canopy of their ship as they avoided a direct hit. The new course placed them in line with an incoming Vindicarn fighter. Assured by Bassa that the first ship was not on their tail, Byron opened fire on the new target. His shots disabled the vessel without destroying it, and he pulled up to prevent a collision. Suddenly, a disrupter beam brushed the nose of their ship.

Left!

Byron yanked hard on the control, catching his breath at the force of the pull. Out of the corner of his eye, another beam flashed. He physically ducked, but the shot did not strike him. However, Bassa's excruciating cry of pain filled the cockpit, and Byron's heart missed a beat.

Bassa!

There was no reply except an agonizing gasp. Fear washing over his body, Byron realized what had happened.

Aware of their exposed position, he turned his attention to the radar. A Vindicarn ship passed below them. With his navigator's painful gasps echoing in the cockpit, Byron's rage consumed him. Without pausing to consider the dangers, he pursued the enemy fighter.

"Damn Vindicarn scum!" he cried, repeatedly firing his lasers.

The ship eluded him for only a moment before one shot found its mark. Byron did not stop firing until all that remained were particles.

Pressing his back against the seat, Byron gasped, too spent to feel any satisfaction with the kill. A moan from Bassa jolted him back to reality.

"Hang on, Bassa!" he exclaimed, locating the position of the Sorenthia.

Using the final traces of his mental ability and what remained of the teleporter's energy, he jumped the fighter to the entrance of the hanger. Control would protest the location of his appearance, but his navigator needed immediate help. He landed the ship and the moment the runners locked into place, he pressed the com button.

"Requesting medical assistance!" Byron shouted. "Senior officer injured by disrupter blast."

Byron powered down the ship as the conveyor pulled the Cosbolt into the transfer shaft. Stripping off his gloves and helmet, he impatiently waited as the outer doors closed.

"Come on, come on!" he cried when the inner doors were slow to open.

Another moan from Bassa distracted him. Byron felt a wave of nausea and fear wash over him as he recalled Corten's fate. He could not lose Bassa now.

"Stay with me!" he called, unable to reach his navigator mentally. "You hear me, Bassa? Stay with me! We're almost there."

Their fighter slid into the hanger and came to a halt. Releasing the canopy, Byron scrambled to his feet and turned to view Bassa. His navigator's head was down, his body curled almost in a fetal position. Byron could hear the man's labored breathing, which was as erratic as the tremors that shook his body. Yet, despite his physical agony, Bassa's mind was silent.

Byron leapt onto the platform as the crew wheeled it into position. Grasping Bassa's shoulders, he forced his body back against the seat. His navigator's eyes were squeezed tight and his face contorted by pain.

"Bassa, I'm right here," Byron assured his friend.

He released the helmet's seal and pried it off his partner's head. Tossing it aside, he reached for Bassa's hands to remove his gloves.

"I just have to unfasten the harness," he explained, pulling off the second glove.

Free at last, Bassa's left hand curled around his own. Byron hesitated, his gaze on the firm and desperate grasp. He felt his chest tighten as a wave of emotion flooded his thoughts. Unable to communicate with his mind and not likely to comprehend verbal words due to the pain, that handclasp was Bassa's only means of contact.

Roused by the tumult in his head, Byron's anger resurfaced. He glanced over his shoulder.

"I need medics now!" he screamed.

Two medical personnel scurried across the hanger, a floating gurney in tow. Byron turned his attention to the harness and unfastened the latches with his free hand. He heard frantic steps on the ladder and a technician crouched at his side.

"Disrupter?" the man asked, lifting Bassa's head to check his eyes.

"Yes," Byron answered, keeping his voice calm despite the panic in his chest.

"Let's get him out of the cockpit," the medic instructed, glancing at his partner. "We need to get him to medical right away."

"I'll help him out," Byron stated, daring the second man to intervene as he reached for Bassa's other hand.

They extracted Bassa from the cockpit, and his navigator sagged against Byron. Positioning himself under his friend's arm, he guided Bassa to the ladder and into the waiting arms of the medics below. Leaping off the platform, Byron rejoined his navigator as his body was eased onto the gurney. Bassa uttered a deep moan, his fists clenched at his sides.

"Hang on, Bassa," he ordered, grasping his partner's hand again.

The senior officer's fingers curled around Byron's as if holding on for dear life. Afraid to relinquish his grasp, Byron trotted along beside the gurney as they moved toward the exit.

They took the first available telepod and entered the medical facility seconds later. Byron's gaze traveled to the set of double doors as they loomed closer with every step. With great reluctance, he pried free his hand.

"You just hang in there," he told Bassa, patting his arm.

The doors opened and Byron stepped aside as the procession continued. The medics guided the gurney to the left and out of his line of sight. A moment later, the doors closed with an audible sigh.

Byron stared at the barrier, his fists at his sides. His rapid breath sounded loud in the spacious entry room, overpowering the other sounds of the medical facility. In a daze, he spun around and surveyed his surroundings.

The bench near the entrance was occupied by a lone, hunched figure. The man met his eyes and then dropped his gaze to the floor. Byron glanced at the wall to his left, noting the large glass windows that revealed a testing lab. The frosted glass was too thick to discern more than shadows in the next room, but the close proximity bothered Byron. Right now, he just wanted his privacy.

Retreating to the other side of the room, Byron approached the wall. Halting just inches from its surface, he dropped his gaze to the floor. Closing his eyes, he attempted to calm his shattered nerves.

All his incredible talent and skill had failed today. His error in judgment had cost his team and now Byron's navigator lay writhing in pain beyond those double doors. That single disrupter blast might mean the end of Bassa's career. If his senses were gone, he'd be unable to continue as Byron's navigator. The one person he trusted would no longer hear his thoughts. The absence of Bassa's reassuring mental voice frightened him. Even now, the silence in his mind was almost deafening. What if the sensation was permanent?

Consumed with fury and unable to convey his hurt in any other manner, Byron raised his fist and slammed it against the wall. His angry and tormented cry accompanied the sound, which reverberated throughout the room. He struck the wall again, ignoring the pain in his hand. With a gasp, he lowered his head against his forearm. Byron now understood Ernx's resolve. Regardless of the outcome, he refused to fly with anyone but Bassa.

He turned around and slid to the floor. Propping his elbows on his knees, Byron let his head drop against the cold, hard surface of the wall. His energy was drained, but his mind would not be still. Locking his shields into place, he contained the anxiety that chewed at his thoughts and bore into his heart. Not even the admittance of several more officers elicited a response from him, and he ignored the other men now waiting in the room.

His mind continued to rehash the events leading up to the disrupter shot. Byron berated himself for allowing Bassa's injuries to occur. After the first disrupter blast crossed their nose, he should've jumped to another location. Byron wondered if his navigator had sensed fatigue and selected the evasive maneuver to prevent the overtaxing of his abilities. Teleporting would've removed both men from danger, though. He never questioned Bassa's judgment, but Byron wished this once he'd taken the initiative and jumped the ship to safety.

A medical officer retrieved the first man, and Byron watched as the pair disappeared through a second set of double doors to his left. He shifted his position, his muscles sore and stiff. The pervading medicinal smell and distant echoes of urgent voices continued to assault his senses. His mind racked with fear and guilt, he doubted he could wait much longer. If he didn't receive word soon, Byron's patience and rationality would come to an abrupt end.

"Officer Byron?"

Lifting his gaze, he noticed a man standing in the doorway to his left. Byron scrambled to his feet, his muscles protesting the rapid movement. Holding his breath, he waited for the medic to speak first.

"We've stabilized Officer Bassa," he announced in a low voice. "He's sleeping at the moment, but you may see him now."

Byron nodded, afraid to trust his voice just yet. He followed the man through the doors and down a short hallway, his anxiety rising with every step. They turned to the right and entered a long corridor dotted with many open doorways. The technician proceeded to the third door on the left and gestured for Byron to enter. Taking a deep breath, he moved closer and peered into the room.

The lights were dim, but he had no trouble discerning the occupant of the oversized bed. Monitors filled the wall over Bassa's head, their functions unknown to Byron. Wires were attached to his temples, the lines snaking up to connect with the various displays. A tube filled with a clear fluid pumped medication into his arm and a gentle beeping signified Bassa's heartbeat. While the sight was unnerving, what struck Byron was the lack of pain on his friend's face.

"Will he regain his senses?" he asked in a hushed tone.

"We won't know until tomorrow morning," the medic replied. "You can stay with him until he awakens if you like."

Byron nodded in affirmation and entered the room. He paused by Bassa's side, his eyes on his navigator's face. At least his friend no longer felt excruciating pain. Feeling his emotions surge, he glanced at the doorway. To his relief, Byron realized he was alone.

A padded stool sat to one side and he pulled it closer to the bed. Once seated, Byron stared at the still figure. He didn't know what to do and felt helpless.

"Bassa, I'm so sorry," he whispered, aware his words would go unheard. Raising his hand, he hesitated before touching Bassa's arm. "You have to be all right, Bassa. Damn it, I'm not flying with another navigator."

Byron swallowed hard, his eyes on the unmoving figure. Bassa had sacrificed so much, giving up a high-ranking position just to follow an arrogant young pilot into space. In the hands of a less qualified navigator, Byron doubted he'd still be alive. As he sat staring at Bassa, he realized the man's contribution extended far beyond the cockpit. The senior officer had become Byron's first real friend.

He remained at Bassa's side while the man slept. Unable to communicate mentally, the lack of sensation would unnerve his friend when he awoke and the physical presence of his pilot might provide some comfort. Byron's stomach began to protest the lack of food, but he refused to leave. He could not indulge his meager needs while Bassa's body was still held captive by pain.

The appearance of a medical officer roused Byron from his thoughts. The man approached the bed and turned off one of the monitors.

"He'll wake up soon," the technician explained as he removed the tube from Bassa's arm. "His head will still hurt, but the burning sensation will have subsided. His senses will remain numb until tomorrow, at which time we hope they will return."

The medic adjusted another monitor and departed. Releasing his friend's hand, Byron stretched his arms. He ran fingers through his unkempt hair, still matted from his helmet.

Shifting his position on the stool, he peered closely at Bassa, watching for signs of life.

After a few minutes, Bassa's breathing changed in pitch. The peaceful expression faded and his friend's eyes closed even tighter. A soft moan escaped Bassa's lips and pain once again colored his face.

"Bassa?" Byron gasped. He cleared his throat. "The medic said your head would still hurt."

His friend did not appear to comprehend his words. Concerned, Byron grasped Bassa's hand once more. His navigator's grip tightened around his palm and Byron realized that physical contact was all his friend understood. Determined to provide a measure of comfort, he wrapped both hands around Bassa's and waited.

Bassa raised his other hand to his face. Byron started to reassure his navigator before remembering that Bassa wouldn't hear his mental voice either. His partner rubbed his forehead and uttered a soft moan. His hand dropped, and Bassa opened his eyes, blinking to focus on his surroundings. Byron leaned a little closer.

"Bassa?" he asked, hoping to reach his friend this time.

His navigator turned his head and met Byron's gaze. His eyes were dull, but he obviously recognized the man at his bedside. Managing a weak smile, Byron nodded.

"Welcome back," he said with relief.

Bassa took a deep breath. "How long was I out?" he asked, his voice faint.

"A few hours. They kept you under during the worst of the pain."

Brows coming together, Bassa appeared puzzled. "Head still hurts," he murmured, "but I can't feel anything else."

"Your senses won't return until tomorrow morning," Byron explained, speaking with conviction. He hesitated, disturbed by the fear now evident on his friend's face.

"Can you feel this?" he asked, squeezing Bassa's hand.

The man's grip tightened around Byron's fingers. "Yes," he replied.

Byron smiled, hoping to reassure his friend. Bassa's gaze dropped and he frowned.

"You're still in your flight suit," he observed, his voice still shaky.

"I haven't had time to change, you know."

His navigator appeared surprised. "You've been here the whole time?"

"Well, of course," Byron stammered.

A smile played at the corners of Bassa's mouth. "Thank you."

The gratitude in his friend's eyes embarrassed him and Byron dropped his gaze. "I couldn't just leave you here alone," he explained, a lump rising in his throat.

A noise distracted him and Byron looked up just as a medical officer entered the room. He leaned away from the bed but did not relinquish his hold on Bassa's hand.

"I see you are awake now," the technician observed, inspecting a monitor. "Head still hurt?"

"Yes," Bassa answered.

The man nodded and adjusted a setting. "It will subside in the next few hours. Unless there is permanent damage, your mental abilities will resurface tomorrow morning.

"In the meantime, I'll have a meal brought to you," the medic announced as he moved toward the doorway. "You'll probably sleep for a few more hours after that."

Once they were alone, Bassa turned to his pilot. "You should go eat, too," he said, his voice a little bit stronger.

"I can wait."

"Byron ..."

Raising his eyebrows, Byron flashed a wry smile. "I don't think you're in a position to give orders right now."

Byron remained at his side until Bassa had eaten and drifted to sleep again. Slipping out of the infirmary, he reached his quarters without being spotted. Requesting a meal in his room, Byron stripped off his flight suit and jumped in the shower. His food arrived as he was dressing and he all but inhaled the contents on his plate in his haste to return to Bassa's side.

He discovered his friend still sleeping. It felt odd to watch Bassa sleep, but after the man's earlier distress, he wanted to be in attendance when he awoke. If his physical presence provided stability, Byron refused to deny his friend that small consolation.

He'd not waited long when a figure appeared in the doorway. Byron's eyes widened as he recognized the ship's commander and he rose to his feet. Kernen nodded at the young pilot as he entered the room. His gaze shifted to the figure in the bed.

Officer Bassa still sleeping? he asked, pausing at the foot of the bed.

He awoke earlier, sir, Byron replied. *He fell asleep again after eating.*

The commander stared at Bassa, his brows furrowed. Kernen's thoughts were guarded, but Byron thought he detected genuine concern in the man's eyes.

Shifting his gaze to Byron, the commander's eyes narrowed. *Bassa's tough, Officer Byron. It will take more than a Vindicarn disrupter to bring him down.*

Byron lifted his chin, buoyed by the conviction in the man's words. *I hope so, sir.*

A faint smile crossed Kernen's lips. *You've certainly given Bassa a reason to recover,* he offered, his tone kind.

Surprised by the man's observation, Byron could only nod in agreement.

Please inform Bassa I came to see him, the commander requested, turning to depart.

Yes, sir, Byron replied as Kernen disappeared from the room. He continued to ponder the implication of the commander's words for several minutes. His presence here might encourage Bassa, but he couldn't imagine his life a motivational force in any situation.

An hour later, Bassa roused again. He seemed far more coherent than his first awakening although still bothered by the lack of mental connection. Byron didn't need to read his thoughts to realize his friend appreciated his presence, either, as it was reflected in his eyes and the tight grasp on his pilot's hand.

Bassa had no difficulty rising when a medic arrived to assist with necessities. Outside of groggy from so much sleep, his physical condition was much improved. He protested when the technician insisted he return to his bed, claiming he was ready to return to his quarters.

"The senior officer must evaluate your condition first," the medic advised, prodding Bassa back into bed.

Annoyed by the delay, Bassa adjusted the bed to an up-right position. He consumed the water left by the technician before fiddling with the controls again. His pilot chuckled at Bassa's disgruntled attitude.

"I see I'm not the only one who questions orders," Byron observed.

"I feel fine," Bassa protested, shifting the pillow behind his back.

"Head feels better?"

Bassa nodded and settled against the pillow at last. No longer distracted by petty annoyances, his thoughts turned to the void within his mind. The lack of all sensation was unsettling.

"Just feels ... numb," he mumbled. "I can't feel a damn thing."

Byron patted his shoulder. "Your senses will return tomor-row," he promised.

Meeting his pilot's gaze, Bassa emitted a sigh. "I never realized how much we rely on those mental links. Even if it's only temporary, now that I find myself without any connec-tion at all ..."

A senior medial officer appeared and he inspected every monitor, asking several questions in the process. Bassa con-firmed the lack of pain and sensation, assuring the man he felt fine otherwise. Unnerved by his condition, he wanted to return to the familiar surroundings of his quarters as soon as possible.

"Your condition is stable," the officer announced, regard-ing Bassa with a patient smile. "However, until we've deter-mined whether or not your senses will return, you'll require observation."

"Observation?" Bassa asked, perplexed. He didn't want to remain here overnight.

"Someone must stay with you until full recovery is achieved. Either that or we monitor your progress here."

The man's gaze shifted to Byron. Catching the implication, Bassa turned to look at his pilot. Byron's eyes widened and he glanced from one man to the other.

"Me?" the young man asked, an anxious waver in his voice.

"Yes, someone must remain with Bassa to assist with the recovery process. Since you share a familiar connection, your presence would be the most beneficial."

Byron hesitated, his mouth slightly ajar. He glanced at his navigator, his expression uncertain, and Bassa wondered if the young man was up to the task. Byron treasured his privacy.

Straightening his shoulders, Byron nodded. "I'll stay with him."

The medical officer nodded and turned back to Bassa. "I'll have a technician bring a change of clothes. He will also instruct your pilot on the recovery techniques."

Bassa remembered to thank the man before he departed. Turning his attention to Byron, he noticed his pilot's wary expression. Bassa's head dropped against the pillow and he offered a weak smile.

"Thanks, Byron."

Crossing his arms, the young man shifted his position. "Well, I'm sure you don't want to stay here all night," he stammered.

"Not really," Bassa answered, amused by his friend's nervous behavior. A total lack of confidence was a rare thing in Byron.

Bassa was allowed to dress in private, for which he felt grateful. However, his lack of mental connection meant he completely missed the conversation between Byron and the technician outside his door. Bassa retrieved his flight suit before stepping into the hallway and discovered his pilot waiting alone. Flashing an uneasy smile, Byron gestured toward the exit.

When the telepod doors opened across from his quarters, Byron poked his head out first. Indicating that the coast was clear, the young man allowed Bassa to exit and followed him across the hall. Bassa passed his hand over the press plate and entered his quarters just as the sounds of heavy boots echoed down the corridor. Byron breathed as sigh of relief as the door closed.

"Didn't think you were ready to be assaulted just yet," he explained.

Bassa dropped his flight suit in the appropriate bin. "Not yet," he admitted, feeling strangely antisocial. All he wanted was a shower and his own clean clothes.

"Let me grab a couple things from my quarters and I'll be right back."

"Be quick!" Bassa called as his pilot darted from the room.

Byron was not long in returning and Bassa retreated to the bathroom. The cold water felt good, but he did not linger. The lack of mental sensation was unpleasant. Bassa couldn't even sense Byron in the next room. He felt disconnected, as if no one else in the universe existed. Dressing quickly, Bassa escaped the confines of the small room before anxiety set into his brain.

Byron awaited him at the table. "Feel better?" he asked, sitting up straight in his chair.

"I suppose," Bassa answered with a shrug. "Could use some food. Are you hungry?"

"I am now."

Bassa requested two meals in his room. The men said little as they consumed their food. The hour was late and he suspected sleep was not too far in his future. Bassa felt as if he'd slept for days, but it still wasn't enough.

"I've done nothing but sleep all day," Bassa moaned, shoving aside his tray, "and yet all I want to do is sleep some more."

Byron leaned back in his chair, his shoulders sagging. "I'm pretty beat, too. We probably both need a good night's sleep."

Rubbing his eyes, Bassa rose to his feet. "I'll request a cot for you."

A portable cot and extra blankets were delivered within minutes. The men each took a turn in the bathroom before retreating to their respective beds. Bassa stretched out on his back, pleased to feel his own bed under his body again. Once Byron had settled on the cot, he dimmed the lights.

"Goodnight," he called.

"Goodnight," Byron answered, stifling a yawn. "If you need anything, let me know."

Bassa's eyes remained open for a few minutes, adjusting to the darkness of the room. His lack of mental awareness was eerie. He could discern the form lying on the cot, but he couldn't sense Byron's presence. Bassa finally succumbed to exhaustion and the opportunity to escape the silence in his mind.

Restless even in sleep, Bassa finally arose. Disturbed to discover he was alone in his quarters, he went in search of Byron. Bassa wandered the Sorenthia and entered the hanger just as the ship was placed on alert. Without hesitation, he joined the officers boarding the Cosbolts. His ship was wheeled into position and shot into space without even a countdown. Alarmed to discover enemy fighters swarming the ship, he instructed Byron to take evasive action.

His pilot didn't answer. Bassa called again, but there was no reply from the pilot's seat. Reaching out with his mind, he realized he was all alone in the fighter …

With a gasp, Bassa awoke. The darkness of his quarters matched the black expanse of empty space in his dream. He reached out mentally, desperate for contact, but no mind returned his touch. Chest tightening as panic swept through his system, Bassa sat upright and reached out with one hand, his mind disorientated.

"Bassa?" came a sleepy voice.

Turning in the direction of the sound, he attempted to focus on the dark form. Bassa detected movement, but his lack of mental connection with the voice's owner unsettled him further. Only an empty void loomed within his mind.

"Bassa, you all right?"

Realizing he was in his quarters, Bassa sought to dispel the darkness. "Lights!" he cried.

He caught a fleeting image of Byron on the cot before the brilliance blinded him. Hand covering his eyes, Bassa requested the lights to dim. Adjusting to the subdued light, his thoughts focused and he recognized his pilot. The reality of his situation became clear and Bassa remembered why he was unable to hear Byron's thoughts.

"Damn, that was bright!" his friend exclaimed.

As his heartbeat slowed, he realized how foolish his behavior must appear. Moaning, Bassa pulled his body upright and swung his feet to the floor. Embarrassed by his display of insecurity, Bassa covered his face with his hand.

"Sorry," he muttered, taking a deep breath.

"It's all right. You just startled me. Are you all right now?"

"I'm fine," he answered, rising to his feet.

Bassa stepped into the bathroom to splash water on his face, taking a moment to clear his head. Once he felt in control of his thoughts, he returned to his bed and forced his muscles to relax. Doubt continued to nag at Bassa, though. What if his senses didn't return?

Chapter Thirteen

In the morning, Byron was pleased to discover food waiting when he emerged from the shower. Hunger overruled all other considerations and the men consumed their meal in silence.

Byron suspected his navigator still felt awkward regarding last night's rude awakening. Bassa's moment of panic had unnerved him. The loss of his senses had frightened his friend in the medical facility as well. This turn of events troubled Byron. The man never displayed fear, not even in the most dire of situations in the cockpit. The most stable and assured person in his life was coming undone and this worried him.

Finishing his food, Byron leaned away from the table. They needed to test Bassa's senses soon. He waited until his friend had set down his fork before broaching the subject.

"Feeling anything yet?" he asked, shifting in his chair.

Bassa's gaze dropped to the table's surface and his brows came together. His frown deepened and he shook his head in disgust.

"Nothing," he growled, leaning his elbows on the table. Bassa rubbed his forehead and sighed.

"Try again," Byron prompted, pushing aside his tray.

Setting his jaw, Bassa closed his eyes to concentrate. Byron watched with a hopeful heart, willing his friend's powers to return. Bassa took a deep breath, his fists tightening. Suddenly, he lifted his head and slammed one fist on the table.

"Nothing!" he exclaimed. "Just damned empty silence."

Alarmed by the desperation in his friend's voice, Byron cringed as he realized what was required. Reviving stunned senses required an open mind. He couldn't shield, as it would prevent connection, thus forcing Byron to sacrifice the one thing he treasured – his privacy. He felt uncomfortable with the process, but he had to try for Bassa's sake. His friend deserved every opportunity.

Clearing his throat, he leaned forward. "I guess we need to work on it together, then. Focus on my voice," Byron instructed, his authoritative tone catching Bassa's attention. "Listen for my voice in your head."

Bassa appeared skeptical, but he dropped his chin and closed his eyes. Byron focused on his navigator, determined to reach his friend.

Hear my voice, he thought. *Follow the sound. Follow my thoughts.*

He repeated his entreaty, his eyes on Bassa. His navigator gave no indication that Byron's voice registered. Frustrated by the lack of response, he closed his eyes and tried again.

Bassa, hear me. I know you can! Follow my voice. Find your own.

Something stirred in Bassa's mind. Eager to uncover any remaining trace of mental ability, Byron followed the echo.

Try again! Follow my voice.

A tiny sound rippled through his friend's mind, but it was not enough to establish a connection. Abandoning all caution, Byron flooded Bassa's mind with his presence.

You have to hear me because I'm not flying with anyone else! he cried, his eyes squeezed tight.

Something stirred within Bassa's mind and Byron grasped at that thread. His friend could not abandon him now …

I … hear … you …

The voice was faint, but his friend had indeed spoken. Byron's eyes flew open as he uttered a triumphant cry. Bassa met his gaze, his expression incredulous. Byron grinned foolishly as relief flooded his entire body.

"You did it!" he exclaimed, slapping the table.

Bassa grasped his arm and Byron returned the gesture as he continued to grin with excitement. His friend appeared equally elated, his eyes revealing a gratitude he could not voice. Sensing the intensity of the moment, Byron decided to press forward.

"Let's get the rest of your senses working," he offered.

Bassa lowered his head and closed his eyes. Feeling apprehensive but a little more confident, Byron did the same. Taking a deep breath, he opened his mind and reached out to his friend. He sought to connect with every aspect of Bassa's mental abilities. He'd never entered another man's mind before, although he endured evasive probing as a child. Bassa's thoughts were faint, but his senses seemed intact. Byron focused on that area of the brain, encouraging his friend to reconnect. As if sleeping, Bassa's mind began to awaken and return to life.

As the man's senses grew in strength, Byron became aware of a thousand different thoughts. A kaleidoscope of images swirled in his mind. Scenes drifted in and out of focus like a dream. He saw Bassa's parents and brother, now just distant memories. Moments from his friend's first tenure as a navigator, as well as his years as an instructor, flitted past his mind's eye. The images were strong and fresh, and the sights he viewed intrigued Byron.

The accompanying emotions carried the most impact, though. A hint of regret colored Bassa's thoughts regarding his lack of mate or family, although it did not run as deep as his feelings regarding Tal. He continued to harbor guilt and blamed himself for ignoring his obligations as an older sibling. That perceived failure weighed heavy on his heart. Byron sensed Bassa's remorse stemmed from those feelings rather than a genuine love for Tal.

The brothers were never close. The realization of this fact caught Byron by surprise. Bassa had never loved Tal, and only thoughts of the man's parents carried any sense of genuine affection. Despite the vast number of partners and friends over the years, Bassa had never connected with any of them.

For a moment, Byron felt confused and betrayed. He didn't matter to Bassa at all …

You're wrong.

Bassa's voice was much stronger now. The deep echoes released a new flood of thoughts. What he could no longer recall from his parents, and had never experienced from his sister, Byron now felt from Bassa. The acceptance and understanding that had eluded him for years filled his mind. Bassa believed in his young pilot and was dedicated to remain as his navigator for the duration. The life of a troubled young man was more important than his own.

Stunned and humbled by his friend's feelings, Byron dropped all inhibitions regarding their connection. He wished he knew how to reciprocate the sentiment and convey the depth of Bassa's impact on his life. And at that moment, with his mind open, he realized that Bassa already knew.

He felt Bassa's grip on his arm tighten and the sound of movement reached his ears. Byron hesitated, afraid to open his eyes. Reaching deep for the courage, he lifted his head and met Bassa's gaze. Bassa squeezed Byron's arm and released his grasp, stretching his back as he leaned away. Byron moved his arm, stiff from resting in one position for so long. Leaning back in his seat, he grinned at his friend.

Keep talking to me, he prodded.

Bassa returned his smile. *What do you want me to talk about?*

I don't know. Pretend we're on Guaard and I just performed a reckless maneuver. You never lacked for words then.

Byron! Bassa protested, leaning forward.

Flashing a mischievous grin, Byron crossed his arms. *It's true!* An idea struck him.

Tell me why you were interested in exploration. I'd like to know.

His question surprised Bassa. With a little prodding, his friend began to elaborate on his fascination with space exploration. Pleased to hear the man's voice in his head, Byron was content to listen to his navigator talk. He now understood Ernx's eager joy when Nintal regained his senses. After the cold silence, Bassa could occupy his mind all day.

They were eventually interrupted by a call from medical. Bassa needed to return for a full evaluation of his abilities. His senses appeared to be functioning on all levels, but Byron was anxious for positive confirmation.

All right if I accompany you? he asked.

Of course! Bassa replied.

Byron was permitted to observe as his navigator's mental powers were tested and measured. Now a full day past the disrupter blast, his senses were operating at ninety percent. Full restoration would occur within the next day. Bassa was placed on injured reserve, effectively grounding their team until further notice. Byron felt he could live with that status, though.

You wouldn't want me navigating right now anyway, Bassa declared as they exited the facility.

I'd take you with limited senses over anyone else at full capacity!

Bassa requested the midday meal in his room and Byron joined him. The endless questions from their fellow officers would just have to wait until later. However, they did need to complete their flight report before the evening meal. Byron thought a change of scenery might be good, too.

The biosphere? he suggested, aware of Bassa's affinity for the peaceful surroundings.

He sensed his navigator's pleasure before the man even spoke. The open connection certainly required adjustment, but if it assisted in Bassa's recovery, Byron would leave his shields down for now.

Retreating to an isolated section of the hydroponics bay, the men focused on their computer pads for the next hour. Bassa appeared to take his time and paused on numerous occasions to contemplate his report. Byron reviewed his flight information several times, ingraining the final incident in his mind, before completing his account. He claimed full responsibility for Bassa's injuries.

No. Don't blame yourself, Bassa instructed.

Tilting his head to view his friend, Byron frowned. *I should've jumped.*

You followed my instructions. You are not at fault.

But it resulted in your injury!

That was my miscalculation, not yours.

Their mental connection revealed more, though. Byron straightened his shoulders and stared at his navigator.

"You knew you'd be struck?" he demanded.

Bassa leaned back against the bench. *You were exhausted. I was reluctant to suggest yet another jump. That maneuver protected you while increasing the odds I would be hit instead. I made the decision and I'm willing to live with the results.*

I know you just want to protect me, but ...

As your navigator, it is my duty to keep you from harm, Bassa stated, his authoritative tone silencing Byron's protest. His expression softened. *And as your friend, I refuse to fail in that obligation.*

Unable to think of an appropriate response, Byron remained silent. He still felt a jump would've been a better course of action. Eliminating the danger to both pilot and navigator was preferable to yesterday's incident.

Bassa smiled. *I'll try to get us both out of danger next time,* he promised.

You better!

At Bassa's insistence, he altered his report.

With that task completed, they returned to their quarters. Bassa stated that he was tired and would sleep for a few hours before the evening meal.

You need anything, let me know, Byron told him as they parted company.

Bassa paused at his door and smiled. *Now that I can, I will!*

The rest was beneficial, as Bassa acted like his old self when he joined Byron for the evening meal. The moment they entered the dining hall, the other officers all but attacked them with questions and concerns. Byron sensed his friend was relieved he'd delayed a public appearance. Several officers had contacted Byron that afternoon, inquiring on Bassa's condition, and he'd told everyone to wait until this evening. The attention was almost overwhelming, but Bassa appeared to handle it with ease. More than once he stated that it was his judgment, not Byron's flying, that led to his injuries. Byron made one attempt to counter that statement, but a private request from Bassa that bordered on an order effectively silenced him.

They finally escaped the crowd in the dining hall only to be confronted by a junior officer in the corridor.

"Officer Bassa, Officer Byron?" he inquired. "The commander would like to see you in his private office right away."

Acknowledging the request, the men entered the first available telepod. Byron shot his navigator an apprehensive glance.

Are we in trouble?

Bassa smiled and shook his head. *Doubtful.*

Arriving at the commander's office, Bassa passed his hand over the press plate. They were told to enter at once and the doors slid aside. As they approached the commander's desk, Kernen arose with a grin.

"It's good to see you up and about," he declared, extending a hand to Bassa. "You had me worried."

"You know I'm tougher than that, sir," Bassa replied, returning the commander's handshake.

Kernen patted his shoulder and turned to Byron. "Officer Byron," he stated, flashing the pilot a friendly smile.

"Sir," Byron answered, unsure what to make of the situation.

The commander gestured toward the empty chairs. "Have a seat, men."

Byron slid into his chair, hoping his movements did not reveal his confusion. Kernen's appearance yesterday had perplexed him as well. However, he sensed only serenity from Bassa and drew comfort from that fact.

"I appreciate that you came to see me yesterday, sir," Bassa said, stretching his legs. "My apologies that I was asleep at the time."

The commander waved aside his apology. "Sleep is the best medicine after a disrupter hit. I just wanted to confirm your status with my own eyes."

Now seated at his desk, Kernen turned to his computer screen. "I've reviewed your ship's data and your reports," he announced, "and everything appears to be in order. I see no errors in judgment, so as far as I'm concerned, the incident is closed."

Kernen leaned back in his chair, the fingers on his right hand still grasping the edge of his desk. "Just glad you're both still with us! Hate to lose one of my best teams."

"Thank you, sir," Bassa graciously replied.

"I still should've jumped," blurted Byron. "Sir."

The commander regarded him with patient understanding. "I respect Bassa's decision not to place his pilot at risk with another jump. According to the ship's data, you were already draining the teleporter. Even you have your limits."

Byron nodded in acceptance, although he was still not satisfied with that assessment. The commander smiled and leaned forward.

"Do not overestimate your abilities, Byron. Even with your unique talent, multiple jumps are taxing. Trust your navigator's judgment. After all, he is one of the best in the fleet," he added with a sly wink at Bassa.

"Yes, sir, I am aware of that fact!" Byron declared, flashing his friend a grin.

The commander nodded and rose to his feet. "You will be on simulators tomorrow," he announced as Bassa and Byron arose from their chairs.

"Yes, sir," they replied in unison.

"Dismissed."

Byron turned away, but Bassa paused for a moment. Glancing at his navigator, he caught Bassa's wry smile and nod at Kernen before turning to join Byron. They exited the commander's office and he wondered at the private words exchanged between the men. Byron decided not to ask Bassa, but he was curious if there was indeed a past relationship.

We used to fly together, Bassa announced once they were in the hallway.

You're friends?

Yes.

They entered the telepod and Byron turned to his navigator. *Must've helped when acquiring this assignment.*

Our skills landed this post, Bassa said firmly before winking at his pilot. *But yes, it helped!*

Bank left!

Following Bassa's command, Byron veered sharply to the left. The enemy ship mirrored their maneuver, although not to the same degree. Byron conveyed his next move to his navigator and the reply was an instant confirmation.

Reversing the thrusters, Byron spun the ship around to face their attacker. He fired at once, hoping to get in a shot before the Vindicarn responded. A laser passed under their wing, but his second shot found its mark.

That was close! he thought, scanning the area for another target.

They're getting crafty, Bassa replied. *Dive!*

Forcing the throttle forward, Byron caught sight of an enemy vessel passing below. It moved with great speed, but the new angle of their Cosbolt provided a clear line of fire. Holding his position as well as his breath, Byron waited for the precise moment. He sent a single shot and the Vindicarn fighter exploded.

Need an easy one like that now and then, he commented. Byron felt weary after two weeks of constant fighting.

Incoming!

Byron swung the ship around to face the vessel. He was forced to jump when the enemy fighter fired before he could respond. Reappearing behind the craft, he accelerated and took aim. The shot missed its target as the Vindicarn veered sharply to the right and returned fire with a disrupter blast. Byron managed to avoid a direct hit and the ship rolled sharply on its side. Recovering from the abrupt maneuver, he pushed the Cosbolt to full speed. The enemy veered again, but this time he kept pace and fired two shots before the ship changed direction again.

Gotcha! he exclaimed as the vessel erupted in a ball of flame and debris.

Muscles tense and stretched tight during the exchange, Byron allowed his body to slump in his seat. His suit felt hot and itchy and he longed to remove his helmet.

No time to relax! Bassa cried. *Wentar's headed our direction and he's in trouble.*

Receiving the image from his navigator, Byron focused on the incoming Cosbolt. Wentar was attempting to shake his pursuer and flying erratically as he dodged laser blasts. Grasping the throttle even tighter, he requested a strategy.

Head on.

A grin crept across Byron's face. That was his favorite trick and Bassa knew he could execute the maneuver to perfection. Feeling his energy renewed, he turned to face Wentar's craft as Bassa relayed their intentions.

What?! cried Wentar's navigator.

Byron heard Bassa repeat his instructions in an authoritative tone and he proceeded with caution. Wentar's erratic flying meant lasers from the enemy ship were flying in all directions. Wentar appeared more focused on avoiding enemy fire and Byron realized he'd better act quickly.

Throttling ahead at full speed, he bore down on the Cosbolt. There was a flash of panic from Wentar and his ship dove to avoid collision. Byron fired one shot and jumped to safety as the enemy ship exploded.

They emerged some distance away and far from the immediate battle. Wentar's angry voice rang in Byron's mind.

Are you insane? he exclaimed, seething with indignation.

You don't have a Vindicarn on your ass now, do you? Byron answered, annoyed by Wentar's tone.

He'll appreciate it later, Bassa commented privately.

The enemy finally broke off their attack but not before Byron destroyed two more fighters. As he landed their ship, he realized he was shaking from exhaustion. Bassa forgave his rough landing.

We just need some rest, he observed.

The ship taxied into the hanger and Byron was relieved he could at last remove his helmet. His hair felt plastered to his scalp and he slicked the damp locks away from his forehead. Once he reached the comfort of his quarters and enjoyed a long shower, Byron doubted he'd possess energy for anything else today.

He descended the ladder and all but slid to the bottom. The moment his feet touched the ground, he heard Wentar's angry voice.

"You idiot! What were you thinking?" the pilot demanded as he approached, his face livid with anger. "You could've killed us both!"

Byron turned to face the enraged Wentar. "I had the situation under control!" he countered.

"That was your error, Wentar. You turned too soon!" Bassa charged as he joined them on the hanger floor.

"That was still a stupid stunt!" declared Wentar, planting his body in Byron's path.

"I instructed him to execute that maneuver and he did so with precision."

Wentar's head snapped in Bassa's direction. "You told him to do it?" he cried.

Bassa moved to his pilot's side. "Yes I did. He's performed that maneuver many times. The only risk came from your piloting error."

Wentar's navigator had joined them at this point, and he stared in bewilderment at the antagonists. No longer focused on Byron, Wentar had turned his attention to Bassa. The man's eyes were filled with anger and Byron wondered if he intended to take a swing at Bassa.

"Maybe we should be questioning your judgment," Wentar spat, his shoulders squared.

"You'd dare question the best navigator in the fleet?" demanded Byron, clenching his fists at his sides.

Wentar shot him a hateful look. "Obviously his judgment has been impaired by a young, reckless pilot!"

Byron reacted without thinking. Lunging forward, he plowed into Wentar's midsection. The man's hands grasped at his back and Byron managed to push the older officer back several feet before he felt a second set of hands grab his hips. Despite his firm hold on Wentar, he lost his grip. The man's fists beat his back as he was pulled out of range.

"No!" Bassa's voice sounded in his ears.

Wentar's navigator and two other officers were now restraining the man. He struggled for a moment, as did Byron. Bassa had wrapped his arms around his chest, making it impossible to move, and Ernx's hands grasped his shoulder. With a gasp, Byron ceased his movement.

"Let go of me!" Wentar demanded, shoving those restraining him and taking two steps back.

Several other officers had gathered, alerted by the sounds of a scuffle. Wentar scanned the faces of those around him with disgust. Sneering at Byron and Bassa, he shook off his navigator's hand and turned on his heels. His partner flashed them an irritated glance before following his pilot from the scene.

Bassa removed his arms from around Byron's chest and his hands firmly grasped his shoulders. *Settle down,* he ordered.

Ernx stepped back, his eyes wide. "What happened?"

"He didn't like the way we saved his life," Byron cried, his eyes on the retreating Wentar. "Maybe we'll just let them blow your ass out of the sky next time!"

Byron! scolded Bassa. "He's tired and not thinking straight."

His shoulders sagging, Ernx nodded in agreement. "I think we're all pretty strung out."

Now that the excitement was over, the men dispersed. Weary from a long day, Bassa and Byron moved toward the exit at a slow pace. Byron continued to seethe over Wentar's accusations.

Forget about it, Bassa thought.

He has no right to question your decisions! Especially after we just saved his ass.

We're all tired right now, Bassa offered. *I'll talk to him tomorrow.*

Tell him I'll shoot him down next time and save the Vindicarns the trouble!

Byron!

Bassa grabbed his shoulder and spun the young man around to face him. Byron frowned at his navigator's behavior, but he did not pull free. Bassa's expression softened.

"I'm not always right you know," he admitted.

Byron stared at his friend, stunned by the self-deprecating disclosure. If there was one person he never questioned, it was Bassa.

"Of course you are," he stated, allowing his navigator to sense his steadfast conviction.

Bassa smiled and squeezed his shoulder. "I appreciate your confidence."

Byron straightened his back and lifted his chin. *I trust you with my life.*

And I trust you with mine.

They regarded each other for a moment. Byron made no effort to suppress the admiration he felt for Bassa, and he sensed similar feelings in his friend. The meaningful exchange drained his last traces of energy.

Bassa patted his shoulder. "Now, get to your quarters before you drop!"

Chapter Fourteen

"Tomorrow we join forces with the Lathella," the commander announced, his eyes scanning the men, "in what will be one of our most important missions."

Beside him, Byron felt Bassa straighten his shoulders. Every squadron had gathered in the hanger for this briefing, and clustered around the portable screen they were packed in pretty tight. Surrounded by so many bodies, Byron felt a bit claustrophobic. His shoulder pressed against Bassa in order to avoid direct contact with the man on his left, and he could feel the warm breath of the tall pilot behind him on his neck. The announcement piqued his interest though, and Byron quickly forgot his discomforts.

"A large Vindicarn vessel has been located in sector 98-163. It is armed with a disrupter a thousand times more powerful than those in the fighters. A recent encounter revealed this disrupter could potentially neutralize a deep space vessel with one blast."

There were several gasps of astonishment and the mood in the room seemed heavy. Byron felt his chest tighten at the thought of a ship possessing that ability. The fleet was no match against a weapon of that magnitude.

The commander waited for the men to grow still again. "We believe this ship also refuels the disrupters. So it is imperative that we discover a way to destroy it."

The display behind Kernen came alive. The screen exhibited the location of the enemy vessel in orbit over a planet. The commander glanced at the display and continued.

"An hour ago, the vessel parked beside this small planet," he stated. "The surface is mostly rock, but it does boast water and a breathable atmosphere. We believe the ship has stopped to gather resources. This is our window of opportunity."

A closer image of the large craft appeared on screen, its shape as unique as its size. Whereas the fighter ships encountered thus far were narrow and streamlined, this vessel boasted a bulky midsection and many protruding components. It was impossible to see details from their position, but Byron wondered how many weapons adorned its surface. If the ship's disrupter was truly that powerful, it wouldn't really matter.

"Several potential entry points have been discovered," Kernen informed the men, those locations now highlighted on the image. "If we can acquire an interior layout of the Vindicarn ship, we may find a way to reach the vessel's core or main disrupter.

"This is the Lathella's assignment," he announced, raising his voice in emphasis. "We are to provide cover and create a distraction."

Byron glanced at Bassa, his eyes bright, and his navigator returned his determined look. After weeks of endless, random battles, they now had a purpose beyond just holding back the enemy.

The commander outlined the plan of attack, which involved every squadron on board the Sorenthia. Joined by half of the squadrons from the Lathella, they were to keep the enemy fighters occupied while teams focused on five key entry points. Once the shields weakened, single-seater Darten fighters would enter the Vindicarn ship and penetrate its structure. Their squadrons would cease the attack when all five Dartens either returned or their destruction was confirmed.

Potential suicide mission! Byron exclaimed, in awe of the men brave enough to take on such an assignment.

Every time we get into our fighter it could be our last, Bassa reminded him.

Kernen concluded by ordering the squadrons to the simulators in preparation for the mission. The squad leaders announced the afternoon simulator schedules and Byron was pleased they would practice first. He wanted to tackle the simulation while adrenaline still coursed through his body.

By the time he emerged from the simulator, Byron was exhausted. The sheer number of Vindicarn fighters they'd face tomorrow morning was far greater than any previous encounter. Byron did not voice his thoughts, but their mission of diversion might degenerate into a frantic fight for survival.

The evening meal was light, its hours extended for those still in the simulators. The mood was one of oppressive excitement, and anxious discussions flowed from one table to the next. The men were eager and ready, but a measure of uncertainty remained. The simulator drills had revealed a grim reality. Coupled with the threat of the Vindicarn's main disrupter, their chances for success were slim.

This battle has you worried, Bassa commented as they departed the dining hall.

Worried? No. Byron was unwilling to show any measure of hesitation in front of his navigator.

They entered the telepod and he turned to face the entrance, his hands balled into fists at his sides. He hoped his stoic expression would conceal his anxiety, but Bassa wasn't fooled.

A little fear is good, Byron. Keeps you sharp.

Gritting his teeth, Byron felt annoyed, but not with his navigator. As the door slid open, Bassa nudged his elbow.

"Come on. I have something that will take care of that nervousness."

Curious, Byron followed Bassa to his quarters. The senior officer gestured toward the table and Byron sank into a chair. Bassa opened a small cupboard and produced a bottle.

"You still have spirits from Spaceport 89?" Byron exclaimed. His two purchases were long since gone.

Bassa smiled and set the flask on the table. "No, not that cheap stuff. I brought this with me when I boarded the Sorenthia," he announced with pride, "and there's just enough left for two."

While Bassa retrieved glasses, Byron examined the bottle. His eyebrows rose as he noted the label.

"Are you sure?" he asked, stunned Bassa would share such rare vintage with him.

"Wouldn't offer otherwise."

Bassa set two glasses on the table and grabbed the bottle. He deftly filled each one before taking his seat. Setting aside the flask, he grasped the closest glass and Byron followed suit. He expected Bassa to toast to victory, but his navigator simply tapped his glass. In the confines of his quarters, the clinking sound was loud. Byron lifted the glass to his lips, his eyes on Bassa. His friend downed half the contents in one shot. Byron attempted to do the same, but the strength of the drink caught him unaware. He struggled to swallow without losing any of the valuable liquid.

Bassa chuckled. "It's probably stronger than you're used to," he offered as Byron gasped for air.

A little, Byron admitted.

"You'll sleep good, I promise."

Bassa took a smaller sip and set his glass on the table. He leaned back in his chair, arching his back in the process.

"Tomorrow's mission will be difficult, but if just one of those Dartens succeeds, it will be worth it," he declared.

"They won't all make it," observed Byron, his voice solemn.

"They understand the risk involved."

"Damn brave," he commented, lifting his glass. He eyed the clear liquid, contemplating his next words. "Not sure I could be that fearless," he admitted, downing the contents of his glass.

He caught his breath as the liquid slid down his throat, its warmth causing him to wince. Byron coughed once, unaccustomed to a drink so robust. However, he could feel his muscles relax as the liquid coursed through his system. He would indeed sleep well tonight.

"Being brave doesn't mean being fearless," Bassa informed him. "It means doing the right thing despite one's fear."

Byron cleared his throat and gazed at his friend. Had Bassa experienced fear when he discarded his comfortable position to follow a young pilot into space?

"Was becoming my navigator the right thing to do?" he asked before he lost the nerve.

"Think that was a brave thing to do?" Bassa inquired before finishing his drink.

"Absolutely!"

He pushed his glass closer as Bassa lifted the bottle and his friend poured the remaining contents into their glasses. Bassa swirled the liquid in his glass before raising his gaze to meet Byron's eyes.

"It's a decision I've never regretted," he stated.

Byron smiled at the sincerity of his words and the accompanying feelings of genuine friendship. He'd protested their pairing at first, but now he was grateful for Bassa's presence. The man had taught him many things, most of which extended well beyond their time in the cockpit.

"I have no regrets, either," he finally admitted.

Bassa nodded and lifted his glass before taking a sip. Byron downed half his glass, shuddering once more at the effects. The warmth of the liquid filled his body, relaxing his mind as well as muscles. An idea he'd mulled over for the past few weeks resurfaced in his thoughts. While his senses still felt the effects of inebriation, Byron decided to voice his plans.

"I was thinking," he began, his gaze on his drink. "Once our assignment on the Sorenthia is done we'd try something new."

"Oh?" Bassa asked, cocking his head. "What did you have in mind?"

Byron shifted in his chair. "Thought maybe we'd transfer to Exploration," he said.

Raising his gaze, Byron caught the look of total surprise on Bassa's face at the same moment his navigator's incredulous thoughts reached his mind. Bassa pressed his shoulders against the back of the chair and scrutinized his pilot's expression.

"Byron, I appreciate that, but I know how much piloting a Cosbolt means to you," he stated.

"Yes, but my goal was just to get off Cassa," Byron countered, unwilling to be persuaded otherwise.

"You trained hard for this."

Grasping his glass, Byron leaned his elbows on the table. "Bassa, I know you won't be able to do this forever. And don't tell me you're willing to try," he said quickly before his friend could protest. "This is damned tough work!"

Bassa regarded him with patience and Byron could sense his doubt.

"Look, you told me space exploration was once a dream of yours," he continued, hoping to convince his friend of his sincerity. "You followed me out here so I'd achieve my goals. Well, I think it's time you pursued your own. And I want to join you. I mean, it'll still be exciting, just not in a kill or be killed sort of way.

"Besides, when you retire, I'll have to find something else anyway."

His friend's eyebrows came together. "Why?"

Taking a deep breath, Byron sat up straighter. "Because, it took me too long to break in my current navigator and I'm not doing that again. Ever."

Bassa's expression softened and he smiled. Byron felt his navigator reach out, testing for the truth. His mind open, he allowed his thoughts and feelings to speak for themselves. His partner had sacrificed so much. Byron wanted to repay his only real friend.

Bassa's smile deepened and Byron sensed gratitude. "If that's really what you want to do," he said in a low voice.

"Absolutely," Byron answered without hesitation.

Leaning forward, Bassa grasped his arm and Byron returned his friend's grip. Feeling confident, he smiled and nodded.

"All right, then," Bassa stated.

They finished their drinks and Bassa told him to get a good night's sleep. Byron returned to his quarters, his anxiety regarding tomorrow's mission no longer an issue. Those weren't the only concerns laid to rest, either. He could finally give something of value to Bassa.

Dodging enemy fire from a ship on his right, Byron shot at the vessel he was tailing. It was not a direct hit, but the fighter spiraled out of control as it headed for the planet's surface.

Let it go, instructed Bassa, indicating the approach of another ship.

Throttling forward, Byron dove to shake their pursuer. Their new course brought the Cosbolt in range of two new Vindicarn ships and they fired immediately.

Jump!

Bassa's coordinates did not take them far. The ship reappeared behind their pursuer and Byron took advantage of their position. Eliminating the target, he was informed of another vessel as well as incoming fire. Veering away from the laser blast, Byron pushed the throttle forward to catch the other craft.

Gotcha! he cried, firing before a disrupter blast forced them to change course again.

The large Vindicarn ship's proximity to the planet had complicated matters. The Cosbolts responded differently in the planet's atmosphere. Byron continued to adjust his approach, frustrated by the conditions. Fortunately, the enemy was struggling as well.

Jump!

A laser blast struck their wing as Byron teleported to the new coordinates. Bassa has taken them much lower this time, and the ship emerged without an immediate threat of danger.

Can we still fly? Byron asked, edging the nose of the ship skyward.

Yes, minor damage, Bassa replied.

Taking a deep breath to clear his head, Byron accelerated, a Vindicarn craft in his sights. Bassa gave him the clear and he fired multiple shots. The enemy ship burst into a ball of flame, and Byron maneuvered out of its way as the fighter fell toward the planet.

Four of the teams have entered the ship, Bassa announced.

Byron shook his head in exasperation. All five teams should've reached their targets by now. This battle was taking far too long.

Bassa flashed the image of an incoming fighter and Byron moved quickly to avoid its fire. He darted under another Vindicarn ship, hoping the vessel would provide momentary cover. Byron was forced to make a hard right when that craft fired a disrupter blast.

Dive!

Byron followed his instructions, and a Cosbolt shot over their nose, firing at the enemy. Pulling up, he took aim at the Vindicarn in pursuit of their comrades. Both enemy ships were destroyed, but there was no time to relay a word of thanks.

Another wave coming, Bassa announced.

Casting a glance skyward, Byron caught sight of another wing of fighters emerging from the enemy ship. He grimaced at the mass confusion residing over their heads.

When the Sorenthia and Lathella first appeared on either side of the massive ship, Vindicarn fighters had poured from the vessel like an angry swarm, filling the sky. That the enemy continued to send out more ships was of great concern, as no squadrons remained on either Cassan vessel. They were already fighting at full capacity.

We've got to keep them distracted just little longer, Bassa stated.

A flash to their left caught Byron's attention and he turned just in time to see a Cosbolt go up in flames. The sight refueled his energy and anger pounded in his ears. Adjusting their course, he flew at the Vindicarn craft as if intending to collide with the vessel. At the last moment, he fired and pulled up on the throttle. The flames from the enemy ship licked the edge of one wing in passing.

Two more! cautioned Bassa, guiding his pilot toward the approaching ships.

Byron dispatched one ship, but he was forced to make another jump to avoid the second fighter's disrupter blast. Aware that he was nearing the limit of his abilities, Byron pulled energy from the teleporter as a safety measure. Bassa's coordinates provided some security, though. They emerged below two Vindicarn ships, and he took a deep breath before rising to meet the enemy.

I'm running out of jumps, he thought, reluctant to admit his ability was just about taxed.

I know, replied Bassa. *We'll just have to do it the old-fashioned way.*

Byron fired at the two ships flying close in formation. He caught one vessel's tail section, sending the ship spinning, but the other escaped damage and returned fire. The laser skimmed the nose of the ship but did not penetrate the hull. Byron executed a twisting maneuver and pulled the ship out of range. He gritted his teeth, frustrated by the situation.

Sorry! he told Bassa, annoyed he could not jump the ship to safety.

I'm the one who's been telling you to jump ...

And you're never wrong! Byron exclaimed.

Eliminating the Vindicarn ship, Byron spun the ship around to face the heart of the battle. Thousands of fighters dotted the sky. They spanned the length of the enemy craft and extended beyond the two Cassan ships parked on either side. Flashes of light marked the end of both friend and foe. Larger explosions dotted the sides of all three mother ships. The scene was total chaos. However, Byron didn't require a status update to know the Cassans were in trouble. Most of the ships above them were Vindicarn.

The fifth team never made it, Bassa announced, cutting into his thoughts. *And one team won't be returning.*

Feeling sweat run down the side of his face, Byron's hand on the throttle tightened its grip. Would this mission fail completely?

He pushed forward, determined to continue fighting. Bassa alerted him to a Cassan ship in trouble. Byron spotted the fighter, three Vindicarn on its tail. There wasn't time to instruct the pilot to maintain his course. However, he could probably take out two ships by approaching from an angle.

Rising quickly, he came up under the Cosbolt as it shot over the canopy. Byron fired multiple shots, catching the first two vessels by surprise. The third adjusted and Bassa ordered him to dive at once. Blasts sailed past their left wing, nicking their tail section.

Hang on! Byron cried as he fought to maintain control of their Cosbolt.

Incoming! Bassa exclaimed, flashing an image of two approaching Vindicarn.

Desperate to escape, Byron tried to jump the ship. To his chagrin, he lacked the mental strength to perform such a maneuver. Yanking hard to the left, he finally brought the ship under control.

A blinding flash of blue light streaked across the canopy. The stream trailed into the cockpit and Byron felt a jolt of pain that traveled all the way down his spine. Fire erupted in his head, consuming all other thoughts. He cried out in pain and fell forward on the throttle, blinded by agony and unable to sense anything.

Byron!

The ship now spiraled toward the planet at a frightening rate. Bassa grasped his controls, fighting to pull the ship out of its tailspin. The whirling motion was nauseating and if

Bassa didn't regain control soon, he'd be unable to stop their rapid decent.

"Byron!" he called, aware his pilot could no longer hear his mental voice. "Byron, pull up!"

Keeping his head despite the urgency of the situation, Bassa finally brought the ship's incessant spinning to a halt. No longer spiraling out of control, he attempted to edge the nose of the ship up and pull away from the planet's surface. If he continued flying low, perhaps they could avoid detection and return to the Sorenthia. Lacking a pilot and unable to jump, they were in no position to continue fighting.

A laser blast skimmed their canopy. Pushing forward, he sent the ship into another nosedive in an attempt to shake their attacker. Glancing at his screen, Bassa realized there were two Vindicarn ships. At the same moment, a blast struck the side of their Cosbolt, jolting its occupants. Before he could take evasive action, as second bolt struck the ship.

Bassa felt the blow tear through more than the metal. His side burned and he caught his breath as the searing pain shot through his body. He fought the urge to look down for fear it would send his mind into shock. Even now, he could feel himself slipping ...

"Byron!' he screamed, channeling his last remaining traces of energy into his pilot's name.

The sound of his name jolted Byron's senses and he recognized his friend's voice. He gasped, his eyes closed tight against the flames licking his mind. There was no ignoring Bassa's commanding tone, though. He had to respond.

Lifting his head, Byron forced his eyes to open. They were no longer plummeting straight toward the ground, but the angle was too steep for anything but a crash landing. Uttering a sound that bordered on a growl, he grasped the throttle. Forcing his body to obey, he pulled back in an attempt to level the ship before impact.

As if moving in slow motion, Byron watched the ground pass in a surreal blur. He detected the horizon as it dropped into view and fought to slow the craft. The ground now raced past the nose of the plane. The boulders leapt at him as if alive, threatening to tear apart the small fighter. Selecting the path of least resistance, Byron pushed the throttle in that direction. Blinking against the searing pain in his head, he braced for a rough landing among the rocks.

The impact bounced the ship in the air. Byron struggled to maintain balance as the vessel struck the ground again. Throwing the thrusters into full reverse, he attempted to dodge the larger boulders as they rose in his path. He was forced to squint even harder as sparks flew from the underbelly of the ship, the rocks scraping against the metal. Byron lost sight of the scene ahead and he felt a sharp jolt as the nose deflected off a rock. His muscles ached from the effort required to maintain a grip on the throttle. About to collapse, Byron suddenly felt another jolt as the ship came to an abrupt halt.

Letting his head fall back against the seat, Byron closed his eyes and tried to catch his breath. In the ensuing silence, he felt himself drift and fought to remain awake. The searing heat in his head made it difficult to think. His name echoed in his head and Byron realized he needed to check on Bassa.

Fumbling with his helmet, he managed to pry it free. Leaning forward, he dropped it in his lap. Forcing his eyes open, he stared at the instrument panel. Everything appeared dark, but he noticed a red blinking light and frowned. The ship had sustained a hull breach.

"Bassa?" he called, his voice cracking as the sound echoed painfully in his head. "Bassa?"

A soft moan reached his ears and Byron realized his navigator was injured as well. He flicked the distress signal and fumbled for the com.

"Two officers down," he stated, trying to keep his voice steady. "In need of immediate medical assistance."

Byron unfastened his restraints and attempted to raise his body. The sensation sent a shockwave of pain through his head and he winced. Craning his neck, he tried to peer over his seat, but he couldn't get a clear view. Recalling the planet boasted a breathable atmosphere, Byron reached for the canopy's lever. He had to pry hard, but the mechanism finally engaged and the canopy slid out of the way. Byron struggled to his feet.

"Bassa?" he called, grasping the back of the seat and hoisting his body upright.

The movement caused a wave of nausea and he paused with eyes closed. Regaining his senses, Byron opened his eyes and leaned over the back of his seat.

Bassa was slumped in his seat, his body motionless. His eyes were closed and his breathing appeared labored. Byron's gaze traveled down his friend's body, checking for injury. It was then that he noticed the blood. A large, red stain circled a tear in Bassa's flight suit, its expanse widening before his eyes. Byron felt fear grip his chest, threatening to squeeze the air out of his lungs.

He lunged forward and clasped his hand over Bassa's side. His navigator flinched from the pain this caused, uttering a short cry as his head rolled forward. Byron steadied his friend before fumbling with the instrument cluster below him. His finger finally came in contact with the communication panel.

"Sorenthia, I need medical assistance now!" he shouted, as if by sheer volume he could entice an immediate response. "Senior officer down. I repeat, senior officer Bassa is down!"

His head pulsated from the effort, but Byron ignored the pain. Reaching under his left arm, he tore at the first aid pack near Bassa's knee. Byron's eyes flicked briefly to the gaping hole in the side of the ship and noted the twisted and burnt metal. His hand came in contact with a large gauze pad and he extracted it from the kit. Tearing the wrapping with his teeth, he grasped the gauze and slowly lifted his left hand. Blood had completely soaked his glove, and he covered the wound with the gauze before the sight of charred flesh and protruding innards caused his nausea to return.

Pulling the glove from his free hand, Byron grasped his friend's shoulder. "Bassa, can you hear me?" he entreated, desperate for a reply.

His navigator's head rolled back against the seat and Bassa opened his eyes. The man appeared tired beyond his years and his breathing was shallow. Bassa's lips moved, but behind the helmet, the sounds were muffled.

"Let me get that off you," Byron offered.

His fingers found the correct latches, but Byron was afraid to yank the helmet from his friend's head. Bassa managed to raise his left hand and Byron positioned it before grasping the helmet from the other side. Together, they pulled it off his head, and Byron tossed it out of the cockpit.

"Bassa!" he cried, taking a deep breath to clear the agony in his head. Byron grasped his friend's head and forced the man to look him in the eye.

"Stay with me now!" he ordered, fighting to maintain his composure. "Stay with me until the medical ship arrives."

Bassa's chest rose and fell as he fought for every breath. Byron trembled, afraid his friend would succumb to his injuries without a fight. Furious he couldn't connect mentally, Byron gave Bassa's head a light shake.

"Don't you dare give up on me! You hear me, Bassa? I'm not letting you give up."

His friend's eyes lay closed while he spoke, but Bassa's lids slowly opened. Tinged with sorrow, they revealed none of the spirited fire that Bassa possessed.

"Byron," he said in a calm voice, raising a hand to grasp his pilot's arm. "I'm sorry."

Those words cascaded down Byron's spine like a river of ice. The excruciating pain in his own mind was forgotten as he stared at his friend in disbelief.

"No!" he gasped. "Don't you dare give up now."

Closing his eyes, Bassa gently shook his head. Byron swallowed hard, unwilling to believe his friend might die. Bassa had survived too many battles to allow death a victory now. Blood continued to soak his glove through the gauze, its warmth seeping out of Bassa's body. The sensation sent Byron into a panic.

"Damn it, you can't die on me! You're the only friend I've got!"

Bassa's fingers tightened around his arm even as the rest of his body began to sag. His eyes opened and he met his pilot's gaze. Uttering a short, desperate cry, Byron leaned closer.

"Please," he begged, his eyes filling with tears.

Bassa's lips slowly parted. "You'll be all right, little brother," he whispered.

Byron stared at his friend, his mouth ajar. Unable to connect or stop the lifeblood as it poured from Bassa's body, he could only watch as the light slowly faded from the man's eyes. Bassa's fingers lost their grip and his hand dropped into his lap. Byron felt his neck go limp in his grasp and Bassa's head dropped against the seat. His navigator was gone.

Byron leaned away, his eyes wide. The pounding in his head shifted to his chest, making it difficult to breathe. No one in Byron's life had ever believed in him until he met Bassa. The senior officer had chosen to stand by a young man no one else wanted, gaining his trust and encouraging Byron. The man had become the one constant in his world of turmoil and uncertainty. Now his only friend was gone. Byron was alone again.

"No!" he screamed, agony bursting from his chest. "No!"

Closing his eyes and dropping his head, Byron shook violently as he sobbed, unable to contain his grief. The writhing, burning knots in his stomach overshadowed the scalding fire in his head, and Byron's body felt twisted to the point of breaking. Convulsing with each racking sob, his lungs ached for air, and the mounting pain threatened to render him unconscious.

Forcing himself to take a deep breath, Byron pulled Bassa's limp body closer. He pressed the side of his head against his friend's cheek, hoping for a measure of comfort as the tears continued to flow. Bassa's parting words still rang in his ears, and only the sound of his own ragged breath penetrated the throbbing in his head. His senses numb, Byron wanted nothing more than for his body to cease feeling as well. Surrendering to his pain, he felt himself slip down that dark hole and into oblivion.

Voices reached his ears and Byron felt hands on his shoulders. He protested the intrusion as his hold on Bassa slipped. He thought he heard his name spoken, but his focus remained on his friend as his fingers were pried free and physical contact broken. Forcing his eyes to open, Byron watched Bassa's face vanish from sight as he was pulled over his seat. No longer able to see his navigator, he closed his eyes and allowed strong arms to lift his body from the cockpit.

The sudden movement and jolt as his feet touched the planet's rocky surface caused his nausea to return. Fighting the restraining hands, Byron broke free. Dropping to his hands and knees, he relieved his stomach of its contents. It eased his queasiness, but his head now pounded twice as hard, and he covered his eyes with his hand. Completely spent, he offered no further resistance as several men lifted his body and deposited him on the floating gurney.

Once inside the medical transport, Byron felt someone wipe his face before placing a mask over his mouth. He opened his eyes and attempted to focus on the figure hovering over his body. Feeling his senses slip, Byron allowed the dark depths to overtake him again.

Chapter Fifteen

When he awoke, his head still ached, but it no longer felt as if consumed by fire. Byron refrained from opening his eyes and returned to the safety of sleep within minutes.

He was roused long enough to consume a glass of water, and the medic escorted him to the bathroom. Once back in bed, Byron ignored the medic's enticement to test his senses, preferring to recede into the depths once more. The lack of stimulus was preferable to the agonizing pain clutching his chest, and Byron drifted to sleep.

We're spinning out of control! Byron, pull up. Byron!

He awoke with a start. His room was dark and devoid of medical personnel. Grasping the sheets in his fists, he forced the anxiety from his pounding chest. Gradually, his breathing returned to normal.

Groaning, he pulled himself upright and leaned forward. Rubbing his forehead, Byron discovered his head no longer hurt. With great reluctance, he attempted to reach out with his mind and found he could hear the whispers of those beyond his room. His senses were returning. However, there was one voice absent in his mind, and Byron would never hear it again.

The reality of that fact dropped like a boulder in his guts. Overwhelmed by grief and fear, Byron let out a sob. Grasping his head, he all but doubled over in agony. Pulling his knees to his chest, Byron muffled his tears in the bedcovers, worried the noise would attract attention. His whole body trembled as the ache in his heart threatened to consume him. Byron's only friend in the world was gone and he was on his own.

Spent at last, he dried his face. His ragged breath seemed loud and unnatural in the sparse room. The surroundings were as empty as his heart, and he closed his eyes. Exhausted, Byron fell back against his pillow and willed his body to return to the void of sleep. If he couldn't feel Bassa's presence, then he preferred not to feel anything at all.

When he awoke, Byron discovered a medical technician in his room. Uttering a soft moan, he pulled himself upright.

"How are you feeling?" the man asked, glancing away from the monitor over his head.

"Better," Byron muttered, rubbing his eyes.

"Everything here looks good." The officer turned to face him. "Senses returning?"

Byron nodded, his eyes averted. He felt the man probe his mind, testing for a response, and Byron locked his shields into place.

"I need to access your recovery," the technician admonished.

Irritated by the request, Byron lowered his shields. He hated the sensation of another man poking around in his mind and did not hide his disdain. The experience was brief, though.

The medical officer straightened his shoulders. "You will recover," he stated. "And since we are in desperate need of beds right now, I see no reason to hold you here any longer. I'll bring you a change of clothes."

Byron was content to put on the clean clothes and retreat from the medical facility. The hour was very late and he reached his quarters unnoticed. Too tired to shower, he crawled into his bed and was asleep within minutes.

He awoke feeling stiff and his muscles protested as he arose. Painkillers probably suppressed the soreness while he was in medical, but those drugs had apparently worn off now. Staggering to the bathroom, Byron went through the motions of showering. He discovered numerous bruises on his body as a result of the rough landing. Considering how hard his Cosbolt had struck the ground, he was surprised his injuries were not more severe.

Recalling that moment caused his chest to ache once again. Unwilling to dwell on such a painful memory, Byron requested a meal in his room. He'd not eaten since yesterday morning and was beginning to shake from a lack of food. When the meal arrived, he forced every morsel into his mouth despite the unappealing aroma.

The unpleasant task of his mission report was all that re-mained. Sitting in front of his computer, Byron cleared his mind. He preferred to forget yesterday's tragedy and wipe it from his thoughts forever. Determined to get through the report quickly, he disconnected all feeling and concentrated on the facts.

His ship's recorder had been recovered and uploaded. He watched it only once, recording the details as it played. Byron could not bring himself to watch the final moments, especially after witnessing the laser hit that ultimately killed Bassa. He completed his report and discovered he was trembling.

Leaning away from the screen, Byron closed his eyes. His mind could not shake the image of Bassa's dying face. He could still smell the blood, mixed with the foul stench of burnt metal and charred flesh. Bassa's final words hung in his ears, mocking him with the implausibility of his navigator's dying statement.

I'm not going to be all right without you, he thought.

Annoyed with the rising tightness in his chest, Byron sent his report and rose from the chair. A message from medical flashed on the screen, requesting his return for a full evaluation. Eager to complete the procedure and be done with medical personnel, he departed at once.

The facility was busy and it was over an hour before he returned to his quarters. His senses had fully recovered and he supposed he should feel grateful the disrupter hadn't hit him full force. Considering what was lost yesterday, he almost wished his Cosbolt had crashed into the planet and ended his misery all together.

Byron had no sooner requested the midday meal when his door chime announced a visitor. He was tempted to ignore the request. Byron just wanted to be alone in his misery. With reluctance, he permitted entry and his door slid open to reveal Ernx and Nintal's anxious faces.

"Byron?" Ernx asked with obvious hesitation.

Irritated by the invasion of his privacy but relieved to see a friendly face, he offered a solemn nod. Ernx entered his quarters and approached Byron with caution.

"We were worried about you," he offered, gesturing toward his navigator as Nintal entered the room.

"I'm fine," muttered Byron, although it was far from the truth. He grasped the back of a chair with one hand and affected a casual pose.

Ernx paused at his side, his eyes full of sympathy. Byron found it difficult to meet his gaze, and he grasped the chair even tighter. Raising his hand, Ernx touched Byron's shoulder.

"Byron, we're really sorry about Bassa," he said in a hushed voice.

Nodding once, Byron's chin dropped and his gaze shifted to the table's surface. His mind remained closed and feelings restrained. Byron refused to reveal the depths of his agony to anyone.

Ernx's fingertips squeezed his shoulder before releasing Byron. The pilot glanced at Nintal and took a deep breath.

"We're on our way to the dining hall," he announced. "Thought you might like some company."

The prospect of facing the other officers caused Byron to feel ill. "I'm still tired. I'll take my meal here."

Nintal appeared about to protest, but Ernx nodded. "All right. Let us know if you need anything," he offered.

Turning to depart, Ernx paused in the doorframe. He frowned, his eyes filled with concern.

"We'll come by before the evening meal, all right?"

Byron did not respond. His friends departed and the door closed.

He choked down half of his meal before discarding the remainder. This morning he'd been starving, but food held no appeal now. His body still ached and he wondered if he could entice it to sleep all afternoon. Slumber was preferable to consciousness at the moment.

Byron was about to remove his boots when a message flashed across his computer screen, accompanied by an urgent beep. His presence was required at once in the commander's office. Sighing with resignation, he indicated that he would comply.

Passing several officers in the hallway, Byron kept his eyes averted and mind closed. Arriving at the commander's office, he was permitted entry the moment he announced his presence. The senior engineer was speaking with Kernen, explain-

ing the figures in his damage report, and the commander indicated Byron was to wait. Kernen finished with the engineer and dismissed the man.

"Officer Byron, have a seat," the commander instructed,
his eyes on his computer screen.

Byron slid into a chair, straightening his shoulders to prevent slouching. The commander completed his task before
turning his attention to the pilot.

"Medical has cleared you to return to active duty tomorrow," Kernen announced. "You are to report to the simulator
for Darten training."

Byron's eyes widened in surprise. "The Darten, sir?" he
asked.

"Yes. You are one of my best pilots and I need you in a
fighter."

"Yes, sir," he replied, unsure how he felt regarding his new
assignment. At least it did not force him into partnership with
another navigator.

"I've been over your report and discovered no errors in judgment," the commander continued. He leaned back in his chair
and cocked one eyebrow. "Actually, I'm amazed you were able
to land your ship in one piece. The course you selected would've
been next to impossible under normal circumstances, let alone
when subjected to a disrupter blast."

Byron merely nodded. The commander's assessment of his
abilities meant little now. His piloting skills had not been
enough to save Bassa yesterday.

Folding his hands in his lap, Kernen gazed silently at the
young pilot. Mental shields in place, Byron maintained a neutral expression. The commander's brows came together, his
eyes scrutinizing Byron. The harsh lines on his face smoothed
away as Kernen's expression softened.

"I lost a lot of good men yesterday," he admitted, his voice
slow and full of purpose, "including Bassa. We are now deprived of his incredible skill and wealth of knowledge, and
that can never be replaced. I lost a good friend yesterday,
Byron. I know you lost even more."

Gritting his teeth, Byron forced the ache in his chest to
subside. However, the lump in his throat remained and he
was unable to respond beyond a curt nod. The commander

leaned forward and pressed several buttons on his computer pad.

"You have been given access to Bassa's quarters. I suggest you spend your afternoon gathering his personal belongings and data files."

"Me, sir?" Byron gasped.

"Bassa had no living relatives and listed you as beneficiary," Kernen informed him, his gaze flicking to the computer screen. "You will have access to all of his files."

Byron swallowed hard. "Yes, sir," he answered with uncertainty. He'd not anticipated this development and felt unworthy to receive all that remained of Bassa.

Kernen leaned back in his seat, his expression thoughtful. "I'll never forget Bassa's request for a special consideration," he said, a smile pulling at the corners of his mouth. "A pilot of incredible talent was completing his training and despite a lack of experience, I'd be a fool not to request his assignment to the Sorenthia. He promised I wouldn't regret the decision. Of course, it didn't hurt that I was acquiring the best navigator in the fleet in the deal as well."

Byron's shoulders relaxed, although he could not bring himself to return the commander's grin. He knew Kernen would've refused had Bassa not accompanied him.

The commander's eyes narrowed. Placing his elbows on the desk, he leaned forward, his expression earnest.

"I asked him why he'd return to flying under such conditions and his answer surprised me. Bassa stated you were the opportunity he'd been seeking."

Byron shifted in his chair. "He was waiting for a pilot who could jump?" he asked, aware his talent was quite rare.

The commander's eyebrows rose. "Son, he wasn't referring to your skills as a pilot."

His controlled expression dissolved, giving way to surprise. Byron felt perplexed by the commander's response. Before he could request an explanation, Kernen spoke again.

"Perhaps you will find the answer this afternoon," he offered. Kernen's gaze flicked to his door as another visitor was announced. "Dismissed."

Retreating from Kernen's office, Byron pondered their exchange. He arrived at the officers' level and approached

Bassa's quarters. What would he discover behind that door? As much as his heart ached, did he really want to know?

Passing his hand over the press plate, Byron watched as the door slid aside without hesitation. Glancing down the hallway to verify he was alone, he entered his navigator's quarters and surveyed the main room.

Bassa's quarters were immaculate, as they had been two nights ago when they shared a drink. It was a trait he and Bassa had in common, although his abode appeared far more sterile. His navigator had decorated the walls with his numerous plaques, and several personal items dotted the room. The table sat empty, but Byron could still see the two glasses and bottle of spirits. The memory of that moment felt like a knife in his side. Their plans to explore space together were now shattered. Byron turned away from the table, his heart heavy.

Locating two travel cases in the closet, he set them on the bed and began to remove the plaques from the walls. Byron cleaned out the cabinets and discovered Bassa's medals in the process. Stunned by the additional honors, as his friend had never discussed his awards, he wondered what else he might find. Carefully packing the medals in the first travel chest, he secured the fragile cargo with one of Bassa's flight suits. He didn't bother with military issued items or clothing outside of the one flight suit. Only personal belongings mattered to Byron.

The last remaining item was Bassa's desk. The workspace was clean, save for one lone photo. Byron picked up the frame and gazed at the image. Taken just before the Sorenthia visited Spaceport 89, the picture showed Bassa and his pilot beside their ship, arms crossed as they leaned against the Cosbolt. Byron recalled trying to present a serious expression, but a private thought from Bassa had elicited a smile from his pilot. Coupled with Bassa's grin, the resulting image was very candid and natural.

Byron frowned at the photo. On Guaard, Tal's picture had occupied Bassa's desk. He didn't recall seeing the photo when he packed and glanced around the room to be sure he hadn't missed it. He'd visited his friend's quarters often but failed to notice the absence of his brother's photo. Shaking his head, he chastised himself on his poor observation skills.

Eyes returning to the image, Byron thought of his friend's fondness for photos. Bassa had often recorded images with his computer pad. There were so few moments in Byron's life worth remembering, but he wished he possessed photos of his time with Bassa.

A thought occurred to Byron and he reached for Bassa's computer. His friend probably kept those images in a file. Since he'd been granted access to his navigator's personal files, it was only a matter of transferring the information to his private database.

It felt odd that he could now view Bassa's personal information. Rather than spending time examining the details, he simply assigned the files to his own. He proceeded down the list, saving each and every document and transcript. He paused to explore a file loaded with images, but the pictures all predated their meeting. He decided to examine the photos later and saved that file as well.

Reaching the last file in the database, he paused. Simply labeled 'Byron,' it gave no indication as to the contents within. Curious, he explored the file and discovered four separate areas. The first section contained information from his official and personal record. His complete history and profile were represented, and he frowned at the discovery. Noting his Cosbolt training record, Byron remembered that as his instructor, Bassa had enjoyed full access to his files. He'd apparently saved them for future reference.

Exploring the next file, Byron opened what appeared to be a journal chronicling Bassa's personal experiences. Confused as to why this was located in his file, Byron scanned the entries. The first one was written not long after his arrival on Guaard. It described a pilot in training whose cocky, indifferent attitude stemmed from loneliness and insecurity rather than malice or rage. Bassa concluded his assessment that all the boy needed was a friend. Byron's eyes widened in disbelief and he scanned the other entries. Every single one was about him.

Uncomfortable with the thought of invading Bassa's privacy, Byron moved to the next file. A prerecorded video flashed on the screen and he leaned back in the chair. His chest tightened when Bassa's image appeared, and he realized the recording had been made from his very position.

"Good day, Byron," said Bassa's image, a faint smile on his face.

Byron's mouth fell open. Bassa had recorded a message for him.

"I've enjoyed flying with you, more than with any other pilot," continued Bassa, leaning back in his chair. "However, I realize that one day we'll be forced to part company. I'm not a youngster anymore and my stamina isn't what it used to be. Therefore, you are watching this for one of two reasons. Either we have parted company, as I refuse to hinder your career as a pilot, or ..."

Bassa took a deep breath, his gaze dropping. "Or I am no longer among the living. Either way, I'm sorry I cannot continue as your navigator. It's been an honor."

Byron swallowed the lump that rose in his throat. Had Bassa known he was going to die?

"I'm not a master with words, but there are several things you must know.

"When my brother was killed, I blamed myself. If I'd been his navigator, Tal wouldn't have died. I felt my only absolution was to prevent other Cosbolt teams from meeting a similar fate. That is why I transferred to Guaard.

"But as time passed, I realized it wasn't my refusal to join Tal that bothered me. It was the fact I didn't even know my younger brother. We were never friends. And it wasn't just Tal. I really wasn't close to anyone.

"I wasn't looking to save a talented young pilot. I was looking for a friend. And I found that in you, Byron. Your friendship is what I needed. There were days I doubted I'd ever earn your trust, but I knew I couldn't give up trying. You'd had enough people give up on you. I wasn't going to be one of them.

"You were my answer, Byron. Your friendship has finally set me free from guilt."

A tear rolled unchecked down Byron's cheek. His breath was ragged and forced. Unable to tear his eyes from the screen, he stared in stunned disbelief as his friend continued to speak his heart.

"I only have one request," Bassa implored, leaning closer to the screen. His serious expression matched the intensity in his eyes. "Whatever you decide to do with your life, be sure the path is your choice. Don't let anyone decide your fate. And don't waste time running from your past, as I have done. You have nothing to prove, Byron. Not to me, not to anyone.

"Byron, you were never a replacement for Tal. He was a stranger to me. You are not. You are the brother I'd always wanted. And I couldn't ask for a better friend than you.

"I love you, little brother. And Byron, I promise; you'll be all right without me."

Bassa leaned forward, his hand outstretched. Before the screen went black, Byron caught tears in his friend's eyes, and that final image burned into his mind.

The ensuing silence was deafening. Byron allowed a soft gasp to escape his lips. He'd leaned closer to the screen during the course of the recording, resting one arm on the desk and clenching his fist so tight that his nails now dug into his palm. The emptiness of the room matched the emptiness in his heart. Unable to hold back the flood of grief, Byron let out a sob as his head fell onto his forearm.

This time, he did not have to contend with a scorching headache. No one threatened to intrude during his moment of pain. Secluded in Bassa's quarters, Byron allowed his sorrow to flow without inhibition. The wrenching agony and frustration that burst forth from his thoughts hurt, but it was a relief to release the painful emotions and memories that filled his mind.

Empty and exhausted from his exertions, Byron raised his head and dried his face. He stared at the dark screen and felt a pang of regret.

"I never told you thanks, brother," he gasped, his voice cracking.

Taking a deep breath to clear his head, Byron rubbed his eyes. When he refocused, his gaze fell upon the numbers in the corner of the screen. Leaning closer, he realized it was the date of the recording. That number felt so familiar and he searched his mind for its meaning. And then it hit him. It was the day after Bassa was struck by the disrupter blast, and the time stamp revealed the recording was made in the late afternoon.

You said you were tired, Byron thought. But you came back to your room to make this recording.

Byron leaned back in his chair, recalling the events of that particular day. He and Bassa had connected mentally that morning as they attempted to restore his friend's senses. Byron had feared that moment, and not just because it would leave him exposed. He'd worried what he might find in his friend's mind. Much to his surprise, he'd discovered understanding, acceptance, and genuine friendship within the thoughts of his navigator.

You knew how I felt, he suddenly thought, realizing that his feelings were equally apparent that day. The recording he'd just watched was proof. Bassa had looked into his heart and found the trust and friendship he so desired.

Byron quickly saved the recording in his own files, determined not to lose the video. It was probably the only recording of Bassa's voice. He checked the fourth file and discovered a gallery of images. There were shots of Byron by himself as well as the two of them together. He even noted a couple photos of Bassa alone. He wished there were more, but at least he now possessed some visual account of the man who'd become his closest friend.

Finishing his task, Byron retrieved Bassa's computer pad from its drawer and surveyed the room one last time. Nothing else remained. Stacking the crates, he carried them to his quarters. There was just enough room in his tiny closet and he set the two crates inside. There would be time later to explore their contents in depth. Right now, he craved sleep.

Before he closed the closet, though, Byron retrieved one item from the crates. Positioning the picture in the exact same place where it had rested in Bassa's quarters, he stepped back and viewed the photo of him and Bassa with pride. Satisfied at last, Byron retired to his bed and drifted into a dreamless sleep.

The announcement of a visitor at his door roused Byron. He swung his legs off the bed and staggered to his feet, his mind still groggy. Ordering the door to open, he grasped the back of a chair for support. Looking up as the door slid aside, he was not surprised to see Ernx and Nintal's anxious faces.

"Were you asleep?" Ernx asked, his voice tinged with concern.

Byron rubbed his eyes. "That's all right. I needed to get up."

Nintal leaned forward. "It's time to eat," he announced.

Byron regarded his friends with caution. The thought of facing the other officers unnerved him. They probably blamed him for Bassa's death. Those who didn't would have a million questions.

"Not ready to go out yet," he explained, reluctant to say more.

"Byron, we'll be with you," exclaimed Ernx, entering his quarters.

His friend's company would be an asset, but Byron still felt hesitant and shook his head. Nintal stepped into the room, allowing the door to close. He stood up to his full height and fixed Byron with a stern expression.

"You can't hide in here forever," he said in a loud voice. "You're still a pilot and a member of our squadron. I know you don't want to, but you've got to face the other officers. And the sooner you do it, the better!"

Blinking in surprise, Byron stared at Nintal. His friends comprised one of the youngest teams in his squadron, but they were still several years his senior. Nintal had spoken with authority and from the look in his eyes, he was not about to back down.

"Byron, please come with us," Ernx added in a softer tone.

Byron finally acquiesced to his friend's request. They allowed him a moment to get ready, and then Ernx and Nintal escorted him to the dining hall. Byron's relief at the sight of a small crowd was offset by the knowledge that many were absent due to injury or death. He felt grateful Ernx and Nintal weren't killed yesterday. He'd have no friends at all aboard the Sorenthia.

Tray in hand, he followed Ernx to the table. It felt as if everyone was watching and he avoided making eye contact. Taking an end seat, his friend sat across from him while Nintal took the place at his side. Eager to escape the dining hall as soon as possible, Byron began to inhale his food.

His friends engaged in idle conversation while they ate, respecting Byron's silence. He sensed their concern, but was afraid to reach out mentally beyond his immediate company. Focused on his food, he managed to consume half of his meal before nausea overtook him. Unable to finish, Byron pushed aside his tray. He retrieved his water and leaned against the table.

"Where are we now?" he asked when Ernx met his gaze.

"Sector 97-161."

"Didn't go far," he murmured. Byron downed his water and set the glass on the table. Feeling self-conscious, he crossed his arms and pressed his elbows against the table.

Nintal cleared his throat. "The Vindicarn ship broke orbit and headed into deep space. The Sorenthia and Lathella remained long enough to gather downed crews before setting off in pursuit. Both ships were damaged, although I hear the Lathella is in far worse condition," he added.

Byron nodded, his eyes on his tray. "Was the mission a success?" he asked. If Bassa had sacrificed his life for nothing …

"Three of the Dartens were able to transmit data," Ernx replied, setting down his fork. "The information is being analyzed now."

"How many Dartens made it back?"

Ernx and Nintal exchanged nervous glances.

"Only one," Ernx answered, his expression solemn.

The news was sobering. Byron decided not to inquire how many men were lost during the course of the fight. He'd discover that soon enough. The teams had gathered information, though. It didn't ease the loss of Bassa, but at least his death held meaning now.

When his friends finished, Byron indicated he was ready to depart. They rose together and he led the way toward the exit. As he passed the first table, a man rose to his feet. Byron scowled as Wentar touched his shoulder. After their previous exchange, he wanted nothing to do with the man.

"Byron," Wentar said, his fingers squeezing Byron's shoulder. The pilot's expression mirrored his sympathetic feelings. "I am truly sorry about Bassa. He was a damned fine officer."

Sensing the man's words were genuine, Byron nodded in acceptance. He felt a hand touch his other shoulder and turned to discover Hannar at his side. Ernx and Nintal moved closer to protect him, but Byron did not feel threatened. The officers surrounding him, and those seated at the nearest table, expressed only sympathy and understanding. He departed the dining hall a little more secure in his position with the squadron.

He scanned through some of Bassa's files, but reading his navigator's words only made the man's absence more pronounced. Byron retired early to his bed and the opportunity to empty his mind. Tomorrow he'd return to active duty alone and he didn't relish the idea.

After the squadron briefing the next morning, he reported to the simulator for training. The Darten handled much lighter than the Cosbolt and he spent the session adjusting to the movement. Navigating on his own was also a challenge. He missed Bassa's guidance. He'd not realized how much his friend's presence bolstered his confidence and he missed the support.

Displeased with his first efforts, he requested an afternoon session and returned after the midday meal. His second attempt in the Darten proved more successful and Byron felt his proficiency improve. One more day of simulator runs and he'd master the craft well enough to rejoin the squadron.

As he finished eating that evening, an announcement came over the com system. The presence of all officers was required at once in the main hanger. Those gathered in the dining hall rose to their feet and Byron followed suit.

"I wonder if they have a plan for destroying the Vindicarn ship," said Ernx, falling in step beside Byron.

"We can only hope," he declared.

Officers had just begun to gather when they arrived. Byron and his friends waited as the men assembled. The commander and senior squadron officer were deep in discussion while squadron leaders and senior officers congregated to one side. Byron listened with interest to the whispered speculations of

those nearby. The buzz in the room grew as more officers entered and soon he could not hear his own thoughts. The close
proximity of so many bodies was growing uncomfortable. He
was about to move toward the side when the senior squadron
leader called for silence.

"The battle with the Vindicarn vessel claimed the lives of
many good men," he began when the room grew quiet, "and
we honor those who gave their lives for this mission.

"Three of the Dartens successfully transmitted data on the
enemy ship. We now have a much clearer view of the inside."

The screen behind Forllen lit up, displaying a transparent
image of the Vindicarn ship. The majority of the vessel was
only a shell, but three areas revealed interior details. The
image enlarged, focusing on one specific area.

"Team Two's pilot managed to navigate to the core of the
ship," he announced, gesturing toward the screen. "He had to
make one jump to clear a vent grating before locating the
disrupter core behind this wall."

The image enlarged again, and the chamber housing the
main disrupter filled the screen. Byron eyed the view with
interest. A ship the size of the Darten would be but a speck in
comparison.

"The chamber can only be accessed by teleportation. The
pilot could locate no direct access from the outside vents and
the walls are too thick to blast through. However, he was
able to scan the chamber and provide us with a clear view of
the interior. From the information gathered, we believe a direct hit on the disrupter core would set off a chain reaction
and destroy the ship.

"Intelligence scouts confirm this is the only disrupter ship
in the Vindicarn fleet," Forllen declared, his voice loud as he
scanned the men. "We take out this ship, we eliminate the
Vindicarn's greatest weapon."

A small commotion broke out as the men murmured to one
another. Byron took a deep breath, his gaze on the disrupter
core. Destroying the ship would tip the scales in their favor
and might even end the war.

"However," the senior squadron leader exclaimed, his voice
rising above the noise. The men fell silent, their attention on
Forllen.

"However, there remains one obstacle. While the heat encountered inside the core's chamber can be reduced by reinforcing the Darten's shields, hopefully protecting the pilot's mind as well, the effects of the disrupter on the teleporter's power cannot. Team Two's pilot reported a slow drain on his device's energy even through the reinforced walls, so we speculate that once inside the chamber, the teleporter's power would be drained instantly. A pilot teleporting into the chamber would have no means of escape."

The mood in the hanger shifted as the budding hope subsided. The senior squadron leader held up his hand to silence the discouraged murmurs.

"Commander Kernen and I are not yet ready to send a pilot to his death without exploring other options," Forllen said in a firm voice, his hands behind his back. "Destroying the disrupter core is our best option, but the Lathella is working on a plan that involves the Vindicarn's engines. We will make a final decision tomorrow morning when the Clairius and the Jentara reach our location."

Urgent conversations broke out around Byron, and Ernx voiced his thoughts loudly in his ear. The words went unheard as Byron continued to stare at the screen. The disrupter chamber provided many challenges, especially as the exact effects of the core could not be predicted. However, none of those details mattered if the pilot was trapped inside. It was a suicide mission. Unless …

"I can teleport in and out of that chamber," he called, speaking mentally as well in order to be heard over the commotion. His words brought a hushed silence over the crowded hanger and those nearby turned to stare at Byron.

"Son, I appreciate your willingness to try, but your teleporter's power would be drained. You'd be unable to jump to safety," Forllen explained, a hint of fatherly patience in his voice.

Sensing disbelief in those around him, Byron's gaze shifted to the commander. Kernen's brows were furrowed, but he gave a curt nod. Byron straightened his shoulders and lifted his chin high.

"I can jump without using the teleporter's energy," he proclaimed.

His declaration was met with astonishment, and a wave of murmurs and gasps traveled across the hanger. Byron felt Ernx grab his arm, but his gaze remained on the senior squadron leader. Forllen frowned and he sensed the man's annoyance.

"Only one Cassan in 800,000 possess that ability ..." he began.

"One in 802,197 to be exact," the commander added, stepping forward. His eyes met Byron's. "But all we need is that one."

A hushed silence fell over the crowd. Those closest to Byron took a step back, as if afraid. Ernx released his arm and he sensed the man's shock. Shielding his mind from the crowd, Byron focused on the commander.

The squadron leader stared wide-eyed at Kernen. "Sir?" he inquired.

The commander continued to gaze at Byron. "You really think you can do it, Officer Byron?" he asked, his eyes filled with concern.

"Yes, sir, I can."

Kernen's expression turned thoughtful. Byron channeled every ounce of confidence into his appearance, forcing doubt from his mind. The commander had to believe that his young, inexperienced pilot was capable of performing such a feat. His navigator would've harbored no misgivings, but Bassa was not here now. Byron had to convince Kernen without the assistance of his friend.

The commander adjusted his position and nodded. "We'll continue exploring other options, but an attack on the disrupter core will be our primary strategy. Inform the Lathella of our plans," ordered Kernen, turning to his senior communications officer. "Squadron leaders, you will receive your assignments momentarily. Prepare your men."

His gaze returned to Byron. "I want to see you in my office in ten minutes, Officer Byron."

"Yes, sir!" he replied.

"Dismissed!"

Voices erupted around Byron, echoing in his mind as well as his ears. Ernx grabbed his shoulder once more.

"You're a jumper?" he gasped, his turbulent thoughts reflected in his wide eyes. Beside him, Nintal appeared just as stunned.

Byron nodded. It felt awkward to disclose the truth. He'd grown accustomed to hiding his unique ability, but there was no concealing that fact now.

Those around him began to press forward, voicing their surprise. Byron was bombarded by questions. Uncomfortable with the scrutiny, he kept his answers short as he tried to move toward the exit. He did not want to keep Kernen waiting. The mass of people surrounding him prevented his departure and Byron felt a wave of panic. More than ever, he wished Bassa were here to protect his young pilot.

"Let him through!" a voice commanded just as Byron felt a large hand grasp his shoulder.

Bassa's friend appeared at his side. Deacer used his free hand to push aside the overzealous crowd while Hannar stepped in front of Byron and forced a path for the pilot. Ernx and Nintal joined them and the group moved across the hanger floor with considerable ease.

As they approached the exit, Byron sent Deacer a word of thanks. Bassa's friend chuckled in his ear.

I always suspected you were a jumper, Deacer admitted, propelling him into the hallway. *You're a brave young man, Byron.*

Bassa's voice rang in his head. *It's the right thing to do,* he explained.

He hastened to the commander's office, but there was no reply to his request for admittance. Moving to one side, Byron leaned against the wall and waited. The full impact of his commitment hadn't hit him yet, and he purposely steered his thoughts away from the mission. He wanted to prevent doubt from entering his thoughts, causing him to appear hesitant in front of the commander. Byron had made his choice and he intended to follow through with that decision.

The light above the telepod across the hall flashed red. Byron straightened his posture as the door opened and Kernen emerged. The commander nodded and indicated the young man was to follow him into the office. Kernen moved toward his chair and Byron stood at attention on the other side of the desk. The commander dropped his computer pad, his expression weary. Leaning against his desk, Kernen stared hard at Byron.

"Are you sure you can pull this off?" he asked.

"Yes, sir," Byron replied without hesitation. "I can funnel my own power into the teleporter. I'll jump in, deliver the payload, and jump out again."

"You'll have to time it just right. The shields might prevent your exit."

"I'm aware of that, sir."

Kernen sighed, his shoulders sagging. "Son, there's a chance the disrupter core might overpower your senses as well."

That thought had occurred to Byron, but he wasn't concerned. "It's a chance I'm willing to take, sir," he stated, holding fast to his resolution.

The commander's chin dropped and he sank into his chair. Leaning back, he stared at Byron.

"I don't like suicide missions," he admitted with candor. "I know you've suffered a great loss, but I don't want you to throw your life away. Bassa was so intent on keeping you alive, son. Be sure you're doing this for all the right reasons."

"Sir," began Byron, his heart heavy. "Bassa gave his life so we might acquire this information. If we don't take advantage of this opportunity, then his death will have been in vain. I couldn't live with that, sir."

The commander slowly nodded, his eyes dark. Leaning forward, Kernen tapped several keys on his computer.

"Your simulator runs with the Darten weren't stellar, but you are proficient enough to pilot the craft," he observed, his eyes on the screen.

"I'd planned to return to the simulator again this evening," Byron said quickly.

"You will be permitted one run," Kernen cautioned, his finger rubbing the edge of the keypad. "I'll have them upload the schematics so you can practice your approach tomorrow morning."

"Yes, sir."

Completing his task, the commander leaned forward in earnest. "If your morning runs aren't one hundred percent, I won't send you," he warned. "I'd rather not lose you in a futile attempt."

"I don't intend to fail, sir."

"I hope not," replied Kernen. "You still have much to live for, son."

Byron did not reply and kept his thoughts on the matter hidden. The commander dismissed him and Byron retreated to the telepod. Once inside the unit, he requested the simulator level.

He understood Kernen's implication and couldn't deny the accusation. Flying held no real meaning without Bassa. Byron didn't know what else to do with his life. If he were unable to jump out of the disrupter chamber, then it wouldn't be an issue. Byron knew Bassa's absence factored into his decision, but he saw no other option.

Risking it all sounded better than living alone and without purpose.

Chapter Sixteen

All squadrons participated in simulator drills the next morning and Byron was permitted unlimited access. He ran through the program a dozen times, memorizing the schematics of the enemy ship's air vent. He had several close calls during the first run but performed his mission without flaw on subsequent attempts. Unfortunately, there were variables the computer could not predict. The exact conditions of the disrupter chamber were unknown, as was the certainty of his escape. However, only the success of his mission mattered to Byron. He couldn't change the past, but he could destroy those who'd taken his friend and prevent others from meeting a similar fate.

His hand ached from clinging to the throttle so tight, but otherwise he felt ready to tackle the real Darten. Byron reported to the hanger and awaited his squadron. Their assignment was to weaken the shields and ensure his safe passage into the ship. Before the four flagships jumped to the enemy's location, Larnth wanted the men to perform a test run. Byron wondered how his fellow officers felt about their assignment and if any still harbored resentment toward the young pilot. His life would be in their hands until he entered the Vindicarn vessel.

His craft sat apart from the Cosbolts, so he did not see anyone before the test run. Ernx conveyed a word of encouragement before the squadron launched and Byron clung to his friend's comforting thought. He hoped the others shared the pilot's sentiment.

The Darten was the last to launch. His squadron quickly took up position around the tiny ship. Adjusting to the lighter controls, Byron followed the flight pattern, and he felt good regarding their approach. The lead fighters fired at a predetermined location in space, veering off to allow the next line to take their place. The first wave circled around to form an outer layer of protection for Byron's vessel and the ships surrounding his Darten formed an even tighter ring. The Cosbolts dispersed and Byron flew through what would hopefully be a hole in the enemy's ship when they performed the maneuver for real. If they didn't weaken the shields enough, his mission would end rather abruptly.

The squadron performed the drill three times. Satisfied with their performance, Larnth ordered the men to return to the Sorenthia and wait in the hanger. The attack on the Vindicarn ship would commence in just one hour.

Byron's small fighter was towed to one side and away from the Cosbolts. He contemplated waiting in the cockpit, reluctant to face his fellow officers. However, the compact cockpit of the Darten was not inductive of a prolonged stay. He could not remain there for the duration.

Retracting the canopy, Byron wiggled his body out of cockpit. As he descended the short steps, he discovered Ernx and Nintal waiting. Their greeting was friendly but subdued, and Byron sensed anxiety in his friends. Ernx inquired of the Darten's feel in an obvious attempt to divert his attention. Byron offered a quick response, his eyes on the gloves in his hand.

When he raised his chin, he was startled to see an audience gathering. Men from several different squadrons approached and he sensed curiosity as they gazed upon the pilot willing to jump into the disrupter chamber. The scrutiny was unnerving, and he shifted his stance. Perhaps he should've remained in the cockpit after all.

Several members of his squadron came to his rescue. Flanked on either side by his friends and surrounded by fellow officers, Byron was guided away from the growing crowd.

"You up to this?" asked one of the pilots, his voice gruff.

Byron glanced briefly at the speaker. "I'm ready," he replied, his gaze returning to the gloves in his hand.

"You've got guts, young man," someone else commented.

Byron shrugged. "I'm just doing what needs to be done."

"What you need to do is come back alive."

Allowing his arms to drop to his sides, he raised his head. Hannar met Byron's gaze, his expression unyielding and thoughts just as rigid. The pilot's sentiment was echoed in

unanimous support, and Byron scanned the faces of his comrades. So many had protested his presence when he first arrived on Sorenthia, but Byron sensed no ill feelings now. They
were all pulling for him.

"We'll get you to the ship," Wentar added. "But you have to
get yourself out."

Byron straightened his shoulders, buoyed by the confidence
in the minds of those present. "I will!' he declared.

It had not mattered before, but Byron realized he couldn't
disappoint his comrades. His squadron wouldn't accept any
other outcome. Byron realized his navigator had never accepted failure, either.

He'd worried his comrades would cause him to feel nervous and distract him from the mission. Their presence had
the opposite effect, though. Byron felt calm as they waited,
his mind preoccupied with the idle chatter around him. He
intended to survive, but it occurred to him this might be one
of his last memories. Spending the moment in the company
of his friends and fellow officers was preferable to spending it
alone.

As the time approached, all officers were ordered to report
to their ships. Every man in his squadron touched Byron's
arm or shoulder before he departed, as if by physical contact
alone they could guarantee his success and safe return. He
accepted their gestures and encouragement with grace.

Ernx and Nintal were the last to approach. Both pilot and
navigator surprised him with a brief hug and thump on the
back. No words were exchanged, but Byron sensed their feelings. They feared they would never see him again, although
the men tried hard to suppress those thoughts. However, their
feelings of friendship came through loud and clear.

Returning to his ship, Byron wedged into the tiny cockpit
and performed the preflight check. Satisfied the Darten was
ready, he closed his eyes and ran through the flight plan in
his mind. Byron knew the exact location of his jump into the
chamber and visualized that point. He would use the
teleporter's energy to reach the core, but escaping the chamber all depended on the strength of his ability. That jump
would be his greatest test.

The first ships were wheeled into position. Warning lights flashed within the hanger as the Sorenthia jumped to the Vindicarn ship's location. Seconds later, the command to launch the first Cosbolts echoed over the com. Byron watched as the next wave was placed into the launch tubes. His squadron would emerge last, relying on the confusion created by the other ships to approach the enemy vessel.

Despite the rapid departure of the other squadrons, Byron found the wait uncomfortable and his anxiety grew. Sweat formed in his palms and his nerves tingled. Annoyed, he gritted his teeth and attempted to clear his mind. Now was not the time to doubt his abilities.

You are capable of far more than you realize.

Byron's mouth opened as he recalled Bassa's words. His friend had believed in him to the end.

I just wish you were here now, he thought with a sigh.

His squadron was called and Byron felt his ship move forward. Grasping the throttle even tighter, he took a deep breath as his fighter wheeled into position. The Cosbolts entered the launch tubes one by one until only his Darten remained.

"Finish it and return home, Officer Byron," a voice commanded over the com as the launch tube doors opened.

"Yes, sir!" Byron replied, buoyed by Kernen's words of encouragement.

The Darten slid into position and he fired up the ship's engines. Byron gazed at the end of the launch tube. Flashes of light were visible from the battle already in progress. Outside his squadron awaited the tiny vessel and their only hope for defeating the Vindicarn. Byron pressed his head against the seat and cleared his mind. He had to succeed.

"Three ... two ... one ..."

The walls of the tunnel raced past his ship and then vanished as he emerged from the Sorenthia. Byron's squadron converged on him at once, providing protection from the enemy vessels. Several of his comrades were already fighting off Vindicarn, but Byron remained focused on their course. His target resided deep within the enemy ship.

Their approach was hampered by the presence of so many ships. Fighters darted in every direction, firing at any moving object. It was almost impossible for the squadron to hold formation as they dodged incoming ships and laser blasts. Even the six ships assigned to remain as his side were struggling to stay in position. Byron followed close to the lead ship, relying on Deacer's commands. He hoped the navigator in the ship behind his Darten was listening as well.

They veered left and into a sharp roll. A laser shot across the nose of the lead ship and Hannar dove at once. Enemy ships appeared on their right and they were dispatched by Cosbolt fire. Byron clutched the throttle tight as they spun to the left again, narrowly avoiding a disrupter blast.

Adjusting their course, Hannar steered the squadron toward the enemy ship once more. Explosions and laser blasts surrounded the ships as they navigated the battlefield. Another blast flew over Hannar's ship and a disrupter shot just missed the Cosbolt to Byron's left.

"Where's our cover?" demanded Hannar, rolling to the right.

The Vindicarn vessel was fast approaching. Flashes of light were apparent as other squadrons pounded his entry point with laser fire. Byron's squadron would deliver the final blows and he hoped it would be enough to weaken the shields.

They dodged several incoming shots and when Hannar realigned their course, Byron realized they were seconds away from the target. Other Cosbolts were now protecting the envoy, and his squadron fired at the weakened shield. His eyes on the open vent, he gritted his teeth and prepared to enter.

Good luck! Hannar called, firing a shot before veering upward.

The Vindicarn ship's shield fluctuated and shimmered. Byron held his breath as he hit the surface, muscles tensed as he prepared for resistance. Without so much as a shudder, his ship passed through the barrier and into the vent.

He checked his speed and slowed for the first turn. The simulator had not exaggerated the tightness of the wall and he almost scraped a wingtip as he rounded the corner. Relying on memory, Byron navigated the long vent. He flew through the tunnel, reducing speed only when forced to negotiate a turn. No lasers fired upon his ship as he passed, but Byron still felt a sense of urgency. He was sure his presence was detected the moment he entered the ship.

Two consecutive turns tested his flying ability. Once clear, he leveled the ship and proceeded at full speed. The vent was dark and the Darten's lights cast eerie shadows on the walls. The schematics of the tunnel were displayed on his screen, but Byron didn't look away from the view outside his canopy. He'd ingrained the route in his head.

Easing up on the throttle for a turn, Byron came upon the grating in the vent. This was the point of his jump into the chamber. He hoped the Cassan ships had cleared the area and were out of blast range. Once he teleported into the chamber, he would have only a few seconds in which to fire upon the core. Adjusting the strength of the Darten's shields, he prepared to enter. Visualizing his destination, Byron took a deep breath and jumped.

The brilliance of the core caused him to squint. Adjusting to the strong light, Byron gazed at a glowing sphere within the massive chamber. Contained within a giant steel orb, the core sparkled with blue electricity. Bolts flickered in a constant pattern from the center, as if the device were alive. The sight sent chills down his spine. That ball of blue fire was responsible for so many deaths. It would end today, though.

Reversing his thrusters, Byron pulled the Darten away from the core. The disrupter's energy beat against his mental shields and he knew he didn't have much time. The heat was already rising in the cockpit and he felt sweat run down his face. Positioning his ship near the wall, he held his thumb over the button that would fire the rockets. Judging from the size of his target, it would release an incredible blast of energy when it exploded. He'd have but a split second to escape and it occurred to Byron that this might be the last thing he ever saw.

Thoughts of Bassa flooded his mind. He'd lost his best friend because of this device. Anger welled up inside Byron as that terrible moment flashed in his memory.

"For Bassa," he whispered, pressing the button.

The rockets flew from his Darten. Striking the orb, the disrupter core imploded, and the metal structure around the sphere crumpled from the blast. In a blinding flash, the force within the structure exploded, sending a wall of blue flame racing toward Byron's ship. The flames licked his canopy, the heat penetrating his mind as he visualized the coordinates.

Jump!

A faint voice echoed in his head, penetrating the darkness.
I'm here because I care about a young man named Byron.
I love you, little brother.
Byron, pull up!
Byron!

Gasping for breath, he opened his eyes. The darkness remained, though. Blinking to adjust his vision, Byron struggled to focus on his surroundings.

After a moment, he realized he could see stars. They glowed brighter as his eyes grew accustomed to the faint light. The view beyond the canopy became clear and Byron was now aware of his ship. He felt the seat below him, its shape contoured to his inert body. The cockpit was dark, save for one blinking light. The voice in his mind had vanished, leaving only cold, empty silence. If not for the pain in his head, Byron would've assumed he was dead.

His head listed to one side, but he was reluctant to move just yet. Scanning the stars, he searched for a familiar object. One star appeared brighter than the others, its rays reaching out into space. He frowned, trying to understand the meaning behind the bright light. The blast of the disrupter core flashed in his mind, and he wondered if he was witnessing the explosion of the Vindicarn ship.

Did I do it? he thought.

His eyelids felt heavy. Succumbing to the weight, Byron returned to the darkness. He really needed to test the ship's engines, or at the very least try the com. He lacked the energy to raise his hands, though. His body felt as lifeless as the Darten and he wanted nothing more than to return to the black void.

Something prompted Byron to open his eyes. At first, he thought he was seeing things. He blinked, but the view beyond his cockpit remained the same. Two Cosbolts were hovering in front of his craft.

His muscles protested, but Byron forced his limp arm to rise. Fumbling with the controls, his fingers brushed the com button. At once, a loud voice filled the cockpit.

"Byron! Can you hear me?"

Forcing his brain to work, Byron realized that he recognized the speaker. "Ernx?" he asked, channeling all of his energy into his friend's name.

"He's alive!" screamed Ernx.

Byron felt something strike his ship and a metallic sound reverberated up his spine. Rolling his head to the left, he noticed a recovery vessel beside his Darten. He heard a ratcheting sound and his little ship shuddered.

"Officer Byron, we're going to side-tow your ship into the hanger," a new voice informed him over the com.

"Hang on!" implored Ernx.

Closing his eyes, Byron listened to the sounds of the recovery vessel securing his Darten. His mind returned to the bright star he'd seen earlier.

"Did I do it?" he asked, unsure if his voice would be heard.

"Did you?" Ernx demanded, emitting a bark of laughter. "Byron, the explosion was huge! You didn't just destroy the disrupter ship. You took out the smaller escort vessels and almost every enemy fighter as well. You took them all out!"

Byron's lips curled into a faint smile. "For you, Bassa," he whispered, his eyes still closed.

"What was that?" asked Ernx. "Byron, just hang on. We'll have you back in the hanger in a minute."

Byron's eyes remained closed until he felt the jolt of the landing. The recovery vessel guided his ship to the hanger door before releasing the tiny Darten. Once in position, Byron's ship was taxied into the hanger. His eyes widened at the scene awaiting him.

The hanger was packed to capacity with ships and bodies. He assumed with so many squadrons landing at once, there'd not been time to wheel all of the Cosbolts out of the way. What stunned Byron though was the sheer amount of men present in the hanger. They couldn't all be awaiting his return.

His ship came to a halt. Spurred by the crowd, Byron managed to release the canopy. He fumbled with his helmet a moment before he felt it lifted from his head. The anxious face of a medical officer came into view and the man unfastened the harness. He assisted Byron with his gloves and grabbed his hand, pulling Byron from the cockpit. A second technician helped him extract his legs and Byron swung his feet over the edge of the ship.

Applause and cheers erupted across the hanger. Raising his head, Byron stared in surprise as the crowd surged forward. He'd not anticipated the eager welcome and felt overwhelmed. Flashing a hesitant smile to those gathered, he allowed his body to slide from the ship to the top step of the ladder. The medics held on to his arms and lowered Byron down the steps.

Clinging to the handrail, his foot missed the last step. Strong hands gripped him before Byron slid to the floor. Raising his gaze to the man's face, he was surprised to discover the commander assisting him. He returned the grasp with hesitation, afraid his actions would seem inappropriate, but Kernen smiled with pride.

"You did it, son!" he exclaimed above the commotion. The noise from the crowd had not lessened in its intensity.

A hand pressed against his back, and Larnth helped steady the shaken pilot. Together the two men led Byron to the gurney. Kernen gave orders for everyone to stand back and give Byron some room. The crowd stepped back although the noise from the men did not subside. Byron's head began to pound again and he was more than willing to stretch out on the gurney. The medics joined them and worked quickly to secure his body before moving toward the exit.

Byron closed his eyes, his energy spent. He could still feel the heat of the blast. His mind didn't feel on fire as before, but his head throbbed from exposure to the disrupter.

He could hear those around him offering words of congratulations and encouragement, and hands patted his arms as the gurney moved across the hanger. The noise was a distant roar in his ears, but one voice rose above the others.

"Let us through!"

Byron felt a hand grasp his shoulder and another one gripped his fingers. When neither relinquished their hold, he opened his eyes. Ernx and Nintal's grinning faces greeted him. His friends' presence was a comfort and he made a feeble attempt to return their smiles. The men remained with him until they entered the medical facility. When he could no longer feel their hands, Byron surrendered to his exhaustion.

When he awoke, Byron was alone in a dark room. There were sounds drifting in from further down the hall, but outside of the ship's gentle hum, it was quiet. His head no longer hurt and after the intense heat of the disrupter, the cool sheets felt good on his body. The monitor over his head was still, and he realized no wires or tubes were attached to his skin, either.

Stretching his arms, Byron discovered his muscles had regained their strength. He pulled his body upright, grateful the confining cockpit of the Darten no longer restrained his movement. Free of the pounding headache, he tested his mental abilities. Reaching beyond his room, Byron heard the internal voices of two nearby medical personnel and the man in the room next door. His senses had returned and felt none the worse from exposure to the disrupter core. With his mind intact and body no longer exhausted, Byron felt whole again.

A peace settled over him and he closed his eyes. He'd destroyed the Vindicarn ship and returned alive. It was more than just the success of his mission or the elimination of a great threat to the fleet, though. Byron felt a sense of vindication and closure. His status left in question by Bassa's death, Byron had still managed to fulfill his obligations as an officer and a pilot. Most on the Sorenthia doubted the young and inexperienced rookie, but he'd proven his worth. Bassa had always seen greatness in his pilot, and Byron wished his friend could've shared this moment. Recalling the voice in his head, he realized Bassa's physical presence might be lacking, but not his spirit. The greatest navigator in the fleet would live on in Byron's mind.

He arose and moved on hesitant legs toward the bathroom. When he emerged, a medical technician was waiting.

"My apologies, Officer Byron," he said, moving to the pilot's side.

Byron protested the assistance "I'm fine now. When can I return to my quarters?"

The man gestured for him to get into bed. "Have your senses returned yet? he asked, glancing at the monitor.

Yes.

The technician flashed him a brief smile. "It's early, but let me see if I can locate one of the senior officers. Are you hungry? You've had nothing but water since your arrival."

"I'd rather eat in my quarters," Byron replied. His stomach rumbled in protest, but he wanted to leave more than he wanted to eat.

"I will return soon," the man promised as he departed. "Glad to see you're awake now."

Guess I've been asleep the whole time, he thought to himself.

A fresh glass of water resided by his bed and Byron quenched his thirst. Returning the glass to the stand, he ran fingers through his hair. He'd emerged from the Darten drenched in sweat from head to toe. Byron expected his hair to feel nasty, but the short strands were surprisingly clean. His skin no longer felt sticky, either.

Did I sleep through a bath, too?

The senior medical officer arrived a few minutes later. He greeted Byron with a smile.

"You're much more alert now!" he observed, tipping Byron's chin back to look into his eyes.

"Did I sleep through it all?" he asked. "I don't remember anything after landing."

The officer turned to the monitor. "You roused several times, but between exposure to the disrupter and the heat, your mind and body shut down while you healed."

"Oh. I feel better now, though. I'd really like to return to my quarters."

The officer smiled again and Byron realized he was amusing the man. However, the senior officer performed a full assessment of Byron's condition, including his senses. Eager to depart, he didn't even resist when the man tested his mind. When told he could leave, Byron sighed.

"It appears your senses have fully recovered," the medical officer announced, "but you'll be on injured reserve for another day or two."

Byron brushed aside his hair. "Don't think I could jump right now anyway."

"That won't be required anytime soon," a new voice stated with authority.

Looking up, Byron realized the commander had slipped into the room. He sat up straighter, affecting a respectful pose, but Kernen merely smiled and nodded. The medical officer repeated his assessment of Byron's physical and mental state in the commander's presence. Satisfied with the report, Kernen dismissed the man.

"It appears your mission was a success on every level, Officer Byron," he declared with a wry grin.

"I didn't intend to fail, sir," Byron answered, grasping the edge of bed sheets. "I hope taking out that disrupter ship made a difference, sir."

Placing his hands behind his back, Kernen straightened his shoulders. "From the reports pouring in from the rest of the fleet, the Vindicarn are retreating from all sectors. We just turned the tide in this war, Byron, and we have you to thank."

Byron just shook his head. He didn't want the glory. "I only did what was needed, sir."

The commander's smile grew, deepening the lines around his mouth. "You did well, son," Kernen told him, patting Byron's shoulder. "Bassa would've been proud of your accomplishment."

The sound of his navigator's name tugged at his heart, but Byron managed a weak smile. "Thank you, sir."

"I will leave you to get dressed," the commander announced, turning to depart. "And I believe you will have an escort to your quarters."

"An escort, sir?"

The commander paused in the doorway. "Several," he said with a wink.

Byron dressed quickly. He was anxious to leave, but the thought of what awaited him once he stepped through those double doors caused him concern. Perhaps it was only Ernx and Nintal, and maybe Hannar and Deacer, in the waiting room.

The doors slid open and Byron pulled up short. The room was filled to capacity. Every member of his squadron seemed to be present. The men immediately began to applaud and

Byron's eyes widened. Before he could move or retreat, someone gave him a rough hug.

"Byron!" Ernx cried in his ear, thumping his back.

He heard several others call his name. Ernx released Byron
and before he could respond, someone else grabbed his arm
and patted his shoulders. Nintal appeared on the other side,
eager to greet his friend. Overwhelmed, Byron backed away
from the crowd and pressed his back against the wall.

Everyone settle down!

Hannar's thoughts brought order to the chaos. The men
kept their distance, although they continued to grin at Byron.
Bassa's friend turned to face him and lightly patted his shoulder.

"Sorry, we're just excited to see you," he explained. "We
thought we'd lost you, Byron."

Feeling his confidence return, Byron stood up to his full
height. "Felt like I lost me, too."

His comment sent a wave of laughter across the room.
Byron smiled as well and realized it felt good. He'd not smiled
in so long.

"You did it, Byron!" someone called from the back of the
room.

Byron shrugged. "I just did what was necessary ..."

Hannar's eyes narrowed. "Byron, it may well end this damn
war!"

"None of us could've done it!" Nintal exclaimed in exasperation.

"Makes you one of the best damn pilots in the fleet."

Byron met Larnth's eyes and realized his squadron leader
was serious. Immediately, the sentiment was seconded by
everyone in the room. Byron tried to hide his incredulous expression, but his open thoughts gave away his stunned disbelief. Embarrassed and humbled, he lowered his chin.

Ernx placed his hand on his shoulder in reassurance. The
pilot's fingers tightened and Byron sensed concern.

Damn, you're shaking.

Byron glanced at his hands and saw that he was indeed
trembling. *Last time I ate was before the mission,* he explained, grateful for a legitimate excuse.

"You haven't eaten since yesterday morning?" Ernx exclaimed aloud.

"Damn, let's get you some food!" Hannar declared, gesturing for the others to clear a path to the door.

Byron had hoped for a quiet meal in his quarters, but the men had other ideas. They marched him down to the dining hall, still voicing disbelief he'd not eaten for an entire day. The morning meal was just now being served and everyone grabbed a plate of food. Byron discovered an enormous amount of food on his plate when he cleared the line, courtesy of Hannar and Deacer. The dining hall buzzed with conversation as the crowd gazed expectantly at the young pilot. Ernx guided him to an open table and Byron's squadron gathered protectively around him. Seated at last, he attacked his food with relish.

His comrades talked among themselves while he ate. Once his hunger was sated, the men began asking questions. A small crowd gathered as he spoke, eager to hear his account of the disrupter core's destruction. When he asked about the explosion, several officers described the scene in detail. Byron promised he would watch the Sorenthia's recording of the blast later that day. If the heat hadn't melted his ship's recording, that view would be interesting as well.

Detecting his growing fatigue, Ernx insisted Byron retire to his quarters. Escort in tow, he reached the safety of his room without further delay. Alone at last, he sought the solace of sleep.

Chapter Seventeen

By the evening meal, the full repercussions of his mission began filtering through the fleet. Their disrupter ship destroyed, the Vindicarn had retreated to their home world. The Cassan fleet had pursued their enemy, engaging stragglers and those who still dared to fight. Several neighboring allies had pledged to assist with the decimation of the Vindicarn if they refused to surrender or acknowledge a truce. Regardless of the enemy's final decision, they would no longer be a threat in this part of the galaxy.

Byron endured another round of congratulations and answered every imaginable question regarding his flight through the Vindicarn vessel. Flanked at all times by his squadron, he felt secure and handled the attention with grace. The mission hadn't been about glory, but Byron found he quite liked his new status as a war hero. The men kept him occupied and he was able to put aside the terrible events of the past week.

Bassa was on his mind when he awoke the following morning, though. Free until that evening, when a victory celebration was scheduled, Byron spent most of the day going through the information in his navigator's files. He read the various entries and notes and examined each image in depth. Byron wished his friend were alive to share his moment of glory. Bassa's thoughts and feelings of pride would carry far more meaning than the endless congratulations from his fellow officers.

Byron donned his best uniform for the evening's ceremony and celebration. He preferred to remain in his quarters, but his presence was required. After last night, his desire for attention was sated. Reviewing Bassa's files had reminded him of his original purpose when volunteering for the assignment. Since he'd survived the ordeal, Byron could only assume he was destined for far greater accomplishments. In light of this revelation, he'd decided to abandon his arrogant attitude. It

no longer suited him anyway. At any rate, Bassa always preferred humbleness. Byron could now accommodate his friend's
wishes.

He arrived in the hanger and discovered the cavernous
room filled with people. Entering with reluctance, Byron's
presence was noted immediately. Every man on the ship now
knew his name and face and his days of obscurity were gone.
Smiling in appreciation of the comments that filtered in his
direction, Byron moved through the crowd. The warm recep-
tion was nice, but he hoped to find a familiar face soon.

Byron!

Glancing around, Byron noticed someone moving toward
him. Wentar fell in step beside him and smiled.

Come on!

He led Byron to their squadron, positioned near the raised
platform. The sight of his comrades came as a relief. Ernx
and Nintal took up station at his side and someone else retrieved a drink for the young pilot. Byron declined a plate of
food, claiming he wasn't hungry. Now that he was among
friends, his anxiety slowly began to subside.

I thought you enjoyed the spotlight? asked Ernx, resorting
to his mental voice in order to be heard over the crowd.

Scanning the endless sea of faces, Byron shook his head.
Not like this. I almost stayed in my quarters.

"What?!" Ernx exclaimed, almost spilling his drink. "Byron,
who do you think this celebration is for?"

Byron's eyes widened. "What do you mean?"

The commander's call for order penetrated every mind.
Larnth prodded the men to assemble as a squadron and Byron
glanced around for a place to deposit his glass. He noticed
others still holding drinks and plates, and decided to hold the
glass at his side. Kernen and his senior officers scanned the
crowd from the raised platform, waiting for the noise to settle.
When some semblance of silence was achieved, the commander spoke, his voice amplified across the hanger.

"Men, during this time of war, we have faced a relentless
enemy. Many gave their lives in battle. Others sacrificed their
mental abilities. Every victory was followed by defeat."

The commander paused, his brows pulled together. "However, we just received word that after a brief skirmish over their home world, the Vindicarn have requested a cease fire."

His announcement was met with a mighty roar of cheers. Byron turned to Ernx and let loose a triumphant cry. Relief and excitement rippled across the hanger. The war was finally over.

Kernen allowed the men to revel in the victory. Eventually the cheers subsided. Byron took a quick sip of his drink and flashed Ernx a smile.

"I cannot say enough about the strength and resiliency of the men serving on the Sorenthia," the commander announced. "There will be many honors and recommendations bestowed when we return to Cassa. I am proud of this crew and your dedication to the fleet."

Kernen glanced to his left and a junior officer stepped forward. The man held a small box in his hands. Returning his gaze to the crowd, the commander lifted his chin.

"The Five Star Medal of Honor is awarded to those whose contributions affect the very course of Cassan society," he stated with authority, his eyes narrowed. "It exemplifies bravery, excellence, and the ability to rise above adversity, regardless of the sacrifice required. Tonight, we have an officer present whose actions more than qualify.

"Officer Byron, step forward."

Byron almost dropped the glass at his side. He'd expected a word of thanks and praise from the commander, but not the highest honor the fleet could bestow. Byron's whole body froze and he stared at the commander in disbelief.

Byron! Ernx exclaimed.

He felt someone remove the glass from his hand. A gentle shove from behind propelled Byron forward. Moving in a daze, he stepped out of the crowd and approached the platform. His feet felt as if made of lead and he all but stumbled up the steps. Byron came to an abrupt halt in front of Kernen. The commander's eyes twinkled with amusement, but only genuine pride exuded from his thoughts.

Kernen nodded at the officer holding the box. Byron cast a sideways glance as he approached. The young man flipped open the dark case, revealing the elaborate, five-pointed medal. Inlaid with golden crystals, the large emblem hung from a short, thick ribbon. The Cassan symbol was embroidered on a background of yellow and gold, and the medal's shape mirrored that proud symbol. It was truly a thing of beauty.

Averting his eyes, Byron realized the commander was awaiting his full attention. Straightening his back, he stood erect and clasped his hands to his sides.

"Officer Byron, your actions, above and beyond the call of duty, have directly affected the outcome of this war," Kernen declared in his most formal voice. "You were the only pilot capable of performing the mission successfully. Your unique ability was crucial, but so were your skills as a pilot. You were willing to volunteer for this mission and executed it with precision just days after the loss of your navigator, Officer Bassa. That speaks volumes of your character as well as your skill.

"Officer Byron," the commander said, turning to retrieve the medal. "It is with great honor that I present you with the Five Star Medal of Honor."

Byron's eyes were on the medal as Kernen raised it to his chest. Breath held to hide the tremble running through his body, Byron's gaze returned to Kernen as the commander pinned the medal on his uniform. The man completed his task and stepped back to give Byron a proper salute. He returned the gesture and Kernen nodded.

The crowd broke into spontaneous cheers and applause. Byron felt his face flush with embarrassment as the noise continued to grow in strength. He remained rooted to the spot, afraid to face the Sorenthia's crew. The commander flashed him an encouraging smile.

Turn around, Officer Byron, he thought. *You've faced far worse than this.*

Clenching his fists, Byron slowly pivoted. The men had surged forward and now crowded around the stage. Feeling incredibly humble, he took a deep breath and searched the crowd for a familiar face. Locating his squadron, Byron finally permitted a smile to cross his lips. Their antics far surpassed that of the other officers.

Those closest to the stairs gestured for him to descend. Feeling apprehensive, Byron rejoined the crowd. He was buffeted with congratulations and words of praise and thanks. Every man had to touch the newly decorated pilot, as if to verify he was real. It was almost ten minutes before Hannar reached him and pulled Byron to safety.

With good food and drink available, the men reveled in their celebrations. Someone brought Byron a plate of food, but he had little opportunity to consume it, as those nearby asked endless questions. Still in shock, he answered in as few words as possible. When entering the fleet, Byron had wanted to be the best pilot. He'd envisioned great glory and standing proud before his peers. Now that he held that honor, he felt only humility.

After a while, Byron needed a break from the attention. Edging toward a side door, he informed Ernx he'd return in a moment. Before anyone could stop him, Byron darted into the hallway and entered the nearest telepod. He could not vanish for long, but he desperately needed a few moments to clear his head. Contemplating his destination, Byron selected the last place his friends would consider.

Exiting the telepod, he was pleased to discover the corridor empty. Moving with haste, Byron slipped unnoticed into the hydroponics bay. Strolling down the familiar, winding path, he came upon the bench where he and Bassa had shared many moments. Taking a seat at one end of the bench, he leaned forward. The silence was peaceful and he felt the confusion in his mind recede.

Glancing at his chest, Byron reached for the medal. His fingers brushed the ribbon, the material silky to the touch. He held it up for inspection and determined the medal was indeed real. Byron considered the honor and wondered what he could possibly do to top this achievement. He had nothing left to prove as a fighter pilot.

Officer Byron?

Startled by the voice in his head, Byron released the medal and glanced down the path. The commander watched from a curve in the path and Byron rose to his feet at once. Kernen smiled as he approached.

"At ease, son," he instructed, gesturing for Byron to return to his seat. "May I join you for a moment?"

"Yes, sir, of course!" Byron replied.

Leaning back, Kernen smiled at Byron and cocked one eyebrow. "You do realize that ceremony will be repeated again on Cassa with our high commander?"

Byron grimaced, "Yes, sir, I suspected as much," he conceded, clasping his hands together. "And sir? Thank you. I still can't believe it."

"The moment the news came through regarding the cease-fire, I contacted our high commander," Kernen informed him. "He recommend the Five Star Medal before I even made the suggestion. You earned that honor, Byron."

Glancing again at his medal, Byron considered his response with care. "I didn't earn it by myself, sir."

Raising his gaze, Byron met Kernen's eyes and saw quiet understanding. He felt his chest tighten as he contemplated Bassa's numerous sacrifices. His friend had worked so hard to get Byron to this point. Bassa deserved the medal even more.

"You brought him peace, Byron."

The commander's gentle but affirming words tugged at his heart. Byron managed a weak smile.

Draping an arm across the back of the bench, Kernen cleared his throat. "What are your plans, Officer Byron? Will you remain on the Sorenthia or seek other opportunities? There's not a commander in the fleet that would turn away a fighter pilot with your qualifications."

"Sir, I ..." began Byron. Leaning further forward, he closed his eyes. "Sir, I'm going to request a reassignment to Exploration."

"Exploration?"

"Yes, sir. Exploration was Bassa's dream. The night before he died, I told him when the war ended, we'd pursue a career in Exploration instead. Now that the war's over, I intend to keep my promise."

"Son," the commander began in a patient voice, "don't do it just because of an obligation."

Byron leaned back and lifted his chin. "Sir, I'm not flying with anyone else. I can't. I thought I wanted the glory and

241

prestige that goes with being a fighter pilot, but it's lost its appeal now. I've nothing left to prove, especially to myself.

"I want to do this for Bassa, and more importantly, for me. I'm ready to live my own life now."

Kernen continued to gaze at Byron, as if contemplating his words. A smile crept across his face and the commander inclined his head.

"The choice is yours, Byron. And I have no doubt you will achieve great success in the endeavor."

"Thank you, sir."

Rising to his feet, the commander straightened his jacket. Byron stood up as well, his body at attention.

"I hope you will rejoin the celebration, Officer Byron," said Kernen, eyeing the young man expectantly.

"Yes, sir, I will return momentarily."

Satisfied with his response, the commander departed. Alone once more, Byron closed his eyes and allowed the peaceful silence fill his mind. The stillness reflected the serenity in his heart. He'd made the right decision.

He turned to leave, but paused after taking a few steps. Byron's gaze returned to the bench and he envisioned Bassa residing in the spot the commander had just vacated. His friend's smiling face and thoughts of understanding and acceptance toward his troublesome pilot brought comfort and filled him with hope. He would hold on to that sensation as long as he lived, too.

"You knew all along," he whispered. "I will be all right, my brother."

Taking a deep breath, Byron turned to rejoin the celebration.

About The Author

Alex J. Cavanaugh has a Bachelor of Fine Arts degree and works in web design and graphics. He is experienced in technical editing and worked with an adult literacy program for several years. A fan of all things science fiction, his interests range from books and movies to music and games. Currently the author lives in the Carolinas with his wife.

http://alexjcavanaugh.blogspot.com

LaVergne, TN USA
14 December 2010
208749LV00002B/81/P